Also by Danny Morrison

NOVELS

On the Back of the Swallow
The Wrong Man
Rudi – In the Shadow of Knulp

MEMOIRS

Then the Walls Came Down
All the Dead Voices

PLAY

The Wrong Man

NON-FICTION

Rebel Columns
Hunger Strike – Reflections on the 1981 Hunger Strike (Editor)

Danny Morrison

West Belfast

Elsinor Verlag

First published in 1989
By The Mercier Press, Cork
Reprinted 1990, 1991

This edition 2014
by
Elsinor Verlag (Elsinor Press), Coesfeld, Germany
e-mail: info@elsinor.de
website: www.elsinor.de

EEOT · Elsinor English Original Texts, vol. 3

This book appears in the catalogue of the German National Library; details
are available on the Library's website: www.dnb.de.

Cover design by Seán Mistéil
Typesetting: Elsinor Verlag, Coesfeld
Printed in Germany
ISBN 978-3-939483-32-8

CONTENTS

To Sue and Big Dan

PREFACE TO THE 25TH ANNIVERSARY EDITION

From my early teens I wanted to be a writer, without having a clue how to realise that – except that I knew I needed to read widely and learn from other writers and that I needed a typewriter! It cost eighteen pounds, money I borrowed from my sister Geraldine. However, the first thing I composed was not a short story or poem but a letter to the *Irish News* protesting against the British army killing of a Catholic civilian, William Halligan, in the Falls area in 1971. The Troubles had broken out two years before and I couldn't ignore what was happening. The tug of Irish Republicanism was overwhelming, so I became an activist and gave up college and further education. Before the year was out I was interned in Long Kesh.

Two years after my release, and now twenty-two, I became editor of *Republican News,* and a few years after that I became National Director of Publicity for Sinn Féin, a post I held for eleven years. Whatever putative talent I had for writing and speaking was devoted exclusively to the republican cause.

In 1986 I secretly began writing *West Belfast*, late at night, an hour here or there, in between funerals, arrests, press conferences, elections. I wrote it in longhand, sometimes in a notebook, sometimes on strips torn from newspapers or on the back of envelopes when an idea, an image, or a piece of dialogue came to me.

I didn't know how to write a novel.

But I wanted to tell the story, in as realistic a way I could, of a fictional family, the O'Neills, and their experiences of life from 1963 to 1973. I wanted to show how some individuals and families in the nationalist community, which was a peaceful people, eventually came to support the IRA and had to grapple with the morality of actions which the Catholic Church publicly condemned. It would be about the loss of innocence at both the individual and communal level. It would cover the 1964 Divis Street riots, the Civil Rights Campaign, the Pogroms of 1969 when the British Army was deployed (once again) on Irish streets, the Falls Curfew, Internment, and the year of 1972 when almost five hundred people lost their lives.

It would also be a love story.

Although I experienced and adapted those spontaneous creative impulses that come with true freedom of the imagination (when one's more fully realised characters 'take over' and 'tell' you what they will or will not do), I sometimes consciously wrote with political purpose. I had yet to learn that distinction so eloquently put by the Israeli writer Amos Oz who said that he has two pens on his desk, one black and one blue. One he uses to tell a story, the other to write a polemic: "I never mix them… Novels for me have never been a political vehicle. When I want to make a statement I write an article."

It would be almost two years before I had the nerve to tell anyone that I was writing a novel for fear of being ridiculed.

Later, I typed the manuscript up on my friend Joelle's 'state-of-the-art' Amstrad computer – which appears prehistoric now. It had all of 512k of internal memory with an accessory dot matrix printer!

The book was eventually accepted and published by Mercier Press in November 1989.

Although it received praise in some newspapers and magazines, other reviewers said of the novel that it was sentimental, that it depicted unionists as stereotypes, that it was propaganda, racist and promoted 'the sexuality of violence'. I didn't agree with the latter and would argue that there is a pacifistic theme throughout the novel, although some of the other criticisms are valid. The work was a product of its time and probably the only type of book I could have written in that period with my then mindset.

It was a beginning; part of a learning curve for me.

Such was the hectic nature of my life back in 1989 that I didn't even have a book launch and never got to do a reading.

Before I had time to promote it through readings and appearances, and get feedback on what worked and didn't work (the type of comments a writer appreciates and can potentially learn from), I was arrested and imprisoned for the next five-and-a-half years.

But I remember the hour when I finished it and that sense of achievement and delight, but also a mood overshadowed with sadness. My close friend Kevin Brady had been shot dead in Milltown Cemetery a few months earlier, just as sixteen years earlier my friend

Jimmy Quigley had died in a gun battle with British soldiers. (Jimmy O'Neill in the novel is an undisguised tribute to Jimmy Quigley but is *not* biographical.)

In October 1981, in the week the hunger strike ended, the British Army raided our street, began a house-to-house search, including my parents' home. My mother, who was fifty-seven, collapsed at the front door, suffered a brain haemorrhage and never regained her memory.

Now, seven years later, as I was writing at the dining table, finishing the novel, I looked over to her sitting silently in her armchair, a shell of the personality she was. Big Dan, my father, was at work in Telephone House.

I was here, living with them, because my marriage was in trouble.

I was proud to dedicate *West Belfast* to them, even though my mother would never know about it or be able to read it.

Thinking of Kevin and Jimmy, in the company and companionship of their spirit, looking out the window of my father's house to children playing along the length of Iveagh Street, I wrote the last pages of the last chapter which is set on a summer evening in 1972 and is part of Jimmy O'Neill's diary as he attempts to make sense of his life and thinks about his life, his girlfriend, his parents, his street, and his place on earth.

I can still remember that evening. The swifts were swooping over the chimneys, sweeping high into the sky, screaming and shrieking. Below them was a street full of raucous, lively children, "each of their destinies a slow sprouting mystery."

That image remains with me. An implied image of the future trying to escape or transcend the past despite all of us being trapped in the 'present' currents of our own small histories.

West Belfast has been unavailable for many years but people kept asking where they could get a copy and so I decided it was perhaps time for a reprint. I would like to thank German publisher Thomas Pago of Elsinor Verlag for re-issuing the novel to mark the 25th anniversary of its first publication. I would also like to thank my friends

9

Tina Neylon (for proofing the final edit) and Seán Mistéil (for the artwork).

In October 2014 an original copy was scanned (it did not exist in digital format) and I thought to myself a week should be enough time to proof it and give me plenty of time to organise a launch. However, reading the text again after so many years I was embarrassed at the flowery language, the ponderous descriptions, which slowed down the pace of the novel. If it were to be published on time for the 25th anniversary I would have to do the rewrites within the space of about fourteen days. Of course, there was some slippage. Neither the plot nor the characters were changed – just some of the language. It was a hectic twenty two days!

So, here it is: my first novel, based on our 'small history', written twenty-five years ago about life on the Falls Road four and five decades ago, about a people and a road that I love dearly.

Danny Morrison, December 2014

CHAPTER 1
BLACK MOUNTAIN

All over Belfast the blistering Sunday afternoon sun drew young and old alike outdoors.

Some people have small front gardens in which to sit and relax. Others have gardens, back and front. But most working-class people, apart from those who have moved out to the new estates, sit at the doors of their brown terrace houses or in their small backyards to be sunned.

There are elderly people on chairs and next door neighbours chatting to each other, resting on their cool, creamy-coloured window sills. A few sparrows, tippling on melting tarmac, enjoy a dust-bath in a small pot-hole. A little girl in a dry bathing suit crosses the road clattering in her mother's high heels. A budgerigar in its cage is hung from a cup-hook in a doorway. A gurgling baby tos and froes in its swing hung in another doorway.

In the doorway of the University of Alabama stands Governor George Wallace blocking the enrolment of two black students. Kyu Sakamoto's *Sukiyaki,* about a man who looks up at the sky and whistles while he is walking, so that his tears will not fall, goes to Number 1 in the pop charts. "All free men, wherever they may live, are citizens of Berlin. And therefore, as a free man, I take pride in the words 'Ich bin ein Berliner'," President John F. Kennedy tells a crowd of half a million Germans. Clouds of smoke darken the skies over the Perfume River near Hue when US planes drop napalm on a little village of fishermen, their wives and children.

And on a street off the Falls, a little girl in a dry bathing suit comes back across the road clattering in her mother's high heels.

On the streets off the Falls, windows are opened wide and radios are tuned to the BBC's Light Programme. The people are enjoying *Two-way Family Favourites* for British forces in Germany which plays old songs and new. Afterwards they switch to the Dublin station, Radio Eireann, to hear the latest Gaelic football results from across the country.

Children aged four and five years go venturing into the next street. Young and older children who had assembled into gangs explore new lands – from the Falls across to the embankments of the River Lagan or into the leafy serenity of the University, Stranmillis and Malone residential areas to admire the palatial houses and villas and their luxuriant gardens.

Those teenagers not off to the parks (where their mothers believe them to be) are away discovering by train or bicycle the delights of Helen's Bay or Bangor on Belfast Lough. In other parts of the city working-class children are sneaking off to the hills which skirt West and North Belfast.

From Antrim Town direction, Black Mountain and Divis Mountain have little shape or form. But from Holywood in County Down they are clearly visible and most striking against a milky skyline at sunset. People look at them, too, from the southern suburbs of the city with perhaps no more interest than for a sign of the weather.

On this summer's day in 1963 five boys and one little girl were resting before they continued their climb of the mountain.

The youngest of the gang, eight-year-old Jimmy O'Neill, was here with his cousin Tony O'Neill and was not a close neighbour of the others. He listened intently to their conversation.

"Shoosh! Listen," said Tommy, the smartest dressed of them all, as the boys sat in their Sunday-best tee shirts and shorts and absorbed the majestic view of Belfast. Sure enough there was a peaceful silence as the buzz of life below fell short of their altitude. Only a low breeze occasionally rustled in their ears and a turn of the head neutralised the sound.

"Hey Tommy," Sean McCann asked. "Where do things come from? Like all this and the sun?"

"From God, of course," he replied. "Everything comes from God. Your mammy and daddy comes from God."

"Our Angela comes from God," chirped in Sean's sister, Mary Ann, as children often do, whose convictions are strengthened through their repetition.

The sun shone from behind her and splinters of light glistened in her auburn hair which was tied with a skinny yellow ribbon in a bun on top. Masses of little red wisps escaped the discipline of the bow and added to the halo effect.

"Hey. Where does our dog Cocker come from?" Jimmy asked.

"Everything comes from God," muttered Tommy. He quickly added: "Stevie. Where do trolley buses come from?"

Before the eleven-year-old had time to blunder, Tommy couldn't restrain himself and declared: "The back of the City Hall!" They all laughed as the trick question and its answer sank in.

Big Stevie Donnelly was chubby but well made. It was his task to trample down nettles, test the ground and help the others up any steep elevations. His head of thick, black hair and round face and his natural reticence disguised a fearlessness when roused. He lived in the street next to Tommy, Sean, and Tony who were aged nine or ten, and who were all classmates when school had broken up for the summer holidays a few weeks previously.

Stevie had come down a weight, so to speak, by playing with these particular friends. Even though he was their elder, he wasn't quite ready to leave behind forever cowboys and Indians and other games which gave him such pleasure. He enjoyed the respect which his brawn earned him. Without him there was no way they would have crossed foreign territory – the Whiterock and Ballymurphy housing estates.

Though the oldest boy led, the navigator remained Tommy. Standing four feet tall, with one hand covering his puffy eyes from the dazzle of the sky, he had been arguing for some time with Stevie that whilst from the ground the summit might appear to rise from this part of the mountain – and they even argued whether this was Black Mountain or Divis – the highest point was actually on the next hill.

Struggling behind Stevie, Sean, Tommy, Tony, and even Mary Ann, came Jimmy, armed with a bow and a quiver full of arrows. He lived in the next district to the others, but just far enough away to sever it off with clear lines of demarcation, even from the adult's perspective of grocery shops, the butchers' and most frequented pubs, their locals. Preferring these friends of his cousin Tony, Jimmy showed a streak of apparent independence and some mettle. But it belied an innocence which found expression within the privacy of his home where he still loved to sit on his mother's lap, in jealous competition with his younger sister Sheila, and be cuddled, or carried to bed in his father's arms after a long day.

When deep in happy thoughts Jimmy normally walked with a determined stride-and-a-half in hopping movements, his longish brown hair bouncing up and down. Now his legs were sore and he was sweating. He could have gone on but was glad to hear the call to halt.

"Your daddy doesn't own ya, ya know."

"Whad you say?"

Sean repeated his claim.

"Whadya mean?" Tony asked Sean, whose dimples deepened as he struggled to explain himself.

"Your daddy doesn't own ya, 'cos ya came from yer mammy."

"But he helped put ya there," said Tony, who had picked up that notion from various innuendoes.

"How'd he do that, Tommy?" asked Sean, turning towards their mentor.

Tommy appeared stumped.

"Eh? Ach, I can't remember... Is yer daddy old, Jimmy?" he asked.

"Naw."

"What age is he?"

"Fifty, I think."

"Gee! Fifty, and he's not old?"

"Naw. He can still run. He can run faster than me. You wanna see him the other night," he added in his father's defence.

"See that cut, Stevie?" Tommy pointed to his knee. "I got that fixing a puncture when a big chisel this size sprung from a spoke. Did ya ever see a scar like that? Did ya? Did ya now?"

Stevie admired it.

"Ya wanna see our Phelim's head," said Tony. "He fell and hit it against the hearth."

"What age is he?" asked Tommy.

"He's none, but he's okay now."

"Whadya call a German bank robber?" said Jimmy.

"Dunno."

"Hans Up!" he shouted and they all laughed, concluding that Jimmy was good fun, okay.

Sean called to his sister to be careful and there was a pause in their incessant chatter. Sean and Stevie kept their eyes on the little girl who lifted high her pleated frock with either hand to avoid getting it caught in the undergrowth. They moved on and encountered small white rocks which soon changed to smooth grey stones. They found themselves on a path on one side of which the thistle-covered ground fell in a sheer drop from the summit. On the other side was a small rampart covered with throbbing green moss. A brood of primroses sheltered in soft soil under the belly of a bush and there was the sweet smell of wild woodbine.

A thick briar, larger than any of them, caught on Stevie's shirt and then shot out from the embankment like the tentacle of an octopus, its thorns like suckers, frightening Sean and causing some nervous laughter.

The path led them past the Hatchet Field – so called because of its shape. In one corner stood an old single storey house. A few chickens pecked around the yard but the occupant was not about. They moved on up the path and came down to the gulley and a small stream, six inches of crystal cool water at its deepest. With his bow and arrows Jimmy hunted for fish the way Lok and Shan did in his school reading book.

"Be careful!" shouted Mary Ann. "If you fall in you'll catch ammonia and yer mammy'll kill you."

"It's okay... I'm learnin' to swim," he said, bluffing.

The other four split into British soldiers and Germans and fought each other until they were exhausted. Then they fell to the ground in a heap. Tony poked and picked in the grass, checking for earwigs before he rested his head. Stevie wondered what the time was.

"Stevie, Kipper Kelly whacked Tony with a stone yesterday," said Sean.

"It wasn't a stone, it was a brick," Tony corrected him.

"And he and his brother hit you with a hurley, didn't they?"

"It wasn't a hurley it was just an ordinary tennis bat," he added, casually.

"Tell our teacher. They go to our school," said Sean, disappointed at not having stirred up some ire.

"Ya should have told Big Stevie when it happened," said Tommy. "You know that Kipper's da's got one leg longer than the other."

"Howdja know?" the others asked, crowding around him, even though it was common knowledge and they had seen Johnny Kelly's limp.

Sean had heard there was a food shortage during the war and he had caught rickets when they had to eat mice and rats.

"Howdja know?" they asked again.

"Kipper told me 'imself. His da comes in drunk and falls into the chair like King Kong," and Tommy flumped into a soft cavity in the ground which acted as an armchair.

"And Kipper has to pull off his da's socks. The first one's easy but then he has to put his hand way, way up into his trouser leg to find his other foot."

"Geee."

"Yea. Johnny Long Leg."

They all giggled mischievously. The conversation turned to handball and football. Tommy, surveying what he thought was their street a mile or two below was a bit pensive about the previous subject, so he added: "Kipper's always chasin' and makin' fun of Mickey Boyle."

Mickey Boyle was called a Mongol although they were not quite sure how to define his handicap.

Jimmy lay on his belly staring into a pool of still water whose smooth surface kept being upset by little whirling abrasions. Sean scratched his head, trying to pull out midge flies.

"What's the difference between fizcley handikep and mently handikep?" Sean asked. There was pondering.

"I know," butted in Jimmy. "When you're mently handikept you're really, really handikept," and they all shook their heads in agreement.

Tony passed around a lemonade bottle which contained orange juice. They all took a swig at the warm drink and vied with each other in identifying landmarks such as the trolley-bus terminal at the top of the Whiterock Road; the Falls Park; Milltown Cemetery; the Ml Motorway, which had opened the year before; the King's

Hall; the large spire of Broadway Presbyterian Church on the Falls Road; and the derricks of the shipyard.

Jimmy was rigidly attentive and was mesmerised at the extent of their knowledge. The city and its geography was beginning to take shape in his mind.

On the horizon was the sea; then on the coast there were the cranes and oil terminals of Sydenham. He studied the city centre buildings, their boxed and rectangular and dome-like shapes; the church spires; the factories and houses – mills, brown terraces giving way to white gable ends; bright roofs; patches of green and the swoosh of trees rising out of the ground. The realness of it all, the Sundayness of it all gave the picture a quality which could only have been appreciated from this height and at this distance. It was breath-taking.

Sean and Mary Ann were supposed to be in the custody of their fourteen-year-old sister Angela. After an early Sunday dinner her parents, Mary and Frank, had left their eldest daughter with clear instructions: she was to wash the pots and dishes, tidy up the kitchen and generally keep house. Paul, who was twelve, had to stay within two or three streets, and Angela had to keep a special eye on the youngest two. There was salad for tea but they would be back anyway no later than six or half-six. She could have one or two friends in the house but that was all. They were off to the christening of the baby of Mary's younger sister, Maureen.

Having a daughter old enough to mind the others was one of the first rewards for all the years of worrying and sacrificing. However, Angela did not settle comfortably into the role of nanny. Mrs McCann didn't feel she could always trust her and could see the beginning of a rebellious streak which needed nipped in the bud. A few weeks before, Mrs McCann had beaten her around the room with a feather duster when a neighbour told her that Angela had been to Mass without wearing a mantilla or scarf.

Angela pretended to be contrite. And why shouldn't they have believed her? She had been the apple of her father's eye. When she was younger she would dance and sing like Shirley Temple for visitors and make adults laugh when she dropped the threepenny bits they gave her down the front of her dress. Although she could exasperate her parents, she could also make them laugh and they were proud of her, her intelligence, her looks.

On this day Angela's job was to mind her sister and brothers, but within half an hour of her parents' departure and of completing the washing-up she had bribed Paul to stay in the vicinity of the house and she would favourably see to him over the next week. He had been obliging but, shortly after she took off, the two youngest also had disappeared and he was conducting a search for them.

Angela lay on her back in the Falls Park, her young brothers and sister the farthest things from her mind. She was dreamily carried away by the attentions paid to her by the teenage boys, all two or three years older, gathered around her and her best friend Patricia. Her physical maturity and risqué conversation both terrified and thrilled them. Privately, the boys unjustly attributed to her a sexual promiscuity of their own imagination. True, she was heading towards disaster, but her reputation was propelled by gossip ahead of her actual experience. To ensure that they got the right message, however, she regularly cast off her shoes and Bobby socks and on would go nylons, garters, high-heels and make-up – "Care of Mary Senior" she would boast – as she took a long drag on a cigarette pilfered from "Frank's packet".

Carefree as ever, she was lying under one of the many beech trees, seeing in its entwined boughs the figures of naked, embracing lovers.

The park's lawn had been mown but shooting through its close-pile growth were clusters of little daisies. Angela flicked the ash from her cigarette into the grass and badgered one of the lads: "Go on; tell us what he said."

The teenager blushed and regretted beginning the conversation. Now he was being cornered and pinned down on the specifics of the sex education he had received from an equally uncomfortable Christian Brother. She revelled in entertaining the others who were falling back in laughter as Patricia kept biting her lower lip, rolling her eyes and giggling.

"We're gonna get nowhere with you, young man," Angela said, already feeling bored. Her ears picked up with the sound of music. She dragged Patricia to her feet.

"Quick! That big hunk has a wireless . . . Must go men. See youse." And linked to her friend's arm they followed behind an athletic-looking figure. They broke into a rock 'n' roll routine which provoked scowls from the old people on the benches around the bowling green, including one disapproving grey-haired man, hands resting on a blackthorn walking stick. He nudged his wife who was eating a sandwich. She was more preoccupied with staunching the flow of salad cream from her mouth with her little finger, and keeping her teeth in. Her old lips simply took up a secret smile at the youngsters.

They had crossed the stream and waded through dense bracken, gorse and the acres of heather which seemed to have a stranglehold over half the hillside. The more they struggled the more the barbs and stems would stick to and exhaust them. Once or twice, Mary Ann and Jimmy disappeared, their cries alerting the others who then rescued them. Finally, they reached the top of the mountain. The boggy soil was black. On a broken concrete base stood a concrete plinth, like an ancient sundial, possibly to mark the altitude but the markings were indecipherable. Belfast was gone from view but through the haze to the west they could see the faint shimmering of Lough Neagh. The back of the mountain was eerie and deserted.

Only the magnificence of Ulster Television's aerial now held the attention of the gang.

"It's big, but it's not that big," said Tommy, ending years of juvenile speculation that every Viscount and DC-3 out of Nutts Corner airport was about to crash into the towering mast.

"Whaddle we do now?" said Tony, wearily.

"We go down again." And everybody looked to Big Stevie who had just spoken.

The two girls followed the music blaring from the transistor radio which belonged to the bronze body in the shorts.

Angela was in two minds about her attitude to "Mr Muscles," as she had christened him, and he knew he was being followed. She had to keep fixing behind her ears her shoulder-length auburn hair which kept falling loose each time she and Patricia bent over with laughter, talking about him. By his swagger he obviously had a high regard for himself. They shadowed him through the avenue of chestnut trees to the small, stone-bridge, and up the path to where the noise of cheering and splashing rose from the open-air swimming pool, the Cooler.

The afternoon session was well under way. A minority, women with their children, and young men with their girlfriends, had paid in. The rest had scaled the fence or scrambled through a hole below it on the City Cemetery side.

"Are youse going for a swim?" Ricky asked Angela and Patricia, having introduced himself. It was obvious that they were only out for a walk.

"Do you work or are you still at school?" His eyes were on the freckles of Angela's face.

"I'm a secretary, though Josie here, my sister, is going back to St Dominic's in September to do her..." – she almost said, "Junior" – "Senior. What do you work at?"

"Do you know McCullough's Pharmacy on the Andersonstown Road?" They had heard of the shop.

"Yeh, my ... my father owns it and I'm the manager, or I will be soon." He waved to several other friends at the pool, excused himself and said he would be back.

The girls sat on the grass outside the Cooler and watched through the railings. Ricky spoke to his friends and they all shared a joke.

"I think yer man fancies you," said Patricia. The incessant splashing laced the air with a coolness which could almost be smelt.

Angela looked to the sky and loved everything: the air still and then breezy, the canopy of rustling trees, the heat beating down on them, her youth, this little game she and Patricia were playing. She felt a rush of serenity; she was suddenly intoxicated with the drug of life and had to restrain herself from screaming aloud her happiness.

With a panache Ricky knelt on his hunkers, dipped his hand into the pool as if it was a font and blessed himself before cutting a neat hole in the water with a dive which ended with his re-emergence three-quarters way up the pool. Small boys admired his ostentation. He returned a number of times and spoke through the railings to the girls, showing off his radio which lay on a pile of clothes.

To one side he probed Patricia: "Would yer, your mate go out with me to St Teresa's dance tonight if I asked her?"

"God, I don't know. She's an awful lot of typing to do – from work, I mean. She brings it home, you know."

Using his hand as a squeegee he wiped the excess water off his legs.

"Ask her for me." Then he was gone again.

"Well, whadda ye wanna do?"

"I don't like him."

"You're crazy. He's gorgeous."

She felt that Ricky was a cocksure bore, three or four years her senior and yet really immature.

"Okay," said Angela with a smile. "But pick me up at a quarter to eight and be nice to my ma."

He was uneasy about this arrangement, preferring instead to see his dates either outside the dance hall or at their street corner if there was no bus journey involved.

"Right," he declared. "St James Road it is, seven forty-five sharp." He was proud of himself for that last touch of finesse, "sharp". He repeated the door number.

"Seven forty-five, now don't forget," said Angela.

"How could I!" he said, and apologised for not being able to borrow his father's car.

"Jeepers, we'd better be going. My ma and da will be back from the christening soon. Let's go, Trish."

Even the aimless talk had gone out of the gang's conversation and they didn't undertake the downward trek with the same enthusiasm as their climb, though the journey was now much easier.

"How long do ya 'hink it'll take?" was the general moan.

Behind some bushes, close to where the Whiterock Loanen met the end of the Ballygomartin Road, grey smoke came belching out, and made them curious. The gang climbed into the field and Stevie lifted Mary Ann over a gate which had been securely tied.

"Aw, awwww!" said Stevie as they found themselves confronted by three hard-looking boys who, it was obvious, owned the fire.

"They could be Orangemen," whispered Stevie, to the bewilderment of Jimmy and Mary Ann; but making Tommy, Tony and Sean nervous. They knew that people called Protestants lived in New Barnsley, even had heard of a neighbour referred to as a Protestant or "a convert," but had no social intercourse or contact with them and so they were a little afraid.

"Let's get out of here," said Tommy, his voice slightly trembling. His stomach was in knots but he attempted to put some spine into his crumbling composure. He told God that he hoped Kipper Kelly's father's leg would grow some more (he just knew he shouldn't have said that about Mr Kelly), and took a deep breath, bracing himself.

The gang was going nowhere. They were surrounded.

"Hey boy. Let's see your bow and arrow," said a tall fellow to Jimmy.

One shot wouldn't harm anybody, thought Tommy, but he wasn't prepared to express that view.

"Nehh," said Stevie. Jimmy began to wish that he too was elsewhere. His mother would be angry to discover that he had been up the mountain and had had his birthday present stolen. Mary Ann was more curious than frightened. She knew convention. She would not be required to do any fighting. It would be resolved between Stevie and the ugliest and biggest of the other gang.

"Hey, Scobie. You lost a bow and arrow just like that one," said Tall Fellow, who was about thirteen, to his companion who had a turn in his eye. He was in long trousers. It was almost men they were up against, they felt.

"Heh," said Scobie. "I think that's mine. Gimme it!"

He moved to take it off Jimmy, whose heart now sank.

"Push off and leave 'im alone," said Stevie.

"Where do youse come from?" Tall Fellow was still sizing up the situation.

"Why?" Stevie wasn't giving an inch.

"Whadda ya call the Pope?" he sneered.

Stevie was expecting a denigrating remark though Tommy suddenly read the situation and realised that they were Catholics, they were *all* Catholics. What was his name? What was his name? He had learnt it so that he could show off on some occasion and it had been recently on the news, though with regard to what, he wasn't entirely sure.

"Pope John the Twenty-third!" he said with a smile.

"Wrong! He died three weeks ago!" And with that Stevie and Tall Fellow were engaged in hand-to-hand fighting, like Sumo wrestlers, trying to bring the other to the ground. Once the atmosphere was smashed things were not so bad and Tommy felt better joining in with the shouting. Most fights were clean and there was no 'jumping on'.

"Go on Big Stevie, punch him!"

Stevie was doing too well and Tommy's heart came to his throat when the third, much smaller, member of the other gang began pushing him, asking him who he was shouting for. He was mortified at being afraid of a dwarf and the next minute he was hurled into the fight. Within seconds there was a melee as Scobie dived in with a terrifying, confident scream pulling Tony in with him. Jimmy and Mary Ann, however, remained uninvolved. Tony's head was covered with his arms. He was on the ground, hardly being touched though bodies were getting pushed and shoved around him and he was seeing stars behind his closed eyes. While members of Stevie's team became exhausted and retired the three strangers pushed furiously and captured Stevie in a head-lock.

"Do ya give up! Do ya give up!" they screamed.

Stevie choked but didn't give up and his companions felt sick with shame as they licked their wounds, afraid for themselves. Something in Jimmy snapped. He yelled and dived into the scrum, adding a few pounds to Stevie's efforts and surprising everyone.

Tall Fellow momentarily released Stevie from his grip and grabbed Jimmy by the buttocks to hurt him and throw him off.

"I farted in your hands!" Jimmy shouted into his face.

"What!"

"I've just farted again!"

"Ughhh!"

He immediately let go of Jimmy, disgusted. Stevie winded Scobie and with a scowl frightened off the small member. Then, in the first critical act of violence he followed up by punching Tall Fellow straight on the nose, shattering his prestige. His nose began to bleed and hostilities were ended as abruptly as they had begun.

"I'll get my big brother for you, ya pig. He's a hard man and will fix you," he threatened, as the two sides slowly parted: the three former attackers hurling abuse from a safe distance. The gang made their way on down the lane. They were in marching mood again. Jimmy had saved the day.

"Me a fart bomb," said Jimmy and the rest of the gang shook their heads as they triumphantly marched home singing:

> *Barney Hughes' bread,*
> *Sticks to your belly like lead.*
> *Not a bit a' wonder, farts are like thunder,*
> *Barney Hughes' bread!*

Angela had arrived home just in time to mollify Paul who was shouting at Sean and Mary Ann for wandering off. She washed their hands and faces, gave them salad and severely chastised them for being up the mountain. But she forgave them, she said, for confiding in her and they weren't to tell their mother or father.

When Mr and Mrs McCann arrived home they were happy to see the house in order. They always knew if there had been a party in progress when they were away as the house was tidier than when they went out. The house was in home-condition: the *Sunday Post* was scattered about the sofa, its comics' page below a chair, and the bathroom towel was lying on the bathroom floor.

It was half-seven. Ricky turned off the Falls and into St James Road, humming to himself. He was quite looking forward to seeing Angela although he couldn't understand this formality. He followed the numbers and then he saw a dilapidated house. The curtains were unwashed, paint was peeling off the door, the windows were grimy and the small, weed-grown garden was full of papers which the wind had blown in. The place looked shabby. His heart went out to Angela. He began whistling as he walked past the house just to check the next consecutive number.

Secretary, my foot, he thought.

He walked up the path and knocked on the door. There was a hollow echo, no sign of life. He knocked harder.

A boy pulled up on a bike. "Hey mister. Nobody's lived there for two years. The oul doll's dead."

Across the street in Patricia's house, Patricia, Angela and another girl, Rose, were hiding behind the parlour curtains, screaming with laughter.

"Oh mammy, I'm gonna wet myself!" said Angela.

Ricky carefully looked from side to side to see if anybody spotted or overheard the wee bastard on the bike talking to him, before he shuffled out of the path and out of the street.

In Sandy Row, on the Shankill, in the Falls, in Short Strand, the children were called in in shifts, depending on how old they were. In the distance a mother's voice could be heard calling "Jimmy! Jimmy!" or some other name and a faint voice would reply: "Wha'?"

"Come on. It's time to come in."

The streets would slowly empty of the very young. Often, hoaxers mimicking the voice of a particular child would answer a call with a deluge of abuse aimed at getting the kid a box on the ears.

Another child in some other street is called and replies: "Wha'? Whadda you want?"

"Time to come in."

"Ach mammy, Rhonda Smith's still out!"

"All right then, five more minutes."

"Ten more!"

"Get in here right now!"

In another street a girl informs a woman: "Mrs McMahon your Gerard's hiding behind that car ... Mrs McMahon your Gerard's only after throwing a stone at me ..."

"Gerard, I know you're behind that car. Get in before I brain you!"

"Mrs McMahon your Gerard's only after giving me the fingers ..." Clout!

"Mammy, mammy, mammy! I got blempt in the wrong!"

Jimmy and Sheila begged their father to stay a few moments longer. The bedspread was light, the bed spacious. They were in their pyjamas, they had had their supper and were being tucked in by their daddy.

"Ach, daddy, tell us a wee story. Go on," implored Jimmy.

"Okay then. *Tom Thumb*. Now, night, night, and go asleep."

"Daaaady!" said Sheila, feeling cheated. "Ach, daddy, tell us another wee story."

"Okay. *Tom Thumb's Wee Brother*. Now there, away you go asleep," he chuckled but the kids weren't for letting him leave.

"Now if I tell you a story do you promise to be quiet and go asleep?"

"Yip."

"Yippee."

"Once upon a time, a long, long, time ago the wee boys and wee girls didn't go to school and just played all day long beside the river or fed the chickens or climbed trees. Their mammies made baskets or sewed clothes and their daddies went fishing or else they planted corn for bread.

"Anyway, they were all very happy and now and again they had parties and everybody sang and danced all night long ..."

"Did the wee girls have to go to bed, daddy?" asked Sheila.

"Don't interrupt me now or I'll not tell you it."

"Shut up, Sheila. Go on, daddy, go ahead," said Jimmy attentively.

"One day when the daddies were out working the bad men came and they burnt down the huts and killed the animals and stole whatever they could. They shouted and roared and chased everybody away ..."

"Geee. Is this true, daddy?"

"Shut up, Jimmy. Tell us what happened next."

"The women ran into the forest and the bad men went looking for them. To stop the babies from crying and giving their hidey-holes away the mammies put their hands over their wee mouths. Everybody was terrified and then the daddies came home and chased the baddies away.

"Everybody went back and built their huts and got something to eat."

"I don't like that story, daddy," Sheila said.

"I'm not finished."

"After a few months all the mammies noticed that the babies had no teeth – they just weren't growing ..."

"Flip me!"

"They didn't know what to do and the mammies were crying and blaming themselves. But then one day a wee boy and his sister were out playing near a white hawthorn tree when they heard someone calling them.

"'Tsst!'

"They looked around but could see nothing.

"'Tsst! Over here! Are you blind or sumpin'. Open your eyes!' It was a little Leprechaun and although the kids were afraid they peeked into the bush.

"'Don't be letting her get too close!' said the Leprechaun who had no clothes on and was covering himself with his hands.

"'What's wrong?' said the boy. 'Why have you got no clothes on?'

"'Do ya think I always go around like this! Catch yourself on. I went for a dip and a bloody big rabbit stole my magic jerkin and britches. If you find them and bring them back to me I'll grant the pair of you a wish. One wish mind you, I'm not a bloody millionaire.'

"The boy and girl searched all the rabbit holes and found a big rabbit lying on its back, unable to get up.

"'Help me! Help me! Can't you see I'm stuck! Pull these things off before I die!'

"They pulled the britches and jerkin off the rabbit who was very grateful and they brought them back to the hawthorn bush.

"'Turn your head away, wee girl, or you'll not get a wish.'

"When the Leprechaun put his clothes back on he leaped into the air with joy and landed at the top of the tree. He somersaulted and danced and shouted: 'Fooled you! Didn't I?'

"The wee boy said: 'You can't go back on your word, you promised us.'

"'No, I suppose I can't. But I drive a hard bargain.'

"'You're a cheat!' the wee girl said.

"'Okay, okay!' said the Leprechaun. 'I'm only kiddin'. So here's what we'll do.' He told them his plan and the boy and girl smiled and grinned and danced with him around the hawthorn tree.

"Wasn't that a nice story? Now, go asleep," said Peter, as he rose from the side of the bed.

"Ach daddy. What was the plan?" said Jimmy.

"If you don't tell us, I'm gonna cry," said Sheila.

"Jeese, I almost forgot to tell you! The Leprechaun told them to go back to the village and to secretly meet all the other wee boys and girls who were five and six and seven years of age. When their baby teeth fell out they were to hide them under their pillows. He would send fairies around to collect them and put money in their place. The fairies would collect the best teeth and polish them brand new and give them to the wee babies.

"Sure enough within a few weeks all the wee babies' mouths were full and they were able to chew sweets and talk and their mammies cried with joy at the miracle."

"That was a nice story."

"I liked that story," said Jimmy, who checked for loose teeth when his daddy went downstairs. He then sat up, pulled the curtains aside, looked up at the mountain and wondered if his friends Big Stevie and Mary Ann were in bed and asleep.

Ironically, at sunset, the more the night fell the more the ageing day flared in the western sky behind Black Mountain. The creeping darkness eventually prevailed, but even when the sun disappeared there was still a comfortable coolness about the grass and the daisies, and the ground was now redolent with fragrances that had been suppressed by the day's heat.

From below garden thickets there came a moistness and an earthiness. From nettle beds rose an alluring sweetness.

From underground, latent spirits crept through tiny, matted roots, into the souls of wildflower, grass and buds, spilling out into the open where the light wind carried them off into the new atmosphere. The rich earth was giving off night.

CHAPTER 2
THE O'NEILLS

John O'Neill awoke to the familiarity of his bedroom ceiling slowly defining before his eyes. A yawn broke the sleep seal on his lips and he chewed over the iron taste in his mouth. He inhaled a large draught of fresh air which came in through the open window. His younger brother Raymond lay next to him, undisturbed.

By the side of the bed was *Greenmantle* which John had read until two or three. He looked across the landing and saw the face of Jimmy who seemed to instantly awaken. His youngest brother took a breath and stretched his curled-up body. Sheila was fast asleep beside him.

"You make me my breakfast?" he asked.

"In a few minutes," said John, smiling. He surveyed the ceiling which he imagined went through seasonal changes: the dulled, original white emulsion paint with its hair cracks now taking on a sharp, creeping depth in the summer's heat. He was sixteen and he longed to get out in the world.

He knew his father was annoyed that he had not made a go of schooling and that he felt that John was a drain on the family's resources. But John had given his mother some money. He had earned a little through delivering leaflets in the suburbs around Belfast announcing carpet sales and he also secretly gambled and was a lucky gambler.

Though he was somewhat streetwise he also knew that he knew little about the big world. That he could be naïve. That there was a lot of badness in people that he never imagined. That you had to plan your actions carefully because otherwise they would have unforeseen consequences. He recalled a bitter lesson, a shameful episode, from three years previously about which no one but he and his teacher knew.

Waiting on the landing to be dismissed for the lunch-break he saw a fellow pupil, a minor bully, lean over the balcony and spit down onto a group of first years. The spittle hit a well-known weakling, a frail youngster who instantly burst into tears and some minutes later became sick. The form master from below ran upstairs to consult with his colleague. John's class were marched back into the room and each was threatened with six strokes of the cane from the teacher. He said he would give them the opportunity to escape punishment: it was impossible that no one out of a class of thirty-two had seen the culprit, and indeed John knew it was more likely true that half a dozen others witnessed the incident. The teacher gave out sheets of paper. They were to write down the name of the boy they saw spit or whom they thought had done it: it was to be completely anonymous.

John was in a dilemma. He despised the bully and didn't want him to get off scot-free. The teacher was capable of carrying out the mass punishment: he had done so before. There were bound to be other witnesses. Why leave it to one of them to shoulder the sole responsibility of naming the guilty one? John might feel better for not having personally fingered the bully, who was so cowardly at heart that he wouldn't even own up to save the rest of the class, but by not showing solidarity with those prepared to name the rogue, was also to act in a cowardly fashion. There was also the chance of someone maliciously naming an innocent class mate, though not even the teacher appeared to have considered that possibility.

John wrote down the name, Paul McShane, and folded the paper which, along with the others, was collected by the smug teacher. The class was released and he hurriedly ran off to his lunch, the boys expressing relief among themselves that they hadn't been caned. Later, as John was going down the corridor the teacher suddenly appeared in the frame of an open door and called him in.

"This is your writing, isn't it? Well, isn't it?"

John was trembling, close to tears, afraid of someone seeing him in the compromising company of the teacher. He was being over-taken by the speed and gravity of the repercussions of his action and never in his naivety did he believe that his disguised handwriting would be recognised. Worse still, it slowly dawned on him that he must have been the only one who had written anything down.

"You're sure he did it? Are you sure?"

"Yes!" he gasped at last, convicting McShane to a dozen strokes of the bamboo cane.

"Good boy. Away you go."

John skulked out of the room and in class couldn't look McShane in the eye. He took no joy from McShane's ill-founded cockiness, the mistaken belief that the teacher had drawn a blank.

There was a knock on the door and the headmaster, accompanied by the teacher, took McShane out. He came back into the room, minutes later, his face completely pale.

"I've been expelled," he said and packed his schoolbag. Head down, he dragged himself from the room.

John was ashamed and felt close to tears. There was nobody he could turn to without the risk of putting his treachery on the record. That night he was depressed and it took him hours to fall asleep. The whole talk in the class the following morning was speculation about who was 'the squealer'. Then, on their way out to the yard for the ten-minute break, McShane was spotted with his mother outside the principal's office. Forty minutes later the principal brought him into the geography class and spoke to the teacher.

John was so relieved he was overjoyed and felt obliged to patronise McShane for months afterwards.

Lying now on his bed he winced at his collaboration. From that moment on the solidarity of the classroom became a principle. Looking back he now admitted that he had grafted noble intentions onto what was really an act of self-preservation. His concern had been really to avoid punishment and even though the class had been spared a heavy caning, and even though the shock of expulsion apparently contributed to the reform of McShane, John still regretted and was ashamed of his action, his and the teacher's secret. That hypocritical bastard, he said to himself, as he watched the erratic flight of a buzzing bluebottle around the ceiling.

"Right! Jimmy, let's go!" he said, coming back to the present.

When they got downstairs John looked at the clock on the mantelpiece: it was twenty-five to nine and the house was still quiet. This was the start of his father's two weeks' holidays and it was the first day in perhaps a year that his mother wasn't the first up. She was always downstairs, even in the dark winter mornings lighting the fire, and it seemed it was nine or ten o'clock at night before she actually took off her apron, signalling her day was done. Raymond was still asleep and Monica was staying with their Granny Stewart.

John opened the front door to take in the milk. A stout boy, not from the locality, stood on the step, just about to knock.

"Is your Jimmy coming out?" asked Big Stevie.

"He hasn't got his breakfast yet. He'll call for you."

"Ach, it's okay, I'll wait here," he said, making John feel awkward and inhospitable.

"Can I stand at the door until my corn flakes are ready?" asked Jimmy.

"No. I don't know where your clothes are and it's too early to be out running the streets. He'll see you later, okay?" said John.

He poured out the cereal but didn't shake the milk bottle as Jimmy liked the cream.

"Want some toast?"

"Na. Just corn flakes. Do you 'hink the wevver's going to be good for the Fifteenth?"

"How do I know. Why? You're not collecting for the bonfire so soon are you?"

"Yeh. Me collecting for two. One here and one wiff Tony O'Neill's gang. We're gonna have the biggest on the Road!" he said.

Someone stirred upstairs and a few minutes later their mother, Catherine, came down: "Morning everybody."

"Hiya!"

"Mornin'."

"Go on in and I'll finish off," she said to John as she put on her apron.

"Would you do the yard sometime today?"

"I'll do it this morning because I want to head downtown later," he said.

John loved going downtown: going from large shop to small shop; the smells of new, expensive furniture in the big stores; the homes and food sections; and then the cafeterias where he and his friends had chips and milkshakes before wandering through the same places Saturday after Saturday. In particular they loitered at the record shops to hear the latest music from Britain and America, and could spend another hour browsing through the dark, enclosed fusty alleyways of Smithfield where almost anything could be bought or sold in the best second-hand shops in Ireland.

He could trace his fondness for Royal Avenue, High Street and Castle Place back to the times, regular occasions, when Catherine had arranged to meet him in town after primary school. Despite his Dexter belted tight at his waist by his teacher Miss Ryan, and his schoolbag slung over his shoulder to ensure he didn't leave it behind anywhere, he felt like a big boy boarding the trolley-bus, paying the conductor as if out of his own pocket, and travelling into Castle Street all by himself. There, he was met and taken by the hand around Sawyers, Robbs and the Co-op, and then treated to coffee and a pastry with real fresh cream. His Granny Stewart saw to Monica and Raymond on those days, before Jimmy and Sheila were born, and as they and the others grew up they too were feted in the same traditional way.

The other children slowly arrived downstairs.

"Would someone lift in the bread, please," said Catherine, and Raymond, wearing just the bottoms of his pyjamas, stepped out the door and lifted a loaf off the window sill.

"Ask your daddy does he want this in bed," she said to Jimmy, indicating breakfast.

"Daddy!"

"What? What is it?"

"Eh ... Eh ... Mammy? What am I shouting for?"

"Ask him . . . Never mind. Peter! Do you want your egg up there or are you coming down for it?"

"No. I'll be down."

She put out the breakfasts and sat Jimmy on the sofa to help dress him. He gently put his small forefinger at the corner of her eye without smarting it: "You've some sleep in it. Me get it. There! It's away now."

She thanked him with a kiss but he was lost in humming to himself the seven catchy bars of *Seventy-Seven Sunset Strip* which he had now almost mastered.

Peter came and sat at the small table, saw John switch on the radio and impatiently adjust the tuning dial.

"Will you wait until it warms up. You've only put it on. What are you after anyway?"

"Some music."

"Just leave it on the Home Service, I never get to hear the radio. How are you fixed for money?" he said, mellowing.

"Okay, why?"

"Maybe you could lend your oul lad a few bob?"

"Well, when will ya give it back to me?"

"Ah, I'm only kiddin'. Sure it's the holidays, isn't it," he said, making his meaning no clearer, but Catherine needed just the intonation of a few words to detect that he was in a good mood.

Before noon the house was clear of family. John had gone into town, Monica would return at her own pace, and Raymond, Jimmy and Sheila were playing about locally.

After his breakfast Peter finished reading the newspaper and had announced his plans for the day.

"If you don't mind, Cathleen, I think I'll nip over to my mother's to see how my da's back is. I promised her I'd fix the clothes line so I'll be about an hour and a half. Is there anything you want?"

"Maybe you could take some of the kids with you. They haven't seen your mammy or daddy either in about a fortnight."

"Okay, that's okay. I'll ask them but they probably won't want to go."

The children were too anxious to get out into the streets with their own kind so Peter left on his own.

Catherine began scrubbing the hall tiles and then the front of the house including a good portion of the neighbours' footpaths on either side. She enjoyed the early afternoon sun. Passing neighbours bid her the time of day and some stopped to gossip.

Everyone thought that thirty-eight-year-old Mrs O'Neill was a very pleasant and friendly woman who ridiculed no one. She would, patiently, take nonsense from some of the nuisances and nosey-parkers outside shops or at their front doors. In short, she was a good listener and her only comments would be judicious and supportive. In the course of hearing really private matters from a wife worried about her husband's behaviour she would act as a mediator, gently hinting, disingenuously, that she had been through a similar experience for which there turned out to be a perfectly reasonable or innocent explanation.

She was resting on the staff of her tough scrubbing brush, waiting on Mrs Clark, an active middle-aged woman, who was clearly in a bubbly mood: "Suppose you heard!"

"Heard what?"

"I won one hundred pounds at Bingo last night up in the Holy Child School. I was sweatin' on number nine for ages and I could hardly shout when it was called."

"Good for you."

"You should come out with us. You'd enjoy yourself."

"Ah, you know me, I'm a homer . . . Hello Peggy, how's the wee lad? I heard he needed four stitches."

Peggy Carson came over and joined them.

"God, I was up to a hundred. You know when somebody tells you, you think the worst. He's running around now, showing off to his mates. It's me that's got the worry. Here, did you see the polis out at Conlon's ..."

"When?"

"Two peelers on foot. I couldn't help seeing them."

"What's that about, sure they're not in any trouble are they?"

"Well, I was talkin' to Rosie," said Peggy. "And she goes in and out of Conlon's. Says I, 'I saw two peelers at Eileen's door.' Says she, 'Sure, wasn't I there in the house when they came to the door and didn't Tommy near fall off the chair, he didn't know what to say.' Says she, 'After they left he came in and said that the RUC had received a complaint about their Seamus playing handball and was warning them to keep him under control.' Says I to Rosie, 'That's not what I heard.' Says I, 'I heard he sent a letter to the RUC lookin' to join and they were out to interview him.' I wouldn't be a bit surprised either 'cause an uncle on his mother's side was an oul peeler.

"Here, did any of you know Tommy Conlon's brother, Martin? Well, he's back from England."

"His wife's looking better," said Catherine. "She used to look awful failed. It must be ten years since I saw her, a wee girl from Lisburn, isn't that right?"

"Lookin' better! No wonder! That's not his real wife. That's his fancy woman! His natural wife still lives in England. The oul blirt left her ..."

"God save us! That's awful," said Mrs Clark.

"Now, you never know," said Catherine.

"I hear you won money last night," said Peggy.

"News travels fast."

"How much did you tell him you won?"

"All of it, of course."

"Well, my mother always taught me, never let a man know how much money you have in your purse. Keep two purses, one always empty. Do you know it's Frank's anniversary this coming Friday. He'll be dead four years, if God spares him."

"Gee, you wouldn't think it was four years. He was a good man."

"One of the best," she said.

Mrs Clark shifted her weight onto her right leg at Peggy's hypocrisy and changed the subject.

"The Murrays are leavin', did you know?"

"No, where are they going? Up the road?"

"A wee bit further than that," said Mrs Clark. "They're headin' to England, though I heard they were trying to get into Australia."

"They'll be no great loss," said Peggy. "She's always out shouting at the kids or tellin' him to go back to his mother's, throwing suitcases out the window and then the next minute they're walkin' up the street, arm and arm, like Romeo and Juliet, big smiles on their faces. It's a wonder they've any cases left to pack."

"Ach, now. She's a nice wee woman, she just suffers from her nerves, that's all," said Catherine.

"I wouldn't live in England, you know. What with all that killin' and sexual attacks. Every week some woman is strangled with her own nylons. It's gettin' as bad as America," said Peggy.

"I know, isn't it awful," said Catherine. "There's that wee girl last month, just outside Manchester, sixteen years of age, left home to go to a local dance and never arrived. She hasn't been found since."

"Well," said Mrs Clark, "I'm sure you're busy Catherine" – she shot a look at Peggy – "so I'll leave you to get on with it. I'll see you."

"Cheerio now."

Peggy also said she must go and then said: "I believe she suffers from her varicose veins. I hope I'm not gettin' them. Must go and get myself a cup a tea and sit down for a while. Here, before I go, what do you think of them?" She showed off a new pair of brown shoes. "Got them in Sandy Row. I'll not tell you the price but they were a real bargain. Toodleloo."

Catherine lifted her handbag and Peter went out to the yard to use the toilet. She looked into John and Raymond and told John not to be reading too long as it would be sore on his eyes. Peter then came up and told him to put the light out as it was late. John protested and felt like rising up against his father when he stepped into the room and switched off the lamp.

I can't take much more of this, thought John.

"Daddy, it's only one o'clock!" and he switched back on the lamp in what almost amounted to a challenge. His father relented but was surprisingly agitated as he shut all the doors.

"You're in the wrong and you'll have to lay off him, Peter. I don't know what's getting into you."

"I know, I know, I just can't help it. I don't think I'm ready for old age," he said, turning to her with a half-smile.

"For God's sake, catch yourself on, granda. You're forty-three. Maybe you're right! I'll have to get myself somebody younger!"

They smiled at each other and turned out the light.

Catherine was warm and kicked off the sheet into the middle. It must have been half an hour before the thoughts in her mind began losing the constraints of consciousness and became slipping images. Each time she turned over brought her back from the border of shallow sleep until she eventually crossed the line and ended another day. Suddenly Peter said something and his words fell like stones from the sky breaking the peaceful silence, striking the skin of her mind, not quite penetrating, but disturbing her. He repeated himself and she awoke cross: "I was sleeping and you woke me."

"Well, I didn't know. Your head's only hit the pilla'."

Her temper though quickly subsided.

"Do you think is he asleep?"

"I heard him switch his light out a while ago," she said.

Peter looked but could see no bright strip at the door saddle in John's room and he closed their door.

"That's nice perfume you're wearin'."

"Aye, I'm sure it is. It's the lard from the frying pan you smell." It was only face cream.

"You really know how to turn a man off!"

She rolled over to him and he gently stroked her hair. She warmed to his affection and kissed him on the lips, the wee lad she had known for twenty years and been married to for seventeen. No matter the difficulties they had, the rows, the disappointments (and there had been many, early in the marriage), nothing could shake the faithfulness between them. Marriage was sacred, a sacrament bestowed from on-high. She may have preferred a more romantic man. She certainly would have liked a more prosperous life. But she got on with things and made do, which was what her mother had encouraged her to do.

So down the years she had grown closer and closer to Peter in affection and had invested everything in the miracle of their children, her beautiful family. To bring them into the world, to see them grow up, strong and healthy, well-fed, good-mannered, to witness their personalities emerge, was an immensely emotional, and sometimes spiritual experience. The process of life never failed to enthral her. She prayed upon waking every morning. She just couldn't imagine what she would do without her religion and faith nor how any person could say they didn't believe in God. To her it was impossible not to believe in God and Jesus. God was the explanation for everything. She was certainly too humble to allow her faith be shaken by the challenges to God's universal goodness from the phenomena of wickedness and evil, natural disasters and poverty, deprivation, famine, poor children the ages of her own starving to death in Africa and India. But all these imponderables only added to the mystery of life, made her grateful that they had been spared such calamities, and placed a duty on everyone to pray for God's intercession for such poor people.

She was a devoted Catholic and she derived from her religion an inexplicable satisfaction and contentment. On such occasions as the Easter ceremonies or Christmas midnight Mass or at the Retreats, the large number of people all in communion with God filled her with pride. But she also loved to be in the chapel alone in the presence of the Eucharist with only the flickering candles. It was at these times that she felt what she could only describe as a form of melancholia. It was a feeling not really of loneliness and certainly not of dejection but one of enhanced communication with her soul, even though there were no answers to the bewildering questions posed beyond the chapel gates.

So she got on with life, learnt a little every day about human relations and believed thoroughly in the idea that all the good you gave out would one day, and maybe not even in this life, be returned in kind. There was nothing to lose by being nice, by being patient, considerate and helpful.

"Are we okay?" Peter asked as he ran his hand up and down her arm, soothingly.

"'Yes, I know my days. We're okay."

"That's good," he said. "That's good."

From mid-August mothers spoke ominously more often about school and the need for new clothes. Days, which to the children in early July lasted forever, were in the week just before the start of September startlingly shorter and shorter until the last weekend was gulped up by some mean monster which, on one dark leaden night, even put a bitter nip in the air.

Suddenly, the lollipop men were back.

From half-eight until just past nine o'clock the footpaths were bulging with little, and larger, brains (on feet shod in new shoes) – none of which had volunteered for scholarship. The younger ones would have been quite piqued to have learned that their mothers, who walked them to the very classroom door because it seemed they couldn't bear to be separated from their babies, actually were glad they were at school again and that a routine had at long last returned.

And with such a routine the days quickly turned into weeks.

"I see in the paper that the gas lamps are to go."

"Where's that? I didn't see that," said Catherine, standing at the kitchen door in her apron.

"Right here. We're getting electric lamps." Peter handed her the paper.

"Does that mean I'll have nowhere to swing," piped in Jimmy.

"No, it doesn't. Just you get on with doing your homework," said his father. "And never you mind."

"Mammy, he's stole my rubber," complained Sheila.

"Naw, I didn't. That's mine!"

Catherine looked at the rubber.

"That is Jimmy's. Where's yours?"

"I can't find it."

"Well I'm fed up buying you rubbers. You can do without. Jimmy lend her yours. Move out of the way so I can put a shovel of coal on."

The two youngest children, lying on the mat, pushed aside their homework books to make a path to the fireplace. Their father was engrossed in the newspaper, his shoes by his side, twiddling his toes, waiting on his stew.

"Where's John?" he asked.

"He's not home yet"

"Where's Monica?"

"I don't know where she is. She's got Domestic Science, but should've been in before this."

"Where's Raymond?"

"Are you quite finished your roll call! You might have put on some coal. I'm stuck out here making your grub and all you can do is sit there with your feet up!"

Raymond's footsteps could be heard on the stairs and he came into the living room.

"Where were you?"

"I was upstairs, where did you think I was?"

"Don't give me cheek."

"Well, I was upstairs doing my homework."

"That's okay, why didn't you just say that."

"I bloody well don't know what's wrong with you today. You're like a beaten bear and you're driving me and the kids mad," said Catherine as she placed his plate of stew onto the table.

"Thanking you," he said, sheepishly. What was wrong with Peter was that he was being laid off at work. The builder he worked for had ran into financial trouble and was cutting back. Although employment was seasonal, he still thought he would have work indoors until February. Now, Christmas was only nine weeks off and he hated the prospect of not being able to hand Catherine the money to see to presents and clothes. Furthermore, he had placed his last five shillings on a race in a wild flutter and that too he had lost. Tomorrow he would have to ask Catherine for the bus fare to work and she would ask questions. He had tried, unsuccessfully, to disguise his mood.

He scattered a whorl of brown sauce over his dinner, dipping his bread and butter into the mince and carrots. His second eldest child, Monica, arrived home.

"Hiya daddy, Hiya mammy," she said. She went out to the kitchen where her mother exchanged sign language about the state of play.

"The heat in here would kill you," said Monica.

"Here, before you get changed, give him his tea."

"And this is for you," she said, handing her mother a dish of apple crumble pie she had made in school.

"Oh, very nice! He'll think this is the Grand Central Hotel," laughed Catherine.

They had their dinner: Jimmy and Sheila at the table where they could cause the least damage; Raymond and Monica on their knees on the settee; and, lastly, Catherine, at the table when Jimmy finished. The dishes were cleared away, Catherine washing, Monica drying. Peter told the kids to keep quiet during the news but even before it was over he draped his head with the paper and fell asleep in the chair, with Sheila giggling at his snoring behind the vibrating pages.

Jimmy stole over to his father's chair in the corner and urged on by his sister he lifted the paper. His presence awoke his father.

"For God's sake!"

"She told me to see if you were asleep."

"I didn't."

"Yes, you did."

"Have youse got your homework finished? No. Well, then do it."

"Daddy, help me do me spellings."

"Come here and I'll do them," said Catherine, sitting down.

"No, it's okay. I'll do them." Peter took the book and asked him questions. He shuffled his feet, scratched his hair, put his finger in his mouth and rolled his eyes at the inscrutability of the letters B and D.

Catherine was going through Jimmy's schoolbag. He had several books – a blue jotter, an exercise book for homework, both of which were stamped Northern Educational Company, and a stapled Catechism backed in brown paper and covered in RAF logos. At the bottom of the small canvas bag was a pencil which was sharpened at both ends and a haemorrhaging blue biro. Outnumbering his academic possessions were three folded, empty, cellophane Smiths crisps bags, a marble, two whelk shells, a wooden ruler with John's name on it and which was chipped so badly as to be of no academic use (it was actually used as a catapult), and a rich mixture of serrated pencil shavings and several hundred crumbs. Catherine could appreciate why Jimmy was the only person who felt really safe putting his hand into the bag.

She removed the homework book and shook her head.

"Have a look at that," she said. "Read what the teacher has written at the bottom."

Peter opened the page at the sums. Jimmy had six sums out of twenty marked correct but underneath the teacher had written with his red pen: "This has been copied from Joe Montgomery!"

Peter had to smile.

"I suppose wee Joe had the same fourteen wrong with the same wrong answers?"

His son put on a bashful look.

"If you're gonna cog at least make sure you're cogging off someone good."

"Peter!" protested Catherine. "Don't be teaching him to cheat."

"Naw, Daddy. It was Joe Montgomery who copied off me. I got those six right meself," he said proudly.

The front door, swollen by autumn dampness, rubbed at the jamb and after a few seconds John entered the living room, closing the hall door behind him.

"And what kept you?" said his father, not growling but expressing mere curiosity.

"Ach, I walked it up. Didn't fancy the queues in Wellington Place, and Castle Street was just as bad."

"Where's my grub? In the oven? It's okay, I'll get it."

"No, go and wash your hands and face," said Catherine, handing Jimmy his book back. I'll put it out."

John ate his dinner in silence and felt fairly tired. Through a friend of his father he had found work in early September and had started in a mechanical engineering firm on the Ormeau Road, close to the city centre. The boss told him he was now an apprentice but John wasn't totally convinced, even though he had recently begun to attend a technical college two nights a week. His work day began at 8.30 a.m. He filled the pot-bellied stove with coke and lit the fire, brushed the floors and then he rode a messenger-boy bicycle around the town to collect crankshafts, pistons, bearings or camshafts. The basket had been removed and replaced with a large box which added to the bike's instability. He cycled into most parts of Belfast but once had to go as far as Lisburn which was eight miles away. Some of the journeys were short: to the railway stations at Queens Quay, Great Victoria Street and York Road. His most routine journey was up to a garage on the Antrim Road.

That day he had had to make the journey three times, including two pick-ups in the Shankill Road. He was feeling fairly jaded and was convinced that at least one of the journeys was deliberately created for him by one of the older mechanics, Bronco McIvor, whose arms were covered in loyalist tattoos. He rarely spoke to John but when he did address him it was never by his Christian name. It was, "Go over to Simpsons'" or "Give-is a rag," or "Go and get milk". John soon became accustomed to the hostility and the resentment. The boss knew it was happening but said nothing as McIvor was too valuable a worker. John was also aware of a coolness in his boss towards him which he couldn't fathom because, after all, he didn't have to employ him, a Catholic, in a firm where the majority of the workers were Protestant. It was as if his boss couldn't come to terms with his own patronage.

When John had tried to discuss his frustration with his father, Peter began to lose his temper. He may not think he was learning anything but he was, Peter insisted. He was told to stick at it. "You have to have a trade," he said. "Otherwise you're going nowhere."

So John stuck at it though he hated it. As soon as he saw the red brick building with the grimy windows he would take a deep sigh and grit his teeth.

The floor in work was permanently covered with a dark slime of grease and oil which John attempted to keep clean. On the wall was an ancient electric clock whose glass was cracked. The hour hand slowly governed the day when McIvor wasn't ordering John about. Even when he brewed the tea for the engineer and the others there was no gratitude from him. McIvor would go off and sit with two or three workers of his own persuasion whilst John ate his sandwiches either on his own or with his father's friend Patsy who, although a Catholic, seemed to get on fine with the others.

"Old Bronco's not that bad, once you get to know him," said Patsy. John rolled his eyes.

He could have shirked his work and taken his time in returning from a collection but he was too proud and saw himself in some imprecise role as a representative of his community, the nationalists. So, when he picked up a parcel he sped back to work, not to win favour but to show that he could do his job just as well as any man and to give no man an excuse to ridicule him. He kept the concrete floor saw-dusted and swept and made sure that there were always rags in stock and paraffin in the tub at the sink for washing hands. He scrubbed the toilet and removed a sludge which had lain for years in the four corners of the small closet. He regularly checked that cut newspapers were in supply from the cord nailed to the back of the ill-fitting door. He found two screws to right the door so that it shut flush and offered some privacy.

He made work tolerable but he still loved to see the minute hand strike 5.30 p.m. And he loved Friday afternoon when they finished at 4.45 p.m. The men went off drinking and he, with his overalls under his arm, headed for home up May Street and round past the City Hall to catch a trolley-bus. Inside his pocket was his wage packet, £3.12s.6d, which he gave unopened to his mother. She gave him back £1.2s. and when he rolled the two 10s notes in his pocket he felt on top of the world, even though next week's bus fares had to come out of it. Furthermore, he gave Monica and Raymond 6d each and

Jimmy and Sheila 3d each and rose in their estimation in the small hierarchy of adulthood.

John finished his dinner and squeezed on to the sofa beside Monica, who was engrossed in some homework, and Raymond who was watching television. His father lit up a pipe and thought about his financial problems.

There was a knock on the door which Catherine answered. One of John's older friends, Felix, was looking for him. He came into the hall and both boys sat on the stairs, clearly somewhat excited.

"I had to queue for ages," said Felix. "But I got them!"

They examined and re-examined the tickets for the Ritz Cinema. John was thrilled. His friend was prepared to accept the money in instalments. They cost 10s.6d each. When John came in and sat down his father asked him what Felix had wanted.

"We're gonna see The Beatles on 9 November! We've actually got tickets!"

"The Beatles, huh! In my day entertainers were real musicians, Beatles. What a name! How much is it costing you?"

John resented the question and ignored it, then something else distracted Peter's attention.

Catherine remembered that Raymond needed a shirt ironed for school, got up and went out to the kitchen. Jimmy was under the sofa with a toy car. The onset of dark nights, especially when the clocks were put back, meant he couldn't go out on the street after half-five. Sheila, who sat to the side of their black and white television, asked her teddy bear what it was getting for Christmas and heard it reply in a squeaky voice that it was getting a small doll dressed in a white wedding dress.

Peter looked at the flames being swallowed by the black chimney. He mustered himself, pulled on his shoes and went past Catherine and out to the yard for a shovel of slack. Pins and needles of frost stung his nose. He worked quickly. Sitting by the fire again he used the poker to break up some coals which had fused together. The fine slack fell into the crevices, flared and sparkled for a few minutes then an even, yellow and orange glow took hold and radiated heat into O'Neills' small living room.

CHAPTER 3
DIVIS STREET

The winter nights had been lonely ones for Catherine. Peter had been the last one laid off work and the family had just about managed Christmas. He told her of his decision on Boxing Day and by the second day in January he was in his cousin's in Birmingham. By the end of his second week he was sending her home more money than he earned in Belfast with overtime. By the third week the homesickness which he had experienced on those other occasions when he had to go looking for work in England gave him a permanent headache. But until his luck changed he had no choice.

At the end of his third month away, his brother phoned to say that he had work for him. He was thrilled. Catherine was also thrilled when he telephoned her to a neighbour's house with the news for she had missed him.

She met him coming off the boat and threw her arms around him.

"Hey now," he said. "You'd think I was coming back from the war!" Jimmy and Sheila had been kept off school for the occasion and they tugged at his coat. They took a taxi home.

"We're rich," said Jimmy to his sister.

He was loaded with suitcases, more full of presents than articles of his own clothing. Raymond and Monica came home at lunch-time to see their father. When John came in from work his father stood up from his chair and put out his hand. It was the first time that John had ever made a serious handshake and he was surprised that it felt so natural an expression of goodwill. They then hugged and John was again surprised by his father's affection and the fact that his eyes seemed to well-up. John thought about how long it had been since he had touched his father. Not since he was a child when he had sat on his knee, or kissed him goodnight had he been really close to him. He still kissed his mother but the sensation he had just experienced, shaking his father's hand, was also warm and natural and intimate.

That night, friends and relatives came over to celebrate the homecoming. Jimmy collected the currency of tin tops from bottles of Wee Willie, Double Diamond, Monk, Blue Bass, Carlings and Guinness for use in exchanges in the street.

Peter had a lie-in the next morning from Catherine still had to get everybody ready.

"Monica, make sure that child is well hopped up," she said, tucking the scarf in around Jimmy's neck and buttoning up his duffle coat.

"Comb his hair, it's sticking up."

"It is combed."

"Then pat it down."

Monica licked the palm of her hand and patted Jimmy's spiked hair as he squirmed and resisted.

"Gonna be sick! Gonna be sick!" he shouted.

"Don't be such a pockill!" said Catherine. "Stand still! Stand still!"

She gave Jimmy a note so that the teacher would release him early for a dental appointment and after she got them all out she went back to bed.

The afternoon sky was clear and a strong, cold wind was peppered with street dust which made Jimmy's eyes run.

Sheila asked him what it was like to get a tooth out.

"Ya think you're in bed. When you wake up it's bleedin'. And then you yap, 'cos it's very, very sore."

The next day Jimmy was sick at school and was sent home early. It was a Friday and when John came in Jimmy was lying on the sofa, a bucket on the floor, and gave John a weak smile.

"Me sick."

John gave him some pennies, then got washed and went to his bedroom to change. He heard Jimmy retching and then Jimmy shouted up: "I was sick there now again. Wasn't I mammy? Do you want to see it John?" he called out as if the world doubted him.

John came, sat beside him, leaned over and felt his head which was cold but damp.

"Me like that smell. What is it?"

John winked at him. He was wearing some aftershave that his father had brought back as a present.

The winter nights had been lonely ones for John also. He and his friends, who had nowhere to go on week nights, stood at the corner, talking, arguing about Gaelic football, soccer, music, attempting to detain the girls who were out for walks because they too were lonely. To sit in the café cost money even though six or seven of them could occasionally push their luck and sit over a bottle of Coke with several straws.

Half of his friends had no difficulty 'getting off' and 'chatting up'. John was amazed that a snatch of conversation with a passing group of girls could result in immediate success for some, while everyone else stayed 'single'.

John had poor luck, was shy, never seemed to strike the right note. So he now decided to pay more attention to his dress and spruce himself up.

"Where you going?" asked Jimmy.

"To a dance," said John.

"Can you dance?"

"No."

"Then why are you going?"

John ruffled Jimmy's hair. "That's a very good question!"

At the dance John caught a glimpse of a girl whom he was sure he had seen before and been immediately attracted to. He thought it had been one Saturday. Two people, perhaps sisters because of similar looks, were in the queue in front of him waiting for a bus. The younger one turned around and after a long glance smiled at him. Because of the angle of the sun he hadn't even been sure she was looking at him, but there was no one behind him, and he was taken by surprise by the gesture which seemed full of promise. So, the following Saturday, at exactly the same time, he went back to the bus-stop, loitered for a while, hoping to see her, but was disappointed.

Now there she was, out on the floor, jiving like an expert, moving and turning, occasionally clapping her hands.

Angela nodded to him. He was very glad they had come to this particular dance. He smiled back. In between every two or three show band songs the Master of Ceremonies, Big Al, would take the microphone and make some inane remark which would send everyone laughing, regardless of its absurdity.

"Here, I fancy her," said Felix to John and Gerard, pointing to Angela. She heard him and replied: "Well, I don't fancy you!"

The two boys slapped him on the back of the head. John was relieved at this rejection but as the night wore on Gerard danced with Angela two or three times.

"I'm leaving her home! John, would you walk her mate Patricia up the road. Angela says there's no problem and that her mate really fancies you. Well?"

At dances there was about a half-hour before the end of the night when – for those who came with no firm arrangements – the wooing went into its last and serious phase. Usually, a girl had a fair idea, from who danced with her, who would be proposing to leave her home. Similarly, a boy knew from the responses he had received who were the girls most approachable. Negotiations could often be critical and misjudgements could be made which could lead to humiliation. Arrogant girls, with too high an appreciation of themselves, could find themselves *spinstered* if they got the arithmetic wrong on contending suitors.

The reason why offers were delayed and decisions postponed was quite simple: the possibility that someone better would become available. And so by a quarter of an hour before the end most pairing-off had been completed. Out of desperation some late offers were made en route to the cloakroom or in the street. And, of course, there were those who weren't asked and those who hadn't got the nerve to ask.

Patricia was attractive but her friend Angela was incomparable. There was only one word to describe her: she was beautiful. Her long, reddish-brown hair was striking as she had danced.

"Well?" asked Gerard. "Will you walk Patricia home?"

"Okay," he replied, but his main purpose was to find out more about Angela.

They bought two bags of chips from a vendor. Angela shared Gerard's and linked his arm. John and Patricia walked behind them, talking about work and school exams. When the couples split up the two young men arranged to meet back in twenty minutes. John was there first.

"How did you get on?" he asked

"Fine," he answered. "She told me she wants to see me again. She's a passionate little girl," he laughed. "How about her mate?"

John shook his head.

At least once a week John was in the company of Angela and Gerard. He was infatuated with her and was jealous. Felix said he didn't like her. John was hurt by this judgment but said nothing. As far as he was concerned she was an incredible girl. Full of life. Her confidence towered over theirs; she was articulate and intelligent and each time he saw her he saw yet another new quality. He found out which Mass she attended, found a pretext for being in that chapel, and then made sure they bumped into each other afterwards.

"Hello John, what has you over this way?"

"Doing a message for my da. It was simpler to go to Mass here. I think I'm going in your direction. Mind if I walk?"

"No, no, come ahead."

She lived in the same street as his Uncle Harry whose son Tony often called for Jimmy.

She seemed to enjoy their conversation and his tales about work. He was more interested in her views and wanted to know what she had been studying and did she think she would do well.

"And what are you plans?" she asked.

"What I'd really like to do is travel and see the world. Sometimes, living the way we do, we have a very narrow view of things. I'd like to see how other people live, how they cope with their problems."

"Are you talking about earning a fortune ... coming back rich?"

"No. Not at all!" he said. "Naturally, I would like to have money but I'm talking about broadening my horizons. In fact, I've put in for the Merchant Navy and have been waiting on a reply for some time. I've heard so much about the sea."

"What I would love," she said, "is to be famous or married to someone famous, or powerful, or wealthy."

"Ah, like Gerard!"

"Like, yehhhhh. I can't stand poverty. In fact, these streets sometimes drive me crazy, they are so dense and dirty. Look at the dogs, they're everywhere. At night there's cats fighting on our toilet roof."

"Would you not like to travel? See London, Paris or New York?" These three particular cities he mentioned as a concession to what he imagined was the notion of cosmopolitan life beyond Belfast.

"Wouldn't mind shopping there. Do you know any millionaires who would take me away?" she laughed. "Honestly, I'm not quite sure what I want but it has to be splendid and unique. I haven't got into tackling the problems of the world, the way you appear to have. Is it worth it? Who cares?"

"But if you don't have a view of the world," he argued, "the only thing you have a view of is yourself."

"That's correct!" she shouted into the summer sun. She said it so disarmingly that he also laughed.

"There's crowds gatherin' in Divis Street!" Gerard said to John as soon as he came to the door. His friend was agitated: "Get your coat! Felix's meeting us at the corner."

John grabbed his jacket and shouted to his mother that he was going up the road for a walk. Gerard had an older brother, Dominic, who had served three years in jail for IRA activities and who lived in the Divis area. He was Gerard's source of information. They met Felix and the three of them went at a brisk pace towards Percy Street. Until then none of them had any interest in the election. The election headquarters of Sinn Féin, the political organisation which had close links with the underground Irish Republican Army, the IRA, was in Divis Street at the bottom of the Falls. Fundamentalist preacher, Reverend Ian Paisley, had addressed a meeting of his followers in the Ulster Hall. He threatened to invade Divis Street if the Irish Tricolour was not removed from the window of the office.

In work that day John had had to listen to Bronco McIvor boasting that he would be marching onto the Falls with Paisley unless the government took action. But then came news that after a meeting with the Minister of Home Affairs Paisley had agreed to a rally at the City Hall instead. Nationalists suspected that some kind of a deal had been done. The Falls community had come under sectarian attacks many times in earlier decades.

The boys arrived in Divis Street at a quarter-past nine. The sky was dark but the weather was mild. A crowd of several hundred had gathered and were standing, mostly on the footpaths, close to the election headquarters. Some were eating fish and chips or standing around smoking and chatting. A large police contingent came on the scene, some in cars which pulled up close to the offices. The people made a passage for the senior officer and three others.

When the police discovered that the door had been locked two of them went to the boot of a car and got two crowbars. The crowd hissed and booed as the door was smashed in. The police seized the banned flag. Although the people were hostile no one took any action, except to shout abuse at the departing vehicles. News of the flag seizure spread rapidly and the numbers now swelled to about 500. A small section of the crowd then verbally abused those in the Sinn Féin office for "letting the police" take the flag.

"We want our flag! We want our flag!" they began shouting.

Over a loudspeaker an official appealed for calm but he was heckled. A man next to John jabbed the air with his finger and shouted: "We want our freedom!"

"We want our flag! We want our freedom!" the crowd chanted, their numbers spilling on to the road, emboldened and defiant. Further down the street the police had to redirect traffic.

"The seizure of the flag by the RUC was an abject surrender to mob law ... But let's not forget that behind Paisley, behind the Stormont government lies the hand of British imperialism," said the official.

Felix rolled his eyes in boredom. The government and what it did to them was tangible; they couldn't see British imperialism. But a cheer went up when it was announced that the Republican Election Directorate had issued an ultimatum to the police that unless the flag was returned by noon on Thursday it would be replaced. The crowd then sang the national anthem before dispersing.

At work on Tuesday Bronco was jubilant.

"Billy? Any of youse see that oul flag knockin' about! I've nothing to wipe my hands on!" Then he laughed loudly and most of the others smiled.

On Tuesday night Paisley held another rally outside the City Hall and demanded that those responsible for the display of the Irish flag be prosecuted. Crowds again gathered outside the election headquarters. John watched as dozens of police pushed people back on to the footpaths and made sure there was no repeat of the previous night's road blocking. John thought that the police were obsessed with even the most minor breach of the law. Keeping open the road had become an excuse: allegedly for the free movement of traffic when in actual fact it was to keep the people on their knees. Most of those when ordered obeyed the police. There was some pushing and shoving and a few bottles came flying from the back, smashing harmlessly in the middle of the road. One of the more senior RUC officers remained unflappable but a few younger ones became agitated and began making threats: "Hey you, I know your face. Move back!"

"What's your name?" said a young officer to an old man.

"Fuck off, you Orange bastard or I'll knock your teeth in," he said.

A sergeant overheard the exchange. He was familiar with the dynamics of such situations and ordered his junior down the row and appealed to people to take it easy. The road was successfully re-opened and much of the crowd felt cheated. Many of the teenagers had experienced police harassment when standing at corners and being ordered to move on or for playing handball or carrying a hurling stick on the way to the park.

As the tension rose Liam McMillen, the republican election candidate, got up with a bullhorn and read to the crowd a telegram he had sent to the leader of the British Labour Party.

"Armed police using crowbars smashed into Republican Headquarters, Belfast, without warning, seized Irish flag. Demand you clarify attitude to this violence against democracy."

The word went around the crowd that they should disperse and come back the following night.

John, Gerard, and Felix, headed down to the Spanish Rooms for some Scrumpy and to discuss politics and women. When John got home he was asked where he had been. He lied and said that he had been playing snooker.

On Wednesday night Felix went into town with a girlfriend. John and Gerard again went down to the election headquarters. It was the place to be.

"Not seeing Angela tonight, then?" John had asked as they walked down the Falls Road.

"Couldn't be annoyed," he said, but John got the impression from other statements that Angela had grown tired of him.

The air was full of excitement and expectation. The RUC had not handed back the flag.

Again there was a heavy police presence below the Sinn Féin offices and as the onlookers swelled in number they had to walk on the road, slowing down traffic. The last trolleybuses of the night picked up their final passengers in Castle Street. Opposite the election offices people began singing rebel songs. Police moved to prevent the singing and there was jostling. John realised that things were rapidly reaching a head.

"Come on," he said, "everybody's blocking the road!" The police appeared startled and withdrew. A bus approached the human road block but couldn't get through. There were altercations between some of the passengers who complained that they had to get up for work in the morning.

"It's well for you has jobs!" a man shouted.

Two tenders of reserve policemen were rushed to the scene to support the original contingent. Hundreds were now involved in the protest. Their mood was defiant but they were in good humour. By blocking the road they had challenged the authorities and achieved a victory. It was a notice to the government that it couldn't walk over people.

The police drew batons.

"Jesus Christ!"

"Run!"

Without restraint a large force of RUC men ran into people, batons flailing, kicking and punching. People fell on the ground and were trampled over. Young people stayed and fought them but the violence of the batons became too much. Flocks of bottles came flying through the night sky and some took their toll on the police. But then fresh police made a second baton charge and chased the demonstrators into the side streets where everything from bottles and stones, vegetables and tins of fruit looted from a shop were thrown at them.

John lost his friends in the confusion and took refuge in a street with about 50 or 60 people. Just as the first of those who retreated stopped and paused for breath, the police reached those at the back. Women were screaming. A policeman caught John by the back of the collar and crashed him into a doorway. He put up his arms to protect his head from the blows.

"Fenian scum!" shouted the policeman who hadn't realised he had outdistanced his colleagues. Gerard appeared and struck him over the head with a bottle. He staggered and both young men fled and made their way home. Gerard was full of nervous laughter and his conversation see-sawed between boasting of the incident – "Did you see him fall! Did you see him!" – to deep dread – "Oh God, John, you don't think I killed him, do you?"

On Thursday when Liam McMillen returned from handing in his nomination papers he and his supporters held a little ceremony which included the singing of the national anthem. Then, ceremoniously, the Tricolour was once again placed in the window. This time they barricaded the door.

Shortly after 2 p.m. a column of RUC men marched out of Hastings Street Barracks and up to the office. The police, carrying batons, brandishing revolvers in their holsters as the ultimate threat, ordered everyone off the street. The people were pushed and made move along. A tender appeared and drove up to the front door of the election headquarters. A number of RUC men tried to break down the door. They used a pick-axe and crowbars but failed to gain entry. They then smashed the large pane-glass window, stepped in and seized the Tricolour. Some women began struggling with the police. One girl was knocked to the ground.

"That's my sister, you bastard!" The young speaker was beaten over the head and then arrested. The flag confiscated, the police withdrew and marched back to their base. Gerard saw his brother Dominic in the crowd and introduced him to John. He was shorter than Gerard, thickset, in his mid-to-late-twenties, and there was absolutely no resemblance between the two brothers. The crowds quickly reassembled and demanded that the stolen flag be again replaced. They were angry and were demanding more leadership than they were getting from the republicans who were calling for restraint and for people to go home.

"What the hell is all this about?" shouted a Sinn Féin supporter who just wanted to get stuck into the RUC for previous humiliations.

"We don't want to get the blame for any trouble," said one of the election officials.

"No, I'll tell you what's wrong," said Dominic to Gerard and his friend. "It's all now about politics and fighting elections and running down the IRA because the border campaign was a major failure. Maybe it was a failure, but it wasn't a failure of the men I was in jail with, but a failure of strategy and of timing."

John was lost but listened intently.

"Things are quiet. Come on and we'll get a cuppa," said Dominic, inviting them over to his flat where he lived with his wife.

After teatime the crowds multiplied. Children were taken indoors and old people stayed at home. Several thousand now gathered across the width of Divis Street. Word reached them that around the corner police riot squads, tenders, water cannon and armoured cars were lining up.

Over the loudspeaker an appeal was made for people to go home. A shower of stones was thrown at the office in disgust.

Then, the police charged. People scattered in every direction. The young ones split up into gangs, raided public houses for bottles and barrels for barricades. They ran into side streets and began siphoning petrol out of whatever cars they could find.

John and Gerard fell in with a group of about twenty who were lifting up the cast-iron metal gratings and smashing them for ammunition. Demonstrators at nearby Albert Street jeered the police surrounding the election office.

Rioters charged the RUC cordon and the police had to retreat under the withering fire of stones and bricks. A bus was hijacked and set on fire at Northumberland Street. The rioters tried to lure the armoured vehicles off the main road, into their terrain, where they could escape into the rows of terraced housing. But the police weren't falling for it. Petrol bombers then moved up to the front of the road. John had thrown his jacket into someone's house. The street fighters were panting and sweating. Water cannon, further down the road, was being used on everyone, including innocent bystanders.

Armoured cars raced up Divis Street and into the Falls Road scattering the crowds. Occasionally the cars would drive slowly and in their wake would be a police riot squad which charged a safe distance into side streets and made arrests. With nobody directing the fighting the police had a fairly easy task breaking up the groups.

A big tank of a man ran over to the burning bus and drew from its undercarriage the bamboo pole used for connecting trolleys to the overhead booms.

"Follow me!" he shouted. "Quickly! Put the beer barrels across the road." John's gang did as they were told. "Get ready. As soon as I charge prepare to let them have it." The hare-brained scheme became clear to all. An armoured car turned the corner and accelerated to crash through the makeshift barricade. But its underside got caught up in barbed wire debris and as it tried to move into reverse the man charged at it with the pole. The pole and its billhook passed through the driver's slit, shuddered for a second and seemed to be swallowed up into the guts of the vehicle. The attacker pulled the pole backwards and forwards looking for heads to catch. The driver had been injured and there were screams from within as a shower of petrol bombs rained down. Suddenly the doors burst open and the steel-helmeted policemen ran down Divis Street pursued by a cheering crowd.

The abandoned vehicle burned with a fierce yellow glow, its tyres melted and exploded like muffled gunfire.

When John arrived home it was 1.30 in the morning. He had completely forgotten the time, and couldn't remember the house in which he had left his jacket. The lights were lit in the living room. His father jumped up when he heard the key turning in the lock.

"Where the hell have you been! Your mother's been worried sick. I've been out looking for you. You were in Divis Street, weren't you? Look at you! Covered in dirt. Think it's great fun, do you? Have you nothing to say for yourself? What have you to say to your mother? Eh?"

"Da, I'm old enough to look after myself. I'm not stupid. I wasn't arrested. And I wasn't hurt. But the cops started it. You saw that for yourself on Monday night and again today."

Catherine sat on the sofa, crying.

"Mammy, I'm sorry but they started it."

Catherine cried even more. Nothing could appease her. As the night had passed and news and rumours came in from neighbours she had pictured her son lying dead in the street. Her lips trembled. Peter went to her and held her tight. He pushed her hair back from her cheeks, wetted by small sheets of smudged tears.

"You should be ashamed of yourself," he said. "Don't you ever, I mean ever, do this to us again ... Come on love. Come on and I'll put you to bed."

John sat downstairs, fuming with this attempt to restrain him, his actions, his freedom. He had no doubt that there was going to be further trouble and he wanted to be in the thick of it. But to do that he was going to come into conflict with his family. To bow to their disapproval meant staying at home, doing nothing. Knitting jumpers, making cupcakes. He was becoming more furious by the minute.

In the past few days, whilst listening to discussions and arguments, he had learnt more about the history of his people than in all his years growing up. He thought about what partition had done to them, living under the same unionist government for fifty years. They had turned in on themselves, abandoned their own dream of freedom as something obsolete, as a liability. They embraced defeat. Tried to justify it. They would end up ennobling defeat, he thought. Then, whenever a person born free, stood up and dared say, "Let's fight!" the people would cower, would be more loyal to their submission, safe with the life they knew. Half-people.

This explained why they would rail against even a minor call to arms, why these vanquished people would oppose – some of them with paradoxical viciousness and energy – the minority who said, "Unless we fight, our spirits are dead."

These thoughts prowled through his mind. He was still sitting in the chair, biting his lip at the upcoming domestic crisis after Friday's dinner, when his father came downstairs. Peter's temper had cooled but he was still angry. He told John he was being used by people, his gullibility exploited.

"Da, would you catch yourself on? I'm over seventeen, I can see what's going on. Nobody's leading me astray."

"But you saw what it's doing to your mother. You've been in Divis Street, you've thrown your stones and we're glad, really glad to have you back safe with us. My parents – your granny and granda – have seen all of this before and it changes nothing. Please don't be breaking our hearts," he said, before going back to bed.

That night and the following day John felt under immense moral pressure. Fortunately, McIvor was not at work.

On his way home he decided that he would be out that night, regardless of the consequences. In the living room the atmosphere was strange. Everyone seemed to know that a clash was looming. The children hardly spoke and there wasn't the usual bickering between Sheila and Jimmy over the space they were occupying. John said hello to his father then his mother. Peter filled his pipe for his after dinner smoke. He had switched the television off so that the main story on the news – the riots – could be avoided.

Suddenly, there was a crash in the kitchen and Catherine screamed. The handle from a pot of boiling peas had caught in her sleeve, spilled and scalded her leg. The kids were crying; Peter and John were panicking.

"Quick! Phone an ambulance!" said Peter, as he put a cold wet cloth to her leg.

As Catherine was being seen to and they waited in the casualty department of the hospital, the first injured civilians from the rioting were arriving in large numbers.

The rioting had spread from Divis Street for almost a mile, only yards from the entrance to the hospital.

Catherine was kept in overnight. At home, John and Peter said little. Out on the Falls Road there were baton charges and scores of people were arrested. In Dublin there was a big demonstration outside the British embassy protesting against the actions of the police.

Saturday night was relatively quiet with just five arrests after a plainclothes detective was struck with a milk bottle. On Sunday thousands of people marched down the Falls to a Sinn Féin election meeting. John told his father that he was going to the march and Peter told him to do whatever he liked, that he didn't give a damn.

The Tricolour was carried at the front of the march and the police – clearly under new instructions – were so thin on the ground that their presence was token. Dominic was cynical and said that some sort of a quid pro quo must have been worked out. The flag was carried through the Falls, and the police backed off, but the flag was not replaced in the window of the election headquarters.

That same night, Ian Paisley addressed a packed Ulster Hall. He warned that Protestant leaders were showing weakness in the face of republican pressure and that, unless they stood firm, their "faith" would be in jeopardy.

CHAPTER 4
COURTSHIP

After the riots, normality returned. The republican candidates fared badly in the election as Bronco McIvor reminded John and all in his vicinity at every opportunity.

Months later, on Ash Wednesday, John arrived in work.

"You've a bit of dirt on your head, mate," said McIvor, and with his thumb quite forcefully smudged the ashes on John's forehead. John exploded and threw a punch which the older man thwarted before they went for each other. John was being pulverised before the other workers pulled them apart.

"Do that again, and I'll kill ya!" said Bronco. John ignored him but he was reprimanded and warned that if there were any similar incidents, any more disruption, he was out. He was almost past the point of caring.

At home there was still friction. That night he said that he was thinking of going to sea. Peter was immediately enthusiastic, singing the praises about the need to broaden one's horizons. Catherine couldn't believe what she was hearing. It would do him good, said Peter. And besides, they couldn't hang on to him for ever: he had to leave the nest at some stage.

A few days later John went down to the Shipping Federation Offices – the pool – to check for news. He had been expecting word almost immediately to go on a six-week course to Sharpness in England where novices were trained. But there was a long delay and he began to despair.

Some weeks later he met seamen from his area who had just come off the Heysham ferry and were about to go on a spree.

"Well Phil, how's it going? I'm still waiting."

"Listen! Listen. You're the very man I'm looking for." He told John to get around to the boat and speak to the chief steward if he was interested in getting a start as a galley-boy.

"Tell him you're the fella I mentioned." John appeared apprehensive: a stranger suddenly showing up.

"Okay, okay, wait and I'll go around with you."

Having spoken not to the chief but to the second steward John was excited. If he wanted to work he had to start there and then. There was no time for indecision. Work in the kitchen would start in a half-hour and the boat was sailing at 9.30 p.m.

John said to Phil: "Jesus I'm dying to go but I haven't been home yet ... Would you tell my ma and da what happened?"

"No problem. Leave it with me."

"Do I not need anything? Passport? Clothes?"

"No, you'll have no trouble. It's only for a few days."

The boat, the Duke of Lancaster, was packed with passengers. John worked in the kitchens which serviced the second class cafeteria. Fish and chips, bacon and eggs, and sausage and chips were the most common orders. He worked at a huge stainless steel sink washing greasy plates which mounted beside him. Knives, forks and spoons lay over a foot deep in the hot, steaming water which had a rancid smell no matter how much soap he put in. Between this and the swell of the sea he felt queasy and had to run to the toilet to be sick. The cafeteria closed shortly after midnight and it was about two o'clock before John, totally exhausted though still exhilarated, got to bed in a small hot cabin. It was so tiny that there was no room for anything but two doublebunks and one tall locker. The churning of the propeller and the vibrations from the engines' pistons made the berth hum. He closed his eyes for what seemed to be about ten minutes when a cabin mate shook him and told him to get back up again. He had been asleep for three hours and it was time to go and prepare the tables for breakfast: the boat was due to dock in Heysham at 6 a.m.

By ten thirty John had finished cleaning the dishes, washing the dining-room tables and scrubbing the floor. His stomach was raw from the pain of retching and he couldn't keep food down.

He had a shower and planned to rest before they made the return. However, he was called again to the cafeteria to help lay out the tables for the crew's lunch and spent another hour cleaning up dishes. At five thirty he then had to help make the tea and sandwiches for the crew again. Trains from London, the Midlands and the North of England began arriving from ten for the midnight sailing and the cafeteria had to be again prepared for those passengers. It was the same routine except he worked until four in the morning and got two hours sleep before he was up again.

It was about eleven on Sunday morning before he, and the majority of the crew who were from Belfast, disembarked. He was exhausted, rid of the romantic notion he had of sailing. He decided he could cope with working alongside McIvor. Things would settle down, would improve, and, actually, relations had started to improve since their fight.

When he arrived home there was uproar. Phil had been so drunk that he only sent word to Peter on Saturday night about the sailing.

"First, you encourage me to go on the boats. Then when I do, there's a bloody row. I can't win!"

"Don't you use that language in front of your mother!"

"For God's sake," said Catherine. "Settle down, you two. It's okay, we were just worried when you disappeared off the planet."

"I was gone one night before you knew where I was."

"Anyway. How was it?"

"It was brilliant," he said, pig-headedly. "Can't wait to go back."

On Monday he went into work but planned to leave without making an announcement. It was ironic that at lunchtime, McIvor offered John a cigarette and called him "John" for the first time.

At sea he was taught conduct and how to dress properly. Personal hygiene was emphasised. He was shown how on a cruise a table must be properly set, how forks and spoons were to be used when serving vegetables, from what side to serve, how to pour gravy, when to remove plates, how to 'work' with the chefs who were like supreme beings.

"Changing your shoes twice a day," said the head waiter, "is a good way of looking after your feet."

Back home he registered at the Pool and then signed on at the Social Security Office for unemployment benefit. Before long he was working on The Buffalo, a container boat, which sailed between Belfast and Preston. A few months later he was on a passenger ship between Southampton and New York.

It was at the end of his first trip from New York when arriving home on a Saturday morning that he bumped into Angela. She was looking at a cosmetic display in a city centre shop. He hadn't seen her in months – since her split with Gerard.

"Booh!"

She jumped. "Well, look who it is! And how are you keeping? I see you've a bit of a tan."

"Yes! High life on the high seas."

They looked in each other's eyes, the gap in the conversation causing a little awkwardness. John came straight to the point.

"Would you like to go out tonight?"

"Sttt, I can't. I've something else on."

"Fair enough, but remember. All you have to do is wink at me and I'll come running. Just like that ..."

He winked at her devilishly, uncharacteristically.

"Okay! What about tomorrow afternoon?"

"Great!" he said. "Hold on. Wait a minute." He searched his bag and gave her a small bottle of perfume, *Youth Dew* by Estee Lauder.

"Here's a little present for you. A reminder of this day."

"Gee, I couldn't. You got that for someone special."

"No, I've another bottle," he lied. She accepted it and they arranged their meeting. John felt a twinge of conscience. He had *another* present for his mother with which she would just have easily been pleased but he knew the only way he would have peace of mind was by getting another bottle. He was taken aback at its price but bought it.

He had some butterflies in his stomach when he recognised her approaching, her sure step, that broad smile on her lips.

"How do I look?" was the first thing she said.

"Do you want me to really tell you?" he said, softly. They went for a long walk. They held hands as they strolled along the Lisburn Road, she picking some flowers from the gardens. He made her laugh.

"You some sort of botanist?"

He felt happy and proud. Later, at the dark end of her street she snuggled up to John. She gave him a wider, a longer kiss before leaving and he was in heaven.

Angela gently coaxed Mary Ann over towards the wall. The little girl resisted in her sleep the cool side of the bed. Angela carefully climbed under the blankets. She heard Mary, her mother, ask Frank how long he would be, she was going on up, and he said he would join her shortly.

Angela lay still. She was tired but couldn't rest. She thought about her afternoon in John's company. She used to think him shy but he seemed shy no longer. She fell asleep but then awoke, not knowing the time.

She rose to go quietly downstairs to the toilet. As she made the turn in the stairs, a few steps from the bottom, she discovered her father at the mirror above the mantelpiece manoeuvring a hand mirror from all angles to examine his receding hairline. He almost dropped the mirror when he heard her and threw a newspaper over it as she came into the living room.

He was a little flustered and she was ashamed for creeping up on him. On her way back to bed she kissed him goodnight. Despite her guilt she spied on him again. He climbed onto the hearth again and rolled his forefinger around his bald patch, perhaps convincing himself that it was still quite small, hardly noticeable, about the size of an egg cup, and not as big as people actually saw it, about the circumference of a soup bowl.

"So who are you going out with now?" asked Angela's Aunty Maureen who sat on a tall stool sipping coffee.

"A strange sort of a fella, Maureen. I used to think he couldn't open his mouth. Very quiet. But he's grown up now," she laughed. "Good looking and kind. Maybe a bit too serious."

Maureen smiled. Only nine years separated niece and aunt but they were almost confidantes. Sometimes they were even mistaken for sisters. They read the same magazines, tried on the same clothes and went shopping in town together every other Saturday. Angela reminded Maureen of her younger self but she was careful not to undermine Mary either. Everyone needs a shoulder and an ear.

Angela picked up Gary, wiped his mouth and grabbed the flab of his belly, squeezing him and making him gurgle and laugh.

"Anja, Anja!" he shouted, begging her to stop but enjoying it.

Maureen was prettier than Mary, and Angela supposed that she took some of her looks after her: the light freckles, the full lips, the proud figure.

Angela's mother saw the real likeness, the kinship in spirit. Maureen had been rebellious and shameless. But over time she settled down, so there was no reason why Angela wouldn't do the same, she was just going through a phase.

Angela would listen to Maureen talk about her past which sounded so exciting and full of promise, yet couldn't fathom her marriage to portly, placid Desmond whose favourite topic of conversation was insurance. She dressed in short and flashy skirts with bright coloured tops; he wore conservative blue suits and combed back his hair with Brylcreem.

But the first thing he always did upon arriving home was go to Maureen, kiss her and ask her how was her day, before taking off his coat and hanging up the car keys. In the evenings they watched television on the sofa, he in his slippers, on his lap she stretched her legs and he massaged her feet, then he routinely smoked one small cigar. The sameness, the tediousness of this domestic bliss actually terrified Angela. They had a full drinks cabinet but apart from special occasions would only take a drink as a night cap once or twice a week. Yet Maureen not only seemed but was unquestionably happy and content. Desmond would regularly bring her presents – usually a record of some popular music which he loathed but she loved. Every summer they had a proper fortnight's holiday outside of Ireland – not like most families who had to make do with a weekend in some town just up the coast.

When Angela called in to see Maureen, and the two disappeared into the kitchen, howls of laughter would erupt. Desmond would simply shake his head and smile. There was nothing for him to learn because he knew his wife's past and what Angela did was Angela's business.

"Do you see much of him?" asked Maureen.

"Actually, he's been away at sea quite a bit."

"You know what they say about sailors – they've port in every girl!"

"Possibly you're right, but I doubt it. He's a mate of Gerry's and when we first met he left Patricia home. All he did was ask about me. So she said. It's a strange feeling for me to be thinking about the one person."

"Sounds as if you're smitten, if you ask me. You should lure him here some night in July when we're away. Pop open a bottle of wine, stick on one of my black lace negligees and scare the bloody pants off him!"

"Hey! You're supposed to be keeping an eye on me, not encouraging me."

"When it happens just make sure it's pleasant and not in the back of a plumber's van up some entry lying on top of a carry-out."

"You speaking from experience! How do you know it hasn't happened already? Eh?"

"Because it hasn't. You've still got that yet-to-turn-the-page look in your eyes and besides I'd be the third person to know."

"That's right!"

Angela and John went to the pictures and went dancing together when he was on leave, though he was bad on the floor and usually just watched from the side-lines. Sometimes they called up to Maureen's and spent the evening there. On occasion Maureen and Desmond would go out and leave them babysitting. John was back home in July when the Orangemen had their traditional parades and on the thirteenth he took her on an Isle of Man excursion. They stood on the deck, kissing passionately and she allowed him to explore a little.

Leaving her home a few nights later they kissed at her corner in the shadows for almost an hour. He laughed at her virtuous stance. He raised her chin.

"Do you know what Mark Twain said?"

"No, what did he say?"

"He said, 'Be good and you will be lonesome!'"

She smiled, kissed him on the cheek and ran up to her door before turning and waving.

John was going to sea the following week, early August, but had yet to tell Angela. He walked to her house. Jimmy asked could he tag along to visit their cousin Tony. Mr and Mrs McCann knew that John was dating their daughter but generally when he called she was ready to go: she didn't want him subjected to a litany of questions.

Tony wasn't at home so Angela suggested they bring Jimmy into town with them where she was to pay some bills for Maureen. They went to the Wimpy Bar for hamburgers and chips. Jimmy sat on the seat feeling very important. When Angela opened a packet of cigarettes the 10-year-old said, "No, thanks. I used to smoke, didn't I, John? But I stopped about five or six weeks ago. I don't drink anymore either." He began giggling and Angela laughed.

"There's something your da could be doing with," said John to Angela, pointing to a man with an ill-fitted hairpiece.

"Jesus," she whispered. "It's like a golden hamster."

"No, it's not. It's a hair helmet!" shouted Jimmy, causing customers to look around. Afterwards, they took Jimmy to the Model Shop and Angela bought him a balsa wood aeroplane. When Jimmy went home John and Angela went up to Coolnasilla to bring in the milk that Maureen had forgotten to cancel.

John sat on the settee. The living room was airy and bright with large windows.

"Do you want a cup of tea? There's plenty of milk," said Angela, indicating the bottles she held in either hand.

"No, thanks." He stood up and walked over to a dining table where fruit was mounted on a silver dish shaped like a tropical leaf. "I'll have one of these, okay?"

"Go ahead. Wait and I'll get you a knife."

He followed her to the kitchen which, again, was very modern, spacious and flooded in light. When he split the orange, the juice immediately shot in a line across the bread board leaving a few dribbles at the tip of the knife. He popped the segments into his mouth and slowly chewed one after the other, the citrus giving off a powerful fragrance and numbing his lips.

"Can I put on the radio?"

"Aye, if you want. She's got some new records."

"Music is always in the background for our generation, don't you think?"

"I hadn't thought about it."

They went through the LPs, commenting on this and that.

"Here's one from that film."

She put on *Theme From A Summer Place* by Percy Faith, took off her shoes and closed her eyes, entering another world.

"I don't think I saw that film," he said, as he browsed the collection. "*Beatles for Sale*! I saw them in the Ritz. They were brilliant. Can I put it on? Do you like them?"

"I prefer the Rolling Stones, but go ahead. I like Paul McCartney but not John Lennon."

She watched as he re-rolled and tucked in his fallen shirt sleeve. She watched him delicately remove the record from its sleeve. It seemed almost as if his movements were in slow motion. Atmospheric specks caught in a bar of sunlight splicing the room sparkled like stardust. She could see he was lost in his own small excitement about the record and she felt the pull of his delight. She dug her toes and curled them into the dense pile of the carpet. They began kissing but before long they were on the floor.

"I think this LP is absolutely brilliant!" he said, momentarily.

She smiled.

"Shush! I know what you're gonna say… You still prefer Mick Jagger."

"No. I was going to say that The Beatles are becoming my favourite group, if you must know!"

He whistled wistfully. There was no conversation, no embarrassment, they were lost in music, now and again looked into each other's eyes between kisses, smiled, sighed, occasionally suppressed laughter at how potentially foolish they might look to a fly on the wall. They grew courageous. They became full of conviction.

Oooh I need your love babe,
Guess you know it's true …
Hold me, love me,
I ain't got nothin' but love babe,
Eight days a week …

Hold me close and tell me how you feel,
Tell me love is real …

Let me hear you say,
The words I long to hear,
Darling when you're near…

Words of "Love You,"
Whispered soft and true,
Darling I love you …

Someday, you'll know,
I was the one,
But tomorrow may rain,
So, I'll follow the sun…

From her little toe with his forefinger he traced the seam of an imaginary nylon stocking, along the side of her ankle, up the calf of her leg. His heart was thumping as she allowed him to continue.

A giggle rang through the rings of her throat as John kissed and bit her neck. Her chin retreated in mock defence to her chest, like a snail into its shell, and he tickled her on the back so that she opened again but this time to his gentleness.

Angela felt strange, strange sensations. Though it was late afternoon and the sun filled the whole house she felt entranced. The tossing and turning had loosened her blouse at the waist and two buttons were undone. Within seconds he was playing with her flesh and feverishly removing her and his clothes.

After he rolled off her and they lay staring at the ceiling neither of them knew what to say, whether to explain or offer an opinion. It was as if they were puzzled, confused, worried, frightened, and desolate, in contrast to their fortitude minutes before, when they were the only two people alive, on top of the world, paradise below them.

It was she who broke the silence. She turned to him and laughed and her brightening had a relaxing effect on him and he smiled.

"Are you okay? I didn't hurt you, did I? I'm sorry."

"Why? What's happened? Have we done it yet?" she said and began laughing again at the pained look on his face. She now felt proud. Her first lover. She cuddled up close to him and he held her:

she staring across the width of the room, he at the ceiling. Their breathing became light and they dozed for about half an hour.

When he awoke she was poking her finger into his belly-button, screwed out some fluff, rolled it into a ball and flicked it away.

"Hey! That was mine."

He forced her down and pinned her arms with his knees in horse-play as he sat across her breasts, irrepressible laughter shaking his rib cage. It was all with a familiarity beyond imagination an hour earlier.

"Ready for round two!"

"Oh, I'm ready. But are you sure you are!" she said, getting the last word.

On those evenings, before Maureen and Desmond returned, John would call up to their house to see Angela. They would potter about like a married couple and on one occasion she cooked him a meal. Before he went back to sea they spent the warm nights going on long walks and having long talks. She had given up cigarettes at his encouragement. She was surprised at her frugality: normally she couldn't wait to spend a boyfriend's money and go on the town.

One night after leaving Maureen's they were kissing below the trees at the corner of Coolnasilla on the Glen Road. There had been an electrical fault and the entire area was in darkness. Above, the sky was teeming in points of colour and light.

"There's a shooting star ... make a wish," he said.

"Where? I didn't see it."

"Watch. You'll see more ... There!" And to where he pointed she saw the faint trail just disappear.

"Yes! Yes! I saw it. There's another one ... and another one!"

"Well, did you wish?"

"Of course, but I'm not allowed to tell you."

CHAPTER 5
DESTINATIONS

Over the next few months John was away on short trips between Belfast and England and on other occasions between Britain and Mediterranean ports. They stayed in touch by letter, every four or five days, she sending him postcards to the Seaman's Mission in whatever port his ship was docking. He could read into them references to their intimacy which no stranger could ever guess at. Although she still went out to an occasional dance she refused all offers of dates. She had passed her exams and had decided to stay on at school rather than take a course in commerce and typing.

When in Belfast John brought Angela to his home where she was made welcome after it was confirmed that her parents knew they were going out together. John played down in front of his mother how committed he and Angela were. To Catherine their relationship was respectable and she would have been shocked to have thought differently. Monica, who was now working, had her boyfriend call at the house. Jimmy would sit at the edge of the sofa admiring his big brother's girl. He had a crush on her and wanted to show her his books.

When Catherine went out to the kitchen to make tea Angela would follow and help with the sandwiches.

Catherine couldn't exactly place her finger on what it was she didn't like about the girl.

Angela sensed her unease and decided to visit less or for long.

John was upset.

"Your mother can't stand me! But it's okay."

"That's not true!" he said, wounded at the thought that the two women closest to him disliked each other.

In December the winter cruises to the Caribbean were beginning and John was anxious to get on one of the boats. He had 'earned' his seaman's book which brought benefits but also meant that he could only turn down one offer of a ship. The companies wanted seamen with commitment, and the committed were those on contract.

Angela could see he was reluctant to be away for too long but she also knew he wanted to explore the world beyond the greyness of Belfast. They bickered from time to time, over small matters. He always took her out for a meal before leaving but then would irritate her by comparing the blandness of the food to a great little restaurant in Lisbon or Ostend.

She missed him. She would sit down to write a letter to which she would add a few more pages each night. She would sprinkle the letter with *Youth Dew* and when he arrived in New York there would be a perfumed letter awaiting him.

In January John reported to the federation in London. He joined the crew on an oil tanker which set sail for the Persian Gulf from where it would draw aviation fuel to South Africa, back and forth for six months.

Most of his friends, acquaintances from Belfast or those with whom he had worked on previous trips, had signed up on other vessels. On his very first day he had a row with the second steward, Chris Hutchinson, an ill-mannered Londoner, about ten years older and several inches taller than him. As a pantry-boy John's responsibilities were very clear – taking the food from the galley to the officers' mess, serving the catering crew theirs and keeping the pantry spick and span. The second steward had to look after the cabins of the captain and chief officer, serve their meals and supervise the other caterers, including John.

They had hardly sailed out of London before Hutchinson called John.

"Paddy, this is your job here. You've to make my bed and clean my room."

"No, I don't," said John. "You do that yourself."

"I'm telling you. You do it."

"Well, I'm telling you I'm not. I'm not a skivvy for you or anybody else."

"You'll do as I tell you!" he said, spittle flying from his lips. John still refused. Throughout the following day he picked fault with John's work. At the end of every voyage each seaman was issued with a discharge in his book with a comment on his behaviour: VG – very good; DR – declined to report; VNC – voyage not completed. A DR was a black mark and made it extremely difficult to find future work.

After John had cleared away all the lunch dishes and scrubbed out the pantry Hutchinson deliberately arrived late with the captain's dishes. John ignored the plates intending to see to them at tea-time and went to his cabin. Later, the chief steward brought him before the captain who fined him two days' pay for disobeying an order. He did the extra work but told Hutchinson, "I'll see you when this is all over."

"Huh! I've heard all you Paddies talk like this before," the big man boasted.

One day when they had set sail from the Iranian port of Abadan John went up on deck to get some sun. The tanker was awesome, like a huge sewing machine churning out a silk fabric of blue waves in its wake, flecks of spume like white cotton stitching holding it all together. A cool breeze disguised the fierceness of the heat. John lay down and fell into a deep sleep and wasn't discovered for some hours by which time his back and shoulders were covered in blisters. He was sent to an American oil company's hospital onshore where he spent two days. There he met an Irish nurse from Belfast who wasn't long out in the Gulf and gave him details of the trouble back home.

There had been petrol bomb attacks on Catholic shops, homes and schools in Belfast. In April the government banned all trains travelling from the south of Ireland to the north to prevent republicans commemorating the fiftieth anniversary of the 1916 Easter Rising.

When John returned to the ship he was fined eight days pay for being absent from work whilst his 'self-inflicted injuries' were being attended to.

As they approached Cape Town alarm bells began ringing. Black smoke was belching from the skylights above the engine room which had gone on fire when a sudden swell overturned one of the oil spillage trays sending fuel into hot pipes. There was pandemonium on board and it took fireboats five hours to put out the flames. The following day they offloaded the fuel at the terminal but the damage the vessel suffered forced it to return to England six weeks early.

Most of the seamen had a cynical view of their union leaders. Their membership form authorised the shipping company to deduct their dues from their wages and pay the union direct. When a ship returned to home port the union man, carrying his brown briefcase, came on board. The first people he went to see were the captain and the chief steward to hear their version of any problems during the voyage. Only later would he ask the crew their side of the story. So cynical were the seamen that they reckoned that the briefcase was especially made for the two bottles of whiskey and the two cartons of cigarettes the captain invariably presented him with.

The boat docked at Teesside. John sought out the union representative. He smiled when he saw the briefcase but wasn't that dismayed. However, when he tried to complain about Hutchinson, the captain, the excessive discipline, his fines, the union man procrastinated. He said he would need to write off to headquarters in London: he would need a full statement from John which he would get the next day or perhaps the day after because he had to see to three ships. But John had already signed off the boat which meant he had no legal entitlement to remain on board. Most of the crew were breaking up and had gone home. To stay and make a statement he would have had to go to the Seaman's Mission or book into a hotel which would be expensive.

"Forget it!" said John, and the union man seemed quite pleased to have "sorted out" another labour dispute.

At the railway station John placed his luggage on board the train, which wasn't due to leave for another half-hour, and went into the bar to have a drink with those crewmen still left. Hutchinson sat in the company and was in great form, loud-mouthed, boasting about his sexual exploits in Durban. When he got up to go to the toilet John followed him. They stood at the urinal.

"Paddy, it was great knowing you. We didn't start out great but we became the best of friends. Put it there …" He stretched out his hand. John hit him so hard that when he fell his body slid along the floor for about a foot or two. He looked up. He was bewildered, angry and deflated.

"You'll think twice about messin' another Paddy about," John said and left for his train.

The man melted into a little boy once she caressed him and rested his head against her breasts. It was one of those moments when silence was music. Their bodies were covered in sweat.

"I could eat you!" he said.

"I know," she replied, with a trailing, tender emphasis on the last word.

At that they closed their eyes and gently swam into a shallow pool of sleep.

"Do you ever take a break?"

"What do you mean?"

"For God's sake! You go on and on and on. You couldn't enjoy America. When you wrote to me it was all about what they had done to the 'poor' Indians. Everywhere you go there's something wrong. I don't even know why you bother going away ... or coming back ..."

"What does that mean?" he said.

"It doesn't mean anything. Look, I'm sorry, I'm just uptight."

"I've been away too long."

"No, it's not that. Ach, I'll get over it," she said and kissed him.

Doubts opened up like deep holes appearing in the path before him. He felt depressed when she went home. Something was wrong.

John Scullion's funeral was relatively small given the circum-stances of his death. The police said he had been stabbed in a street fight. People said they had heard shots. Then a 17-year-old Catholic was shot dead and two friends wounded, coming out of a pub in the Protestant Shankill area. His funeral attracted large crowds. Scullion's family demanded that John's body be exhumed. The fresh post mortem showed that he had been shot. A Loyalist paramilitary group, the Ulster Volunteer Force, had carried out both killings.

John carefully planned his day with Angela. What was eating her, he thought, was uncertainty in their relationship. He was away too often and for too long. She had been honest and told him about being out to dances. How could he have been so naive as to expect her to sit in seven nights a week while he was seeing the world? But now everything would be okay.

It was a beautiful, sunny August Sunday and he had borrowed a car to take her for a drive through the Glens of Antrim. He was going to propose that they get engaged on her next birthday and that he get a job, any job in Belfast.

During the journey from Cargan village over the mountains, down past Glenariff Forest and down the steep, twisting road, he found it difficult to read her mood. Although initially quiet, Angela became lively as they drove, but turned up the radio so loudly he couldn't hear the replies to his questions.

Then she became distant and cool. She picked on some innocent remark he made about a couple they saw holding hands. She sounded cynical. He kept trying to find an opportunity to put his proposal.

They now sat in silence at the harbour facing the small seaside village of Waterfoot. In Cushendall, over a lunch which she did not eat, she told him it was over. Just like that.

"Listen John, there were times when it was good, really, really good. And there were times when it was not so good. Please, let it go. Let it be."

"But I don't understand. We were getting on really, really well. Is there somebody else? Tell me, is there?"

"You know there's not! But I need the break, I need to look at things more objectively, have some time off to consider things, which I can only do if I'm free ..."

The last word pierced him. Free? As if he would ever imprison her! Or curtail her!

"All I want to do is put the world at your feet."

"After you've seen it," she said, sharply.

"Do you want me to stay? Is that it?"

"No, do what you want. I'm not stopping you. And I wouldn't want to."

"Then, what did you mean?"

"Oh nothing. Just forget about it."

He thought about what she was saying. He went over every word they had spoken or not spoken. In their silence he retraced every inch of the journey before they reached here. Then he recalled their conversation and her moods the day before, the week before, what she had written in her letters. He remembered the expensive watch she had bought him for his birthday and the card she had hidden in his suitcase which simply said, "Thinking about last night!" Try as he might he was at a total loss to explain her behaviour. When they had made love he knew from her total commitment and involvement that it was *love* she was making. If she was unhappy she certainly gave him no indication, gave him no warning, no opportunity for him to mend his ways if he was to blame.

He must have done something wrong or hadn't pleased her and he was about to promise to do this or that but his pride got the better of him.

She saw the anguish in his face and felt a bitch but knew no easier way of breaking it off. The truth would have wounded him even more. She was even selfish enough to have entertained the thought that if she had been honest he may have thrown her out of the car, right there, and that would have been a real inconvenience. She cried a few tears and he misinterpreted them as a further sign that he was troubling her and he comforted her.

"There, there, now," he said, and put his arm around her shoulder.

The windows were rolled down and the brine from the sea below hung in their nostrils. John stared at the U-shaped glen. The hills on either side appeared to merge two or three miles up the valley. He imagined the scalping of the mountain sides, the soil being unpeeled and the almost silent screeching of the rocks as the unrelenting, grinding glacier made its melting retreat to the depths over a thousand years. All of that powerful but inanimate violence was of nothing compared to the scraping of his heart.

"Can we go now?" she said, dabbing her tears.

He pressed her to reconsider, to think things over. He kept up with the appeal until she felt as if she had to make him that promise just to get out of there.

When she closed her front door she breathed a huge sigh of relief. She was out of his clutches and took a few minutes before she looked out the window to be certain that the car had left, that he had gone from her door.

I'm free! she said to herself as she ran upstairs to lie on the bed and take deep breaths of relief. I'm free!

John went through a rough week. He couldn't stop thinking about her. The thought of her holding hands, walking with and kissing someone else was unbearable. He felt he could have coped with the pain so long as he was assured that at the end of it all they would get back together.

He could take that, he could wait, provided there was a sign.

He remembered the ways he had relentlessly pursued her in the past, the stratagems he had employed to 'accidentally' bump into her. For weeks, perhaps months from the time she had made that first impression on him he had been planning how he in his awkwardness would approach the ideal girlfriend.

I wonder had she seen me before I saw her or were the same invisible forces working to bring us together? But as soon as I saw her, I knew, I just knew, I had to meet her, be with her, he thought.

A black cloud descended and he suddenly experienced an inexplicable ache inside. He had had arguments with Angela before, minor rows, some harsh words, but never like this to cause such a haemorrhaging of hope.

Clearly, there had been some mistake. He took a deep, deep breath and thought to himself, how best can I win her back? What can I do to demonstrate that I love her and can give her the type of affection and attention which none other can give? He stared out the window overlooking his back yard. A declaration, inside a heart, had been etched on the entry wall opposite: "SP loves JJ, 1.8.53".

Whoever they are, where are they now? A crowd of children came running up the entry, banging doors and generally making a racket. They were shouting, "Any oul wood for the bonfire! Any oul wood for the bonfire!" He recognised Jimmy and Sheila carrying off between them and three others one of those obsolete stuffed armchairs with threadbare armrests.

They are completely oblivious to the pain and pleasures of love, he thought. They have all this suffering before them.

He had the idea of writing Angela a love letter which he would pass to her at the dance that night. It was daring. He considered the risk of being rebuffed but he couldn't continue like this and, besides, he had faith in her. He mustered all his emotional energy and powers of imagination and sat down to write words of love so persuasive that they would sweep her off her feet. He read the letter. It was brilliant. He read it again. It was awful. But he had no other ideas.

Shit, but it's how I feel.

He read it again.

Damn it, I'll give it to her.

"Angela, dearest. Let me know through a shooting star, or the buttercup yellowing my throat, if you are for me! You showed me heaven and passion and the lights of love. Now you have gone and every day is dark and is literally killing me. I'll be here tomorrow, waiting, your obedient pet, waiting for you to return to the arms of the one who loves you. But tonight just give me a sign, please look at me, give me that wink, and tomorrow, a new, bright day, I'll come running, running into your warm, heavenly sunshine. I love you. John"

The hall was packed, the lights dim and the band music loud when John, Gerard and Felix arrived. They were instantly thrilled by the atmosphere. Most girls were dancing with other girls, a few with boys. Seats around the walls were filled to capacity. Seams of heavy smoke swirled in the light each time the door to the gents' or to the ladies' cloakroom swung open.

Big Al, the MC, was on stage cracking jokes.

"Knock! Knock" he shouted.

"Who's there?" the audience roared back.

"Siobhan!"

"Siobhan who?"

"Shove on your knickers , your da's coming!"

Boys cheered; fewer numbers of girls giggled.

John braced himself for the opportunity to hand the letter to Angela and his heart sank when he saw no sign of her.

But she was there. Earlier, she and her friends had drank in a city centre bar before loudly tumbling into the hall and joking with the bouncers at the front door. John had passed her table twice and failed to see her. He was expecting to see her sitting in her usual company, expecting to find her still upset at their break-up.

He hadn't seen her sitting on her new boyfriend's knee, her lips buried in his, her arms locked around his neck, as she rolled back and forth on his lap. Only when she got up to go to the cloakroom did Patricia stop and warn her that John was there and was looking for her.

"Shit!" she said. "Why can't he leave me alone?" She looked around but couldn't see him. She crossed the slack end of the floor and saw him in the distance, standing transfixed. His eyes lit up when he recognised her and he beamed an innocent, desperate smile in her direction.

He noticed that she had had her hair cut and curled.

There was something of an underdog about his simpering pose which she despised. She moved the sides of her lips into a barely defined smile, but it was booby-trapped with meanness and contempt.

He read her smile as a sign of hope.

In the cloakroom Angela found it difficult to restrain herself. She thought her hostility to him had plumbed all depths but she now found herself drawing upon new reserves of untapped hatred and she was disgusted at herself for ever having seen anything in him. He was boring, serious, unattractive ... an oaf.

She came out from behind the attendant and John was standing in front of her.

"Hi!" she said giddily, as the alcohol raced through her.

"I've something for you," he said sheepishly and handed her the letter. Before she could respond he disappeared into the sultry heat of the dance hall. She went back into the cloakroom.

She appeared to be gone for a long time. Felix wanted to know what was wrong, why didn't he relax, get a girl up to dance, show Angela that she wasn't the only fish in the sea. Gerard, who had gone out with Angela first, was always careful about what he said. He asked him was he feeling all right, he was extremely quiet.

John said he was okay. He had never been so nervous, not even when facing a fight against someone bigger and stronger. He was in a cold sweat and said that he would be back in a minute.

Angela came out, looked around, paused and shot a smile over to where John had been standing in the half-light with his friends. She had read the letter.

The band went on its break and the lights were turned up.

In the toilet John patted his face with cold water, then gulped down several mouthfuls. By now she has read it, he thought. She has read my words of love, the expression of my feelings for her. His fear was gone. His composure returned, his confidence was restored.

The letter, that magic letter! He drummed his fingers on the edge of the sink and joined the throng.

The MC was back on stage entertaining the crowd. There was loud laughter as Big Al continued reading John's letter aloud.

"I'll be here tomorrow, waiting, your obedient pet ..."

Somebody barked like a dog and there were more howls of unrestrained giggling. John's heart died on the spot. His eyes found hers as she swung around on the arm of what was clearly a new boyfriend. He stood staring at her. For a second he wanted to wilt and cry like a child. Not everyone there knew him or knew that he was the author, but one person more than her was one person too many. Some people stared at him, some laughing, others with mixed feelings, some feeling sympathy.

Through her alcoholic swill she saw his stare, saw him stand his ground, and in defence of the action she chuckled hollowly to drown out the faint voice of remorse struggling somewhere inside.

"Let's get out of this fuckin' place and leave these morons," said Felix, taking John by the arm.

John hesitated briefly, looked down at the floor and glanced at her again with eyes that said: You did this to me. You did this. Then he walked out.

John's decision to suddenly leave Belfast took his family by surprise but Catherine guessed that it was to do with Angela. But then she had had doubts when Angela called two weeks later to get an address for John. Angela had stopped visiting regularly anyway and so when the weeks passed and she didn't call back and John's letters made no reference to her Catherine supposed they had just gone their separate ways.

"There daddy. That's for you. I made you that in crafts."

Peter looked at the glazed clay ash-tray which was in the shape of a pipeholder.

"I came first in the class. The teacher said he had never seen a design like it when I started but he let me finish it."

"Catherine! Have a look at this!"

"That's wonderful," she said.

Jimmy looked pleased. He had started secondary school. He showed no academic flair but his real qualities were his humour, his generosity and his general demeanour which meant he was liked by just about everyone. Each time John went to sea he hated to see him leave. If Peter and Catherine argued he would mediate with, "Now, now, you two. Behave yourselves," which had the desired effect and brought them around.

Catherine got up early but hadn't time to light a fire before getting Peter his breakfast. When he left she knelt before the hearth and opened the grate. Fine white and grey particles rolled down the slope of a little mountain of ash below the dead cinders. She stoked the cinders before discarding the useless bits of flake but retrieved the odd honeycombed half burnt coals which made good kindling. She opened the back door, made a quick dash to the bin which was full of refuse and had no choice but to leave the lid full of ashes sitting upright. The heavy rain pulverised the dust, leaving it with the appearance of heavy, wet cement.

Jimmy heard her call but rolled over onto his side. He had a terrible sore head even though he had slept soundly. Though often she would relent, he had been off sick the previous week and she saw nothing in his condition to justify another lost day. She remained firm, assured him that when he got to school he would feel better and then would be glad because afterwards he could go out and play. She sent him off and then felt a bit guilty.

That night they sat watching the news.

"At 7 a.m. this morning," said the reporter, "Tip 7 had sunk by ten feet. At 9 a.m. it slipped another ten feet. Then at 9.10 a.m. the fine tailings from the coal washing plant began to move: slow at first, until it gathered speed and raced like an express train. The wave of black mud ripped its way through two farms, crossed the canal and railway and crashed with full force into Pantglos Junior School where over 100 children were gathered together for morning assembly.

"Some children were able to escape, but 116 were killed, along with another 28 adults. People of Aberfan have said that if the disaster had struck a few minutes earlier, the children would not have been in their classrooms, and if it had struck a few hours later, the school would have broken up for half-term."

Jimmy set his fork into his unfinished dinner. He burst into tears and ran upstairs, crying, leaving everyone in the living room bewildered and embarrassed.

"What's all that about?" said Peter.

Catherine told him not to go up, to leave Jimmy on his own. The others were ordered not to say anything to their brother either by way of sympathy or jest. When she was making tea she shouted up to him: "Jimmy? Jimmy! Do you want a cup of tea?"

"Please," he said, and she knew from his tone that he had regained his composure.

Some weeks later it was Halloween. From after tea-time, children, dressed up in old frocks and clothes as witches, devils and monsters, their faces painted, knocked on doors singing, "Please put a penny in the old man's hat!" The first half a dozen callers were genuinely welcomed and the coppers kept aside for the occasion were soon exhausted. But as more and more called at doors patience wore thin and soon the children realised that the begging was over for another year. Then they went on a tour of the streets to watch small fireworks' displays at different houses.

Jimmy was out early collecting with friends from his own street in his own and neighbouring streets. Later, they counted their separate earnings and boasted of what they would buy. He said he was going to get a book on wild birds but he bought a stamp and envelope and sent the money he had collected, three shillings and seven and a half pence, to the Aberfan appeal fund.

CHAPTER 6
LONDON I

After the school holidays Angela resumed studying A-Level English and French but with little or no enthusiasm. She had fallen a year behind Patricia and classmates and felt frustrated and lonely in a class amongst pupils a year her junior. She eventually lost interest. Her 'new' boyfriend lasted a month; her next boyfriend, two weeks.

On Saturdays she worked as a packer in Lipton's supermarket and gave two-thirds of her pay to her mother. Even so, on one occasion as punishment for coming in late, her parents refused her the extra money she needed to go to a Donovan concert. She sulked in her bedroom and recalled that back in May when in a letter to John she had casually mentioned that Bob Dylan was coming to Belfast he had sent her the money and told her to enjoy herself.

He had never replied to the two letters she wrote. If only he hadn't been so serious and old fashioned, she thought.

In November things came to a head and she was expelled from school for repeated truancy and misbehaviour. One lunchtime Angela had gone down town with others, changed her clothes in a toilet and then went dancing in the Plaza Ballroom. She then returned to school but was caught climbing through the science classroom window and was brought before the Mother of Discipline. She felt it wasn't fair, since her friends who hadn't bothered coming back in the afternoon weren't detected as having gone missing.

Her parents somehow found the fees to send her to Orange's Academy where, they had to admit, she worked hard, conscientiously bringing home with her at night notebooks full of Pitman's Shorthand. They bought her an old Olympia typewriter on which she battered away in the evenings. It was proof, they said, that she could achieve anything once she set her mind to it. In January she began working in a record shop and couldn't believe her luck – getting paid for listening to pop music and meeting interesting boys.

"Listen man. London's the place to be. Everything's happening there ... the music ... fashion," said Eddie, who had his hair in a ponytail and a roll-up dangling perpetually from his lips. He spoke about the "pads" they had stayed in, the "joints" they smoked, the "swell" parties which lasted days on end. Angela was intrigued, though Patricia was sceptical.

"No, man. You're wrong!" Eddie insisted. "I've been, you ain't," he would argue, trying to sound as if he were from the American west coast.

"Well, I'm going," said Patricia, to Angela's surprise. "But I'll be nowhere near you and your mangy mates," she laughed. "Here, go into the booth and listen to this brill record."

"What's the song he's listening to?" said Angela.

"*Something Stupid*, by Nancy and Frank Sinatra!"

"Why'd you say you're going?"

"You don't listen, do you? I told you that a couple of classmates are going to London to work for the summer or to Kings Lynn, in the canning factories, or wherever we can get a job."

"Gee! You're so lucky! When did this all happen?"

"Rose's older sister, Bernie, who's at Queens University answered an ad from students in London who were looking for some people to rent out their flat while they're away picking grapes in France. We're all heading over at the end of next month if things go according to plan."

"Oh Patricia! You're so lucky. I'm dead jealous!"

"I knew you'd be. There's still a chance that one of the others will pull out. I can see no reason why, if you were chipping in your fair share of rent, you couldn't come with us."

Her eighteen-year-old heart was pounding at the thought but it was impossible. Her mother would never let her go. Besides what would she work at? In Belfast there were contacts for jobs and one could always fall back on family. But the idea of such freedom made her dizzy: strolling through the leafy suburbs of London, lying on the grass in Hyde Park, boating on the Thames with some nice boy, frequenting boutiques, bistros, dances, bars! Drinking without having to worry about your father smelling your breath, falling in love!

"I know you from somewhere?" said John to the new galley-boy.

"Yeh, I used to knock about with your wee brother, Jimmy, but I'm not from around your way. I live just around the corner from the O'Neill's. They're cousins of yours, aren't they? And near the McCann's. You used to go out with Angela, didn't you?"

"Yes, I used to. I remember you now! You used to get us up out of bed in the summer holidays to see if our Jimmy was going out! What's your name?"

"Stevie Donnelly."

"Is this your first ship?"

"Yeh."

"Well, I'll look after you. You'll have no problems though I'd say you could look after yourself"

Stevie smiled.

"Who the hell is that at the door!"

Angela was upstairs but still heard her mother's voice raised in disbelief.

Frank looked out the window.

"He looks like your man, the singer, P.J. Proby," he laughed. "He's probably looking for a few coppers. Have you any change, love?"

Mary Ann opened the door.

"Hello little girl. Is your big sister in?"

"What do you want?"

"Angela. Tell Angela that Eddie's at the door."

"Mary Ann! Come in!" Mary pulled her daughter in. Behind her, Sean stared at the amazing figure in the colourful clothes and with hair longer than any girl's in the street.

"Who are you looking for, son?" Mary asked.

"Is Angela there? I've to see her."

Angela came running down the stairs, panting. "It's okay mummy, go on in. It's Eddie, a friend of mine."

Her mother glared at her. "Come here, till I see you a second."

Eddie was left at the door, seemingly oblivious to the shock he had caused.

"Is he on drugs! What the hell are you doing going out with the likes of that! Well? A bloody screwball."

"That's it," said Frank. "You're not going out. I've had enough of you. Tell him you can't see him."

Angela felt tears well up. She was mortified at their narrow-mindedness.

"No, I won't," she shouted, grabbed her coat and ran out the door. Her father made a dash at her but stopped short so as not to cause a public scene.

"Listen babe," Eddie comforted her. "They're all old bags. Mine were the same. Didn't respect me till I got a pad of my own. Here, have a smoke. Wanna stay the night with me?"

"No, let's walk," she said, and poured her heart out to him, though he was talking about other things.

"Angela's up in our house in case you're worried," said Maureen to Mary. Desmond gently closed the door behind him and they came into Mary's house.

"I'll kill her, Maureen. I'll kill her!"

"Now, now. Calm down. She knows I'm down here. She's looking after Gary."

"You've no idea. You should have seen the tramp that called here tonight for her. I'm just sick, sore and tired of her. I give up, I honestly do."

"She's talking about going away and getting a job. It mightn't be a bad idea."

"She's going nowhere with that thing!"

"She wants to go to London. I think you should let her."

"Where they murder people and take drugs? Maureen, are you out of your mind!"

"Listen. Listen," said Maureen. "I don't mean with your man. I mean with student friends, just for the summer holidays. The experience would do her good. Going away helped me."

Mary shook her head and sat in silence. Perhaps there was something to Maureen's suggestion, she thought. They had tried everything else.

The long train journey from Heysham in the north to London in the south gave them the impression of England being a vast place.

The three of them – Angela, Patricia and Rose – had been warned not to talk to strangers but it was Patricia not Angela who broke that rule with the first man to engage them in conversation. Rose's older sister, Bernie, had flown over before them because the English students would be leaving that Friday for France.

The girls fought for the windows as the train pulled into Euston. "Gee 'Tricia! Where are we?" The platforms were full of black people who appeared to outnumber the whites.

They had never seen such a busy place: it was more hectic than Donegall Place in Belfast during Christmas shopping, said Rose. They decided to walk to Holloway Road and spent an hour trying to find the Thames in the belief that once they established their bearings the rest would be easy.

But then they became frustrated at the size of the city and, so, by buses and experimenting with tube routes and asking directions, they eventually made it to Archway around tea-time on Saturday evening.

"Where were you?" said Bernie. "I was worried."

"We got slightly lost!"

"We're starving!"

"Well, there's been a little mix-up and the people here aren't leaving until Sunday afternoon," said Bernie. "There are no beds, but we'll manage for one night. Go straight up the stairs ... Here, give me some of your bags."

After they had something to eat they were introduced to the English students, none of whom were from London. They were the daughters of solicitors, doctors, teachers and vets, although the odd one out, Jane, was the daughter of a Durham miner. Angela thought she was the most down-to-earth of them all and they talked at length about family and friends and home.

In the large living room they sat on sofas, bean bags and the wooden floor. A Persian rug hung from a wall. Traffic hazard lamps had been improvised as lighting on one side of the room. Candles burned from wine bottles on the mantelpiece. There was a dining table and chairs in a small back room. They played Otis Redding and Righteous Brothers LPs and the company talked about Martin Luther King, the Vietnam War, women's rights, nuclear disarmament, UDI in Rhodesia, and germ warfare.

The Belfast girls, apart from Bernie, were completely lost, and even Bernie not always seemed sure of her facts. Angela felt that they, from Belfast, were from a backwater, and hadn't the confidence to explain or argue about their relevance or their experiences. They were, she felt, excluded from this life.

But when someone mentioned The Beatles playing the 'Our World' concert, and the band's new LP, *Sergeant Pepper's Lonely Hearts Club Band*, Angela thought to herself, John O'Neill would be in his element here, would be master of ceremonies!

"Do you have television in Ireland?"

"Pardon?" asked Angela, in disbelief.

"I mean, do you have a television back in Ireland?" said the girl, more tactfully.

"Yes, we have colour," she lied. "And we have running water."

When the English girls left and they took possession of the two upper floors of the four storey house they all felt more relaxed.

Angela got a job close to The Cut at Waterloo as a telephone clerk in a bookmakers which took on summer workers during the racing season. Walking to work each morning she was shattered by the sight of alcoholics and the homeless who had been turned out of the nearby Salvation Army Hostel until dusk.

It was the same at Charing Cross: vagrants old and young, the alienated, outsiders separated by a slither from general society, where separated by a gulf which was the contempt of the privileged and those on their tailcoats – the marginally privileged. Into the cloth caps, the broken cups of the poor, Angela gave whatever loose change she had.

There was an incident in her neighbourhood one night when a woman leaned out her window shouting, "He's going to kill me, going to kill me!" but no one intervened. Angela became agitated and said to her neighbour, who had also been alerted by the commotion, that the priest should be called, but the neighbour laughed at her and offered instead to phone the police. The police replied that the couple fought all the time and refused to come out.

Angela expressed disgust at the Irish who would be drunk and fight among themselves coming out of the nearby dancehall. Bernie agreed with her but Bernie's patience with her guest was also wearing thin. On the one hand Angela complained about the drunken Irish, while she herself would bring back the unwashed, "low-life" Eddie, who had moved from Belfast to a squat in Kensington.

Bernie said: "He can smoke whatever he likes over there, but he's not smoking his swag in this place. Right?"

"Don't be so old-fashioned!" said Angela, before storming out.

As the summer passed she became more restless, thought little of home or family.

Eventually she did phone her mother and said that although Patricia and the girls were going back to Belfast she was going to stay on a while longer and had found somewhere else to live. No money would be in the next letter, she explained, because she had to make some basic household purchases.

From the Trucial States they sailed to Durban then to Cape Town. The chief steward told the crew of an earlier incident when an Irishman, disregarding all rules, was caught with a black girl, was arrested and given twelve lashes of the birch. He warned them to stay away from all blacks and not to interfere in anything they saw.

John and two of the galley-boys, Stevie from Belfast and Dave from Southampton, went on leave. They were some distance from the city centre, and, unable to afford a taxi, they hopped on a passing single decker bus. All the passengers were black and they were stared at. Some moved seats to distance themselves from them.

"Where are we going?" said John.

"To this night club!" said Dave, excitedly, showing him a postcard.

They found the bar which was packed with sailors of different nationalities, drinking, smoking, playing cards and singing. Prostitutes, all coloured girls, with patently false smiles, hung around the shoulders of the sailors. John understood, but didn't like the place.

"Ach, stay a while. Just for me," said Dave who ordered three 'brandy squares', a local drink. The only way John could tolerate it was by getting drunk, but still the misery of the place sobered him up. As he drank, he thought of what his mother would think if she could see him here. Finally, he snapped and he got up to leave.

"Where's Dave?"

"Gone off to see 'a friend'," said Stevie. "You know I've never been in a brothel before!"

"God's sake, keep your voice down. Don't let anybody hear you call it that."

Dave returned a few minutes later, smiling, tripped on the leg of a chair and fell into John's arms.

Outside, the evening was still bright and the light hurt their eyes. An old black beggar, an amputee from some war, stood in the shadows, hidden by a wall. To catch their attention he had no choice but to show his face in the evening sun, limped out and stretched his hand.

Stevie gave him some change.

"What you think you doing? Eh?" screamed a white policeman who appeared from nowhere and stuck his chin into Stevie's face. "Fook off out of here, I tell you. Git now!"

A black policeman joined his colleague.

"Whad you told before?!" With a sjambok he flailed the beggar who stumbled and fell and, yet, despite the beating, and despite falling, continued to pick up his few coins like a famine victim grains of wheat.

It was pitiful.

Dave soon sobered up and held Stevie by his arm.

"Don't be a fool, man! This isn't England! Come on, let's go!"

John was seething but parked his feelings: he had witnessed similar things before, in other countries.

Stevie made a fist to smash the white policeman's face but John stopped him.

"There's nothing we can do," he said. "Not now."

The policeman clearly heard John, so he slapped Stevie across the back of the head as a schoolmaster would do to a late boy and ordered them out of the area.

"Where's Mandie Anjie?" asked Eddie's friend, Jonathan.

"What?" answered the girl with long, plaited hair, trying to understand the question above the music.

"Where's Mandie Anjie?" the tall figure in grimy jeans asked again. Tiny bells sewn on to his frayed, cuffed legs jingled around his sneakers.

"Out."

"Out where, honey? In space?" he laughed, though he sounded menacing.

She at first ignored him and, using a mirror, continued to paint a garland of flowers across her forehead. Then, realising who he was, she said: "She's gone to market to sell a suit, Jonathan."

It was late September. Angela wandered through Kensington Market, strolling through the clothes and knick-knack stalls. She found her contact at a denim jeans and jackets stall, didn't haggle and simply handed over the suit, a present from her mother – which her mother was still paying off through a monthly catalogue. In return she received a capsule of Mandrax tablets and she sang on the way back to the flat.

In the 'pad' some recited poems by William Blake or wrote lyrics or strummed a few bars of their own composition on an acoustic guitar whilst the others listened in awe.

> "One moor, one moor
> A tree did fall
> Upon one moor, one moor."

The poet then fruitlessly searched around for a pen and paper to write down his poem before it vanished forever.

"Astonishing."

"Incredible, man."

They sat on mattresses scattered around the floor, sharing joints. Incense from joss sticks perpetually hung in the air. On one wall was a poster of a head peering through a big toilet seat.

"Hey, that was a bad scene back there, yeh?"

Jonathan was referring to an incident in a pub when one of their company was refused a drink because he wore a suede waistcoat with no shirt which revealed his armpits. He was barred for showing "pubic hair" and they all left in solidarity, having first drained their glasses.

Jonathan tried to interest the squat in his samples.

"What are they?" asked Angela.

"Tabs of acid, Mandie. Acid tabs for special-paying friends. And other samples."

She had an aversion to needles and recoiled.

"This is for you because you are one of the beautiful people. This unlocks the mysteries of the human mind." He placed a tab on her tongue.

Before long she was smiling and able to predict the future and knew exactly what her friends were going to say before they opened their mouths. She felt euphoric.

"Come with me," said Jonathan.

She went upstairs with him.

She wasn't sure what time it was when she awoke. Jonathan was in bed next to her. She got up to get something to drink, unsteady on her feet, and moved as if in slow motion. She went to the front door and waved to the milkman but he ignored her and she couldn't understand why. She found an empty sofa, lay down and went back to sleep.

"Hey you guys, someone's ripping me off!" Jonathan shouted. "We'll have none of that. Come on!" he said

"You're wrong. You'll find it," he was assured.

"You're right I'll find it. Starting with you," he said to Angela. "Stand up!"

"What?"

"Stand up!" He pulled her up. "Turn out your pockets."

"What are you going on about?"

He shoved his hand into her jeans pocket and triumphantly pulled out his pouch.

"Bitch!"

"But I didn't…"

He slapped her across the face. The others looked on in disbelief but didn't intervene. Angela was afraid of Jonathan.

She was on the verge of tears. She turned to Eddie.

"Are you coming," she said.

"You just slept with him and you ripped him off, and therefore us, and you ask me am I coming with you?"

"Yeh, and you've been with no one else," she said, looking over to a girl in the corner.

Angela walked out.

The girl at Archway opened the door.

"Who are you?"

"Do you remember me? I'm Angela. I stayed here during the summer?" Jane, hearing her flatmate in conversation at the door, came out.

"What's happened to you, Angela? What happened your eye? You look awful! She can come in and she can stay in my room for now," Jane said to the other young woman who scowled at her.

"If I could just borrow some money to get home, that would be of great help, and I promise to send it back to you right away."

CHAPTER 7
THE POGROMS

John and his father stood on the beach, looking out to sea. Behind them on a blanket sat Catherine, and around her, munching sandwiches, picking out grains of sand, and thirstily drinking orange juice, were the rest of the family. John had come back to Belfast after finishing a course at Ruskin College on trade union and maritime law, on trade regulations, how to conduct meetings, take and log complaints. As a result of a strike three years earlier seamen had won shipboard recognition and had pushed aside corrupt trade union officials, replacing them with their own representatives.

The family had rented an old cottage in Downings, County Donegal, and now their holiday was coming to an end. Their cottage had no television or radio and Catherine cooked on an old range, Jimmy acting as the chief stoker feeding the range lumps of turf.

One day they had driven to Gweedore and Burtonport. On another day John took Raymond and Jimmy to Errigal, the highest mountain in the county, and they had to climb to the top to earn their lemonade and chocolate.

A couple of nights Peter, Catherine and John walked to the Singing Pub, a thatched house which was tucked up a lane behind a few trees, where they had a few drinks and listened to traditional music.

Catherine watched John and Peter talking, as if man-to-man. John skimmed a stone across the water, his longish hair flicking with each throw. He was twenty one but he was still her child.

"This holiday was a great idea. I really enjoyed it."

"So did I, da. It was a good break and I think my mammy's had a nice time too."

"Tea up!" Catherine called again.

They had decided to leave early because trouble was expected in Derry where the Apprentice Boys were marching. For almost a year marches organised by the Civil Rights Movement, demanding justice and reforms for Catholics, had been attacked and a number of civilians had lost their lives at the hands of the RUC.

When they crossed the border they were stopped by police who said there was trouble ahead and they should take a detour. Back in Belfast, before even unpacking, John switched on the television. The rioting was serious and widespread. The next day he met up with his old friends and the only topic was the Bogside where the police had lost control, couldn't gain access to the area and were being resisted by young people throwing rocks and petrol bombs from behind barricades and from the roof of Rossville Flats. It was becoming an epic battle and one so serious that the Irish government was calling for the UN to intervene.

Stormont, the seat of Unionist power, announced that it was drafting in reinforcements. The civil rights organisations called for rallies and protests in towns across the north to demonstrate solidarity with the Bogside and to tie down police resources.

After three days of continuous fighting the government mobilised a paramilitary force, the B Specials. Within hours, 'B' men had opened fire on an unarmed Catholic crowd, wounding three people. More protests were organised in reaction.

John and Felix met up with Gerard, then joined with several hundred people who marched to Springfield Road barracks to hand in a petition about police brutality. At every street they were joined by people defiantly singing Irish rebel songs. When the sergeant refused to accept their petition they smashed some of his windows before marching back down the Falls to Hastings Street Barracks. There, three policemen kitted in riot gear, stood at the front door. The weather was mild but the policemen shuffled from one foot to the other as if from cold.

"That's the bastard that arrested me during the riots!" someone shouted from the back. "The one with the Buddy Holly glasses!"

There followed a fusillade of bottles and bricks. The policemen retreated and radioed to nearby mobile patrols. Armoured cars turned from Millfield into Hastings Street and drove at the crowds, scattering them. John and Felix ran into side streets.

At eleven trouble broke out in North Belfast where Catholics and Protestants fought each other with stones and bottles. Around the same time youths on the Falls broke into a car showroom, pushed Volkswagen cars into the street and set fire to them. At other points tyres were laid across the road in defiance of the authorities; but still the RUC stayed away.

"What do you think?" said Felix.

"Looks like they're just gonna leave us alone. Most of them have probably already left for Derry and there's nobody to take us on," said John.

"I hope so," said Gerard. "Our Dominic says that if Derry falls, then we're finished."

"Ambulance driver just told me that loyalists are gathering in their hundreds on the Shankill," said Felix.

"We'll have to keep our eye on them," said John, aware of how vulnerable this area had been in the past.

"We're gonna attack Springfield Road Barracks, okay?" said Dominic, Gerard's brother. "You want to join us, get milk bottles and start siphoning petrol."

It was after midnight when the crowd crept up the street before rushing onto the main road. Their petrol bombs mostly fell short of the barracks although large flames momentarily licked the front of the building. A policeman on the first floor fired his revolver at the crowd and wounded two people. Police vehicles then raced towards the barracks and the crowd ran back into Colligan Street before stopping in McQuillan Street where an informal conference was hurriedly held.

"Jesus! Did you hear that!"

"Were they real bullets or blanks?"

"The bastards!"

"Let's get more petrol bombs."

They returned to the scene and attacked the barracks but were warned off when an officer opened fire with a machine gun over their heads. They scattered but were satisfied with the night's activity.

John was due to go back to sea on Sunday night but was undecided. The next day's news was again dominated by events in Derry where the RUC was suffering serious defeats.

A soft blue mist hung over the Falls Road that night as protestors again gathered at street corners. News that British soldiers were replacing the police in Derry had not reached the crowds.

John, Felix and Gerard went to Dominic's flat. Dominic tuned a radio and they were able to eavesdrop on police transmissions. These reported large crowds of loyalists gathering on the Shankill Road.

The three young men went out to the forecourt of Divis Tower where people were congregating, some armed with hurls. Many families who lived in streets between the Falls and the Shankill boarded up their windows before moving out for the night.

"Our Dominic's quite worried about the situation," said Gerard.

"Aren't we all," said John.

"No, I mean about the IRA. He said it isn't ready. Because of disagreements and rows a lot of them have fallen away. Everybody's running around in a panic trying to find guns."

"That sounds a bit paranoid, if you ask me," said John.

A crowd marched on Hastings Street Barracks. Those at the front pelted the building with stones and bottles. Two men rushed from the street behind the barracks and warned the crowd that armoured cars were coming.

"Jesus, they've got machine guns mounted!" said John when he saw the first vehicle.

Crowds from the Shankill Road began advancing on Dover Street and Percy Street, smashing windows. Hand-to-hand fighting broke out as people tried to defend their homes. A rough border was established behind which each side retreated, exchanging stones and bottles. Two shot-gun blasts were fired from the loyalist side and then a line of uniformed B Specials appeared with batons and charged at the nationalists who turned and ran until joined by reinforcements.

Loyalists, supported by the police, were now invading Cupar Street and Conway Street. They tore boards from windows, smashed the glass and set fire to the houses. Some families who had stayed, believing the police would protect them, fled down the streets in their pyjamas, lucky to escape with their lives.

A burst of gunfire from an armoured car scattered nationalists who tried to turn back the petrol bombers. The rattle from the Browning guns could be heard for miles around and tracers could be seen in the night sky. Two people were shot in Conway Street, two others in Balaclava Street, and one person was wounded in Raglan Street.

John and some men were trying to erect a barricade to protect the houses of Ardmoulin Avenue when the police launched a baton charge. Humber and Shorland cars from the direction of the Shankill broke through. But behind them was an army of civilians carrying sticks and hatchets and petrol bombs and Union flags. They overpowered the locals and burst into Divis Street, singing and shouting. They looted the local bar, the Arkle Inn, before torching it. All around, burning homes and shops lit up the night sky.

"They're coming for the flats! They're gonna burn the flats!" screamed a woman. John looked down towards the city centre. A phalanx of Shorlands, Humbers and Commers were lined up across Divis Street. Behind them were riot police. If they were able to join up with the loyalists at Dover Street the flats themselves could be attacked and burned with catastrophic consequences.

"Where the fuck is the IRA?" shouted a man.

"Never mind that, start moving! You lads, get onto the roof of Whitehall! You crowd, form a chain and start passing up anything you can!"

Stones, bricks, petrol bombs, pieces of gratings and scaffolding tubes were transported up to the fighters who hurled the missiles at the advancing ranks of the riot police. The defenders were relieved to see that the police were starting to pull back.

From Gilford Street fire was directed at the loyalists. One man fell dead and three policemen were wounded. Police returned fire and some moments later a Shorland sped up Divis Street, slowed to a steady cruise, trained its heavy machine gun on the flats and let loose with a burst of automatic fire. John couldn't believe his eyes.

"Jesus Christ! They're mad!"

"They're gonna kill us! They're gonna kill us all!" people were shouting from the balconies. A young boy with a bullet wound to his head was carried out to an ambulance at the back of the maisonettes. John made way for those carrying a wounded man down the stairs in Whitehall Row. He was laid on the ground and a priest, having read him the Last Rites, then announced that he was dead.

It all seemed unreal, nightmarish, terrifying and apocalyptic. The night sky aglow with the burning of houses, shops and factories.

Hysterical shouts and screams, the noise of heavy gunfire, the acrid smell of smoke poisoning the air of a summer's night.

Crowds gathered to protect St Peter's Chapel. John ran with others to the front of the road where a school, St Comgall's, was now coming under attack.

Felix shouted, "Here comes the IRA! They've got guns!"

John was expecting to see a Flying Column, not a middle-aged man carrying a machine gun along with two others.

"Any of you know how to get into the school?" the man asked. John said he was familiar with its layout. He broke a window, unfastened the latch and let the men into the corridor.

"Right. You can leave now. Go on, get out!" he said. John was disappointed, a bit angry, but they knew their business. Petrol bombs continued to crash against the solid walls of the school. From the roof of the building the IRA man opened fire towards Percy Street, wounding eight people. The loud roar of return fire from a Browning cut chunks of masonry out of the front walls and brought them back to reality. The IRA man reappeared a minute later and said, "Right, that'll do." Then he disappeared. He moved to another part of the district and opened fire to give the impression not just to the loyalists and the RUC, but also to the nationalists that they were well armed.

"Have you heard the news?"

"That kid, Rooney, has died in hospital. About fourteen've been shot in North Belfast, two dead."

"And The Specials shot dead a civil righter in Armagh. Houses are on fire on the Crumlin Road… There's rioting all over the North."

In the back streets the injured were being nursed in rudimentary 'field' hospitals. Others were making petrol bombs or feeding the menfolk who returned every now and again for a short rest.

Around 3.30 a.m. the last gunfire of the night was heard from Divis Street where an armoured car again opened fire on St Comgall's School though the IRA men had left there long ago.

"What a night," yawned John. "Thank God, it's over."

"Pray we never see another like it again."

The rival crowds, apparently drained of all energy, kept their distance. Up towards the Shankill the RUC and the B Specials sat on the kerbs among the loyalists. They were being given tea and cigarettes. It was an eerie peace.

Families who had lost everything stood in shock. Many houses had survived and during the lull men came to retrieve whatever bits of furniture or belongings they could.

John sat down and someone gave him a cigarette, the first he'd smoked in six years.

"There's the gypsies!" shouted Felix. "With lorries!"

A big, stocky man, who looked unperturbed at the 'war scene' before him, climbed out of the cab of the first lorry and a local man ran over, shook his hand and thanked him.

"We'll never forget this, I promise." He came back and said, "Come and help us take stuff out of the houses." He could see that people were reluctant to go back down the street. "Don't worry. They've realised what they've done. They'll have been given orders to do no more shooting. They're bloody well ashamed of themselves."

All public transport had been withdrawn. Those walking to work from other districts stopped and were appalled at the devastation. Though they had heard the gunfire they hadn't realised that the Falls had been under such sustained, violent attack. People were loading pieces of furniture on to the lorries provided by the gypsies. They were loading items onto handcarts, prams, or simply carrying chairs, tables and cardboard boxes of clothes by hand. Hundreds of others were prising up street flagstones and building barricades.

Some people gingerly went to inspect their homes despite being within striking distance if the loyalists so wished. Their windows had been broken but they hadn't been torched. Amongst the opposing faction were even neighbours whom they had grown up with.

As more people joined with families to lend a hand the loyalists got restless – as if they thought it was now their homes that were to be attacked. Scuffles and vicious fighting suddenly erupted. The police fired shots into the air and marched towards the Falls. As they advanced, a few yards at a time, people turned and ran. But behind the police came the loyalists who began setting fire to the houses, bit by bit, until over two-thirds of the dwellings were ablaze. There was nothing anyone could do.

In the nearby Clonard area, two men with a shot-gun and a sporting rifle were in the monastery after it had received threats that it was going to be burned down. The attacks began that afternoon. Shots were first fired into the streets to clear them, then the mobs came in with petrol bombs and began burning Bombay Street. A fifteen year old boy who was defending his home was shot dead.

The situation was completely out of control. The Stormont government formally requested the intervention of the British Army, which was on standby, and by that night a small party of soldiers led by an officer made their way to Clonard Monastery where he met the rector and inspected the situation.

Further down the street the loyalists attacked the soldiers with petrol bombs and the British Army ran away. The mob then burned down the remainder of the houses in Bombay Street. When the soldiers returned they were again fired on, but this time they stood their ground and the trouble died down in the early hours of the morning.

CHAPTER 8
THE HONEYMOON PERIOD

"You're wrong!" said Dominic. "You've got it entirely wrong."

The men were in the upstairs bedroom of a supporter's house. John was invited along to talk about smuggling and what he could do for the Auxiliaries, a branch of the IRA which he had joined in the aftermath of the pogroms.

"Dominic, listen. You see for yourself. The people are giving the British Army tea and sandwiches. I had to stop my own bloody wife from cooking for them. The wee girls of the area are even going to dances and discos in the mill. Generally, the British are welcomed and we have to take that on board. Without them on the fifteenth and sixteenth of August the rest of the Falls would have been burned out."

"That's nonsense. We would have been okay from then onwards. Bits of gear were starting to arrive from the Free State. The soldiers weren't sent here to protect the people but to protect the Stormont government. Listen carefully to what General Freeland said about the soldiers and the community enjoying a 'honeymoon period'. He's not a stupid man. They'll protect us, then they'll police us, then they'll persecute us and it'll end in divorce and funerals. You're forgetting what you told us down the years about 'British imperialism' being ultimately responsible for our plight. Besides, by the fifteenth we had started a rumour that we were gonna invade the Shankill because of what they'd done the night before. That stopped them."

"Will you let me finish? Okay?"

"Okay. Go ahead. I've heard it all before."

John sat and listened. He didn't know what to make of these arguments amongst old comrades disputing the way forward. Others confided in him that there was no faith in the leadership. They had let people down and they were going to be ousted.

"We are in a very strong position. The B Specials are going to be phased out and the talk is that the RUC is to be disarmed. With the spotlight on this place we can get all the reforms we want pushed through."

"That's fuckin' nonsense," said Dominic. "Stormont hasn't been suspended, the unionists are still in control. There's no chance of the RUC being disarmed because if they were unarmed there wouldn't be a unionist in the North prepared to join such a Boy Scouts organisation. We are in a prime position but for different reasons. For 50 years the British have been able to ignore this place, they've internalised it and it's been forgotten about. Now we've got British soldiers back on the streets . . . British soldiers! Here is 'British imperialism' confronting us, even though it's in a peace-keeping guise. We should get organised and get stuck into them."

"Same old dreaming. Same old dreaming that's cost us dearly down the years. No strategic thinking. All emotion."

"I fuckin' resent that. I wasn't emotional when your brother was shot and I pulled him to safety, was I?"

"I didn't mean that. *Tá brón orm*. But let's go through it. First, the soldiers are popular. Second, we still haven't enough arms even to properly defend the areas. Third, there's plenty of people supporting us whilst we defend our own areas but would soon turn on us if we turned on the soldiers. Fourth, we haven't the right kind of equipment. Fifth, we've no money. Sixth, the British Army is very professional and would steamroll us in about a week. Seventh, we'd lose sympathy, I mean international sympathy and right now the whole world is behind us. Eight, do you think the unionists would take it all lying down? You saw what they did because we wanted one man, one vote. Nine ... for Christ's sake the reasons are endless and you want to get stuck into the British Army! Everything is against what you say. Besides, the leadership is opposed to going down that road and that's that," he said, attempting to conclude the discussion.

"Dominic's right." The next speaker was an old republican who had been interned in the 1940s for a time, and again in the 1950s. He was a small man, a handsome man yet he had remained a bachelor.

"We've got the British by the balls," he said, taking a long draw of his cigarette. "Nobody can persuade me that they're here to protect the Catholic community. I've prayed for this day all my life. If we miss this opportunity we may forget about everything. You say the soldiers are popular. Not in Clonard they're not. Those who are supporting them will get stung, sooner or later. It's in the nature of this army, wherever they've been, wherever they go. They will take this hospitality for granted, come to take the people who show kindness to strangers for fools. Guns and money? We'll get guns and money. All those people who had to leave here because there was no work or who suffered discrimination? They'll arm us, from the States, from Australia, the Irish around the world who despise the British and what they have done to Ireland. For that corrupt, stinking, sectarian government up at Stormont, it will be a case of the chickens coming home to roost. The sight of all those refugees having to move south and live in camps will result in guns and bullets and explosives to our cause. Regarding support, it'll be the people around here, it'll be the people of Ardoyne, the New Lodge, the Strand, the Bogside and Creggan who'll support us. Working-class people, the ones who always do all the suffering and sacrificing to bring change. Not the guy in the suit. If he gives us support, well and good. And it will certainly not be the guy in the collar. You can cue his sermons right now."

"It's a minority of oppressed people who always fight wars…"

"Yeh, but you'll be making *all* our people shoulder that war and suffer regardless without prospect of winning."

"Then pack up and go home. Apply for your British passports, celebrate the Twelfth, pin on you poppies and vote for the Unionist Party. I, for one, will not!"

John could see truths on both sides but could in no way visualise the goodwill which the nationalists showed the British Army being overturned. That would take a mental revolution in attitude, he thought. When he considered the Vietnam War and other struggles he had a romantic notion of guerrilla warfare and revolution, and these Belfast streets just did not fit the bill.

The words of the speaker kept ringing in his ears: "this isn't 1916 and the British Army of today is not the Black and Tans." That was so true.

Stevie had been at sea, on his way home, when he heard about the Belfast pogroms. When his ship berthed at Las Palmas in the Canaries he borrowed £80, a big sum, from a Scottish crew member. Having made some discreet inquiries he met with a shady character in a bar who sold him two .22 pistols and 500 rounds of ammunition. Back in England he smuggled them ashore. At Heathrow Airport before boarding, and while in the queue at the ticket desk, he got to know the name of another Belfast-bound passenger. He tagged the small bag which contained the guns in that person's name and sent it through. When he landed at Aldergrove Airport he simply reclaimed the baggage as his own.

Back in the Falls Road he showed John the weapons which both of them turned over and over, loaded and re-loaded and endlessly admired. It was these two weapons which had helped cut through red tape and 'bought' them their IRA membership.

Behind the barricades both young men had received weapons training in mostly old guns, training given by local men who had spent a few years in the British Army or Royal Navy. On one occasion John brought Jimmy down to the headquarters in Leeson Street where they had a pirate station, Radio Free Belfast, broadcasting rebel music to its listeners.

Four weeks after they had been erected the barricades were taken down. Church leaders had assured local people that the British Army would protect them. With the barricades down a sort of normality returned even though another army was being built in the shadows.

Each night a British patrol would call into Stanley's bar on the edge of the Falls.

"You'll have another beer," said John, encouraging the soldier. "Sure, your patrol's over for the night."

"Okay, Paddy. Just one more."

"And what do you call that part?" asked Stevie.

"Ah, that's the safety catch and that's the magazine release. I showed you already how it works. Are you stupid, mate?" he laughed.

"Yep, I'm Paddy Irishman."

"He's mad about guns," said John, "and would love to be in the army, take part in war and parachute into dangerous territory under fire and get the girls. Have you any medals?"

The soldier drank from his pint, then produced a coin and showed them how to begin stripping the weapon. About a dozen other IRA Volunteers had received similar 'training' in this rifle and in the Stirling submachine gun from the same man.

After some weeks John and Stevie became frustrated by the lack of action and republicans arguing among themselves. The uprising, the revolution appeared to die through want of a crisis or intolerable repression.

John asked Stevie what he thought of the situation.

"What do I think of the situation?" Stevie said, after long thought. "Well, it's a bit slow for me. I can't see anything happening in the near future and I'm thinking of going back to sea. What about you?"

"I think you're right. We'll not be missing anything. And if we do, we can always come back."

The IRA asked them to watch out for other opportunities to buy arms while they were away and to keep in touch.

They had only been gone a short time when there had been more trouble, this time involving young people in the Falls clashing with the British Army. Soldiers, with whom they had been friendly just a week or two earlier, were deployed in 'snatch squads', would come charging out of the barracks wielding batons and attack those involved in protests or throwing stones. In another incident loyalists burned Catholics out of their homes just yards from Hastings Street barracks and opinion was that the army made little effort to defend them.

When in October the British government published a report announcing the disbandment of the B Specials and that the RUC was to be transformed into an unarmed police force it looked like reform was possible, after all.

Loyalists rioted in protest and fought a gun battle with the British Army in the Shankill area where they also shot dead a policeman.

In November John and Stevie joined a shipping line and set sail for the east coast of North America to pick up passengers for the Caribbean winter cruises. A deck-hand, Andy McLean from Clydeside, was the seamen's convenor and he congratulated John who had been made catering representative, which was the biggest single section of the crew. There were trade union representatives also for the deck-hands and engineers.

The cruise was to begin on the Hudson in New York but two hours before they were due to sail one of the engines developed a fault and the passengers had to disembark. The crew was just as disappointed as the passengers – they relied on tips to survive, tips which usually amounted to more than their wages. It appeared that the crew was to be ship-bound in New York over Christmas. The Irish had no great difficulty going to relatives but it would be a difficult and lonely enough time for the rest, most of whom were English.

John went off for a couple of days to spend Christmas with cousins of his father. When he returned to the ship he discovered that there had been uproar. As their money ran out the sailors had gone to the chief purser to get subs to tide them over, a standard practice. Under orders from the ship's captain the money was refused on the grounds that it hadn't been earned yet. John thought this nonsense: there was a North Atlantic bonus available to men working out of east coast ports to help compensate seamen for the cost of living. John saw Andy McLean and suggested that they pursue this line but Andy wasn't enthusiastic.

"Look!" said John. "We're gonna have to do something. These men are going crackers. We're gonna be held up here for another two weeks. As the men's reps we have a duty to examine every option and drawing on the North Atlantic bonus is the answer and will keep everybody happy."

"Okay, okay," said Andy. "I suppose we'll have to go and see Kellner."

Twice they were palmed off with the excuse that Captain Kellner was busy. John was getting angrier and Andy told him to keep his cool. Eventually they got their meeting.

"Look, Captain. There's a lot of bad feeling among the men. They've been here three or four days over Christmas with no money …"

"What! What has that got to do with me? If they were more frugal they would have savings. I can't be held responsible because they fritter away their money on beer and women."

"Well," said John, remaining patient. "What we were thinking was that the men could have a sub on their North Atlantic bonus. That would maybe help them out and get us over this hump?"

"No, no, no! There's no such thing, no such thing! There's no North Atlantic bonus, South Atlantic bonus or South Pacific bonus …" he said. For all the use that Andy was, John felt he was on his own.

"That," said Kellner, "only applies when you are leaving an American port. Since we haven't left, it, therefore, does not apply. Thank you gentlemen." He stood up from the table and Andy rose but John sat on, feeling the psychological disadvantage of being towered over.

"No," insisted John, who knew the law, customs and practices. He was confident of his position. "It applies when you arrive."

"It doesn't apply until you are leaving and that's final. I'm not listening to you people, anyway. Get out! Get out!"

"Hold on a minute, Captain. We are the elected representatives of the men. We've been appointed by the Shipping Federation and by the seamen. You can't adopt that attitude. You'll have to at least listen to us."

"I do not have to listen to you or recognise anybody. I'm the Captain on this ship …"

"So, let's get this right," said John, his dander rising. "You're not recognising the National Union of Seamen?"

"No!"

"Ach, hold on, lads," said Andy, trying to pacify both men. "Take it easy."

The captain had re-taken his seat and began to fill a large pipe.

"You know my position. I have made it clear." His words were as clear and smooth as they were contemptuous.

Andy wanted to stay on and talk but John was finished. "No, let's get out of here. This man's a complete blockhead."

A general meeting was summoned and the situation explained. When they were told that the captain refused to recognise the union there was much shouting and yelling, they were in an angry mood.

"We were supposed to have shipboard representation," said John, referring to the gains of a previous strike which were still very slowly being realised. "And the first time an issue arises that Captain just totally refuses to recognise us …"

"Then we'll refuse to recognise him!" someone shouted from the back and received loud cheers of support. The union representatives were mandated to fight the captain, though Andy appeared uneasy. He had been around much longer than John, he argued, and knew the power of the ship owners. The 1960 strike had started on passenger boats out of Liverpool on the Canadian/Pacific line, and had spread to the Union Castle boats and Cunard. After a few months it was successfully broken by the companies. John told him not to be so despondent. He was their overall convenor, their leader, and shouldn't have a defeatist attitude: it could rub off on the men and the whole protest would then crumble.

After two days John went to the chief purser.

"There's going to be serious trouble here if something's not done about this."

"The Captain has made his position clear and that's his position."

The NUS in London was telegrammed and made aware of the situation. When the men received no reply they telephoned and were told by a union official that the company was being lobbied and that they were trying to do their best to ease the situation.

"Ease the situation!" John shouted down the phone. "We want it fuckin' resolved in our favour!" He slammed the receiver down.

As the days passed and there was no progress the captain became confident that soon the men's representatives would be knocking on his door. It was true that the men were getting a little uneasy. Repairs to the engine were almost completed, the ship would be ready in two days' time and the returning passengers were shortly due to arrive. At Ruskin College John remembered being told about the value of always keeping the men informed of what was going on. Even if nothing was happening it was important to call meetings and gauge the degree of commitment to the positions which they had adopted and to know, before the employers, if a strike was going to collapse. He urged Andy to call a meeting and was pleased with the response. It was, as Stevie had told him, unanimous. The men were not sailing under Kellner and that was that. Nor were they leaving the ship to allow on board another crew – that is, if scabs could be found.

The occupation was now making news in New York and the company was getting nervous and anxious that passengers might switch to other cruises and sue them or that the strike would spread. John was interviewed on radio and by several newspapers. The captain also publicly tied his colours to the mast and a deadline was looming.

Throughout, John had a number of friends and advisors in whom he confided. The two most important ones were an elderly seaman, Peter Osborne, a communist from Liverpool, and, surprisingly because of his youth, Stevie Donnelly, who John joked, had a serious disease called stubbornness.

"Let's hope you catch it!" said Stevie.

He met both in his cabin.

"Did you get the meetings set up?" John asked.

"We've to see the tug men at nine," said Peter.

"I've seen the rep from the ... the ..." Stevie smiled, "the Stevedores. We've another meeting in a bar on the wharf at 10. They're behind us all the way. The leader's a guy called Farragher whose parents are from Mayo. He says that none of his men will handle the baggage, of that we can be definite."

John now knew they were in a very strong position. The men were ecstatic when they heard the news but he told them not to breathe a word of it. Early the next morning Stevie received a message and left the ship. He was gloomy when he came back.

"Our brothers in the Stevedores are being put under big pressure by their national leadership. They're annoyed that the element of surprise has been lost, or given away, to be more accurate. They said Kellner had wind of what was discussed at our meeting fifteen minutes after it broke up."

"Some bastard is squealing. But who is it? When have you to see them again?"

"Farragher will be talking to his men about now. He thinks he can carry them."

"Let's hope so."

By the afternoon things began to move. The Stevedores stood firm. An NUS official from London flew out. When John saw him with a black briefcase he asked him where the brown one was but the well-dressed Londoner gave him an inscrutable look and asked for a complete blow by blow account of the dispute. A senior management representative, Mr Van Eyck, flew in from the company's headquarters to join the New York manager. All sides were to meet in a restaurant that night. Before the meeting John met the men, clarified the demands and received a fresh mandate not just from catering staff but from deck-hands and engineers. He, not McLean, had emerged as the natural leader.

Very quickly John established that the company – despite the protestations of the captain – would bend on the issue of the bonus and they also proposed, unsolicited, that the men be given £25 each for the disruption they had experienced over the Christmas period.

"That's no longer the issue," said John to the dismay of Andy who was whispering that they must compromise.

"This Captain refused to recognise the duly elected representatives of the National Union of Seamen. The men themselves have decided that they are not going to sail under him! Take it or leave it but the ship stays until he goes."

The captain stormed out.

"But this has never been done before. This is unheard of," said the New York shipping manager, disbelieving his ears. "This is mutiny!"

"Call it what you want," said John, stretching casually back in his seat.

"I'm afraid we can go no further. The disruption offer is withdrawn." He pushed back his chair to rise but his bluff was punctured by John who rose first and was quickly out the door.

"Well?" asked Stevie, excitedly. "Have we a new captain or not?"

"Not yet," smiled John. "But we will, by the time passengers arrive in the morning."

Just after midnight the trade union representatives were sent for again. Kellner was absent.

"We've thought things over," said Mr Van Eyck. "In the interests of common sense, in the interests of the seamen who have suffered enough hardship, and of our passengers who would be extremely disappointed for a second time if the ship fails to sail, we have come up with a proposal which we sincerely believe will resolve the deadlock."

"Fire away," said John. "We're listening."

"We propose that Captain Kellner, Mr O'Neill and Mr McLean would stay off the ship, let it sail as normal. They will be flown to the company's headquarters for further talks, would be booked into a first class hotel and would be generously compensated for their loss of earnings."

"That's not happening," said John. "I'm not going off the ship … I came here to earn my living and that's what I'm going to do. There are no negotiations about it. Andy and I are not leaving the men."

"Listen, John. You go ahead to the headquarters. We need a good man talking for us if this is to be resolved. I'll stay behind and keep things right," said Andy. The London NUS official agreed with Andy.

"No, I'm not leaving the ship but I'm leaving this table right now."

At 5.30 a.m. they were all called to a further meeting.

"Okay," said Van Eyck. "The Captain goes, but we want a joint statement. Will you go along with that?"

"You can say what you like. You can say he won the pools or ran off with another woman. As long as he gets off this ship! We're not worried about saving face so you can say what you like."

"We are saying that Captain Kellner has been promoted to take over one of the company's biggest super tankers …"

John started laughing. "Very good, very good. I like your style."

"You handled that well, like an expert," said Andy, congratulating John.

The new captain – who had flown in from London two days earlier in the event of a company climb-down – was introduced.

"We'll meet every day," he promised. "There'll be no communications problems, I can assure you."

Up on deck John bid Van Eyck goodbye.

Van Eyck turned to him.

"I never thought I'd see the day when this would happen. You are a very pig-headed man."

"I'm not pig-headed. There's the pig-headed man going down the gangway now. He created the situation. He's a Captain Bligh. He could not live with the changes that are happening today. He couldn't stomach it."

When the ship sailed the seamen were euphoric and there were no other incidents during the cruising season apart from one. Andy McLean suddenly disappeared off the boat after the first trip and later John learnt that he had been a company plant all along.

In April the ship returned to England to resume the regular Liverpool-Montreal-Liverpool run. Stevie signed off and went home. On the second trip John took a sore throat, he presumed from paint fumes from the freshly painted living quarters. He didn't want to go to the doctor in case he was paid off sick. In a few days' time they would be docking in Liverpool and he was due a week's leave.

What he noticed most, back in Belfast, was the high level of troop activity in Catholic areas and the way they were ostracised. They were no longer the British Army but were now called "the Brits." Confrontations were regular and people complained that the soldiers were worse than the RUC, assaulting young people and firing tear gas into streets at any pretext.

When John reported back to his IRA contacts, as Stevie had some weeks before him, the much-anticipated split in the organisation, and the establishment of a Provisional Army Council to reorganise the IRA, was explained to him.

The British Army announced that petrol bombers would be shot and the IRA issued a statement which said that in the event of this happening, "retaliatory action will be taken by our units in occupied Ireland."

After a meeting John took Stevie by the arm.

"My good man, you and I are going back to sea!"

"I'm not running away," said Stevie, surprised. "I now even have a girlfriend."

John explained his thinking. And Stevie agreed.

"You have to see the doctor. You got paid off sick."

"I didn't get paid off sick. I went home on leave," said John.

"Nothing to do with me, chuck," said the Liverpool woman behind the glass. "There's a medical report here says you got paid off sick. You have to see the doctor."

"Okay. Okay"

"What's up?" said Stevie.

"I have to see the doctor. Some mix-up."

He went to the ship's hospital where there was a stranger, a middle-aged man, sitting in a three piece, pin-striped suit, waiting to examine him.

"You're not the ship's doctor!"

"I know. I've been sent from the shore."

"I never heard of that before."

"Oh? It's happened quite often enough."

"How many people are you seeing today?"

"Just yourself."

John knew something was not right. Out of every crew it was usual for about ten or twelve men to have been signed off sick. When they returned they had to report to the doctor to be given the all-clear before signing on. The examination was usually cursory – "open your mouth, stick out your tongue. Drop your trousers, cough. Okay. All clear."

His suspicion that something was unusual was confirmed when the doctor began a lengthy probe of his medical history, asking about parents and grandparents, then took blood and urine samples, did eye and hearing tests, checked his scalp, even measured him. It took three-quarters of an hour. He's going to find something wrong with me and pay me off this ship for all the trouble I've been causing, thought John.

"Doctor. See before you fill in your report and comment whether I'm fit or unfit I'm going to tell you something. You've been brought here to do a specific job and that's to find me medically unfit. That's not because they are concerned about my health. There was a trade union dispute on this ship as I'm sure you heard on the news or through the grapevine.

"The company wants me off and if you are going to do their dirty work for them I'm going to insist that the same medical examination, the same standards that you apply to me, be applied to everybody on this ship, and before she sails. And I mean captain, officers and crew. That'll take you and several other doctors – on overtime – about eight days."

They looked at each other.

The doctor snapped close the file.

"Perfectly fit! I've never seen a fitter seaman in all my life," he said.

The captain and the officers were surprised when they saw John head for the cabins.

"How long have you got to live?" Stevie shouted, laughing, so that they could hear.

The ship sailed up the St Lawrence River and docked in Montreal. Some weeks earlier John had noticed guns for sale in a large sports store in the centre of the city. On the ground floor were fishing tackle, nets, heavy clothing and camping equipment. Upstairs were row upon row of weapons. John had discovered that the regulations were lax – all you needed was a name and address within the state which was easily gleaned from the telephone directory.

"Have you seen anything you like?" asked the floor manager, a fat man with a bushy moustache.

"Could I have two M1 Carbines please and a 1,000 rounds of ammunition."

"Certainly. Have you decided which of these you'd prefer?"

"Yes, that one and that one there, sir," said John.

Stevie was amazed.

"Huh," said John, out of the side of his mouth. "Two fuckin water pistols from Las Palmas!"

"That'll be $120 please," said the manager, handing him the wrapped package.

"Pleasure doing business."

"Call again, thank you."

"Where'd you get $120?" said Stevie.

"You know that wee post office on the Donegall Road? Well ..."

They had no problems getting on to the boat and hiding the weapons in air vents to escape the customs men back in England, the rummaging squad looking for contraband. From there the weapons were easily smuggled back to Belfast. By the third trip they were so well organised that they were buying and smuggling ten rifles and several thousand rounds of ammunition, telescopic sights and cleaning equipment at a time. Their boat tied up in Liverpool just across from the sheds near where the Belfast-to-Liverpool ferry docked so the weapons didn't have to be shifted any real distance.

At the end of June there was a major outbreak of sectarian violence following Orange parades which led to deaths and serious injuries. The IRA had been careful not to become involved in any confrontations with the British Army.

The following weekend, on a Friday afternoon, British Army trucks drove into Balkan Street in the Falls and sealed it off. The soldiers began raiding and in one house guns were seized. Locals were angry because, as far as they were concerned, these guns were there for their defence and had never been used against troops. A few stones were thrown at the soldiers as they withdrew and they replied with a fusillade of CS gas.

In other barracks across the city, General Sir Ian Freeland had 3,000 troops waiting to go into the Falls on the pretext of a riot. An armoured car knocked down and killed a local man who was an invalided ex-serviceman. Gangs of youths then began hijacking buses and lorries for barricades. The soldiers continued to fire gas and call for reinforcements.

John was back in Belfast. He was summoned to a meeting in Servia Street of D Company, his IRA unit. About fifteen young people were present.

"Our information is that the Brits are going to curfew the area and search every house, every shop and school and community centre," said his unit leader, Charlie Hughes.

"They're out to take all our weapons off us. We don't know what the Sticks are going to do," he said, referring to the rival group, the Official IRA, "but we are going to fight them."

"With all we've got?"

"No, not with everything. Sealed dumps should survive provided they *are* sealed," he said, looking over at the quartermaster.

"The Sticks have a couple of rifles in a house in McDonnell Street. Do you know which house I'm talking about, Charlie?" said Dominic, who had wanted to steal the weapons but had been refused permission for fear of causing a feud.

"They've quite a few dumps," said Charlie. "I expect they'll fight. We'll see. We'll bring out about nine or ten weapons. Improvise if you can. Move about. Come together. Use the nail bombs. Nobody's to stand and fight, hear me? That's what they're trained for. Hit them at the top, from the sides, from the bottom. Use the derelicts. These are our streets, you know them.

"Paddy, you're organising the incendiaries. The girls'll get them into town. Big shops. As many as you can. But you need to move before it becomes impossible."

They discussed their ideas and then the weapons were distributed. Brendan, an ex-marine commando, left first, across to the bottom of Bosnia Street. He was armed with a .303 Lee Enfield rifle.

British soldiers were at the other end of Servia Street and Albert Street. Brendan gave cover fire while the others dashed out of the house in formation, close to the brick walls. They headed towards Cyprus Street, carrying several bolt-action rifles, a Thompson and Sten sub-machine guns, three short-arms and with blast bombs and matches in their jacket pockets. In Cyprus Street the soldiers poured concentrated fire at them, pinning them down in open doorways. They returned fire. John went through a derelict house, climbed up on the yard wall and tossed a blast bomb over the roof, towards a stationary Saracen. The bang shook the whole area and was followed by a sudden peace as everyone gathered their wits about them.

The IRA men then pulled back into Servia Street. A woman peeping from behind an upstairs window shouted down to her husband to warn them.

"Charlie!" the man shouted from his doorway. "Soldiers are in Varna Gap!"

One of the Volunteers fired blindly into the gable wall at a sharp angle.

"What the fuck are you doing?" said Charlie.

"Ricochets. We might hit them with ricochets."

"For fuck's sake, catch yourself on and pull back!"

At the far end of the Falls not everyone had heard the British Army helicopter or the troops with loud-hailers announce that the area was under curfew. In Marchioness Street an elderly, asthmatic man, went to his front door for some air, believing that the night's troubles were over. He was in his shirt sleeves and bedroom slippers, was spotted by a British Army sniper and was shot. His nephew risked death to summon a Knights of Malta ambulance but the soldiers wouldn't let it through and the old man died.

The soldiers then entered his home and quartered themselves there for the curfew, used his bed and ate his food.

More armoured cars poured into the area, followed by hundreds of soldiers.

After an hour, John's unit had exhausted most of their ammunition and grenades. The shooting, however, continued. Soldiers were firing at imaginary targets or in response to the gunfire of their colleagues in adjacent streets.

John got separated from his comrades as the encirclement got smaller. The place was saturated in a mist of gas. John vomited several times and couldn't imagine how families with children were coping. At last he made his way into a supporter's house, an old widower. He cleaned his Luger, wrapped it up in a tea towel and hid it in the rafters of the toilet shed outside in the yard. He and the old man sat there, nervously talking, smoking, wondering what would happen next. They waited on the door being broken in. The soldiers took their time coming, clearing and searching one street at a time, finding some weapons but not the arsenals they had been anticipating.

News of the curfew began filtering out. Stories of widespread beatings and arrests, including children as young as thirteen; stories of soldiers preventing a couple from getting married, stopping Mass being said; of soldiers using machine-guns against a first-aid station and then using explosives to blow their way into a school where people were sheltering; of them killing a freelance photojournalist from London as he tried to get back to his hotel.

The Catholic Cardinal expressed alarm and concern. Journalists began to arrive but were barred from entering the Falls. The army announced that shops inside the sealed zone could open for two hours but that there was to be no movement of people or supplies inside or outside the curfewed area. The army, under pressure to complete its task, now began selecting at random a quota of houses in each street or, in some cases, on just one particular side of the street. On Sunday a military helicopter hovered overhead and announced that people could go to Mass. However, the first families to make their way outdoors were ordered inside again at gunpoint.

John could hear the noise of engines outside. He looked out from the upstairs window and saw two Unionist government ministers standing in an open back army lorry inspecting the military operation like overlords. He wanted to get his gun and shoot them, he felt so angered.

The soldiers began building sandbagged emplacements at the corners of the streets. More hours passed.

John heard a noise in the distance of chanting, singing and cheering. It got louder and louder. It reminded him of the previous August.

Was it loyalists coming in behind the troops? People began opening their doors despite being ordered inside. Thousands of women from Andersonstown, Turf Lodge, Ballymurphy, Rodney, Beechmount, Clonard were marching on the British Army's cordons.

"Come out! Come out! The curfew is broken! The curfew is broken!" they shouted. Soldiers took aim and warned them they would be shot but they continued marching right up to the barbed wire barricades and after a short standoff they began pulling the fences aside. They carried bread, milk, vegetables, meat parcels and biscuits. Some pushed prams, some were elderly people outraged by the curfew and who had never felt compelled enough to act so defiantly.

John turned to the old man who joined him at the front door. The old man was crying.

"Can you believe it," he said. "Can you believe it!" he then laughed.

At every corner the soldiers were being booed and swept out of the way. As the women marched, their numbers multiplied as those who had been under curfew joined with them in a triumphant march around the Falls. John retrieved his Luger and mixed with the crowd. He saw Dominic and found members of his unit.

"We've to shift the dumps," he was told.

"But the area's still surrounded," said John. "How are we going to get them out?"

Dominic smiled and pointed to the prams in which the food had been brought in.

"Fuckin' brilliant!"

"And now we will begin to take them on," said Dominic, as they marched past soldiers who looked downcast. The IRA had lost some weapons and some men but had also retrieved weapons belonging to the Officials.

They emerged from the curfew stronger than before.

"Just one question," said Stevie to the guns salesman. "How come when I first came in here a while back the carbines were only $40 a piece and now they've doubled in price?"

"Ah," said the man, smoothing down the thick bristles of his black moustache and smiling. "These weapons are now in great demand.

Everybody is after them! We've even had the Black Panthers in, the Weathermen, and then there's your crowd – the IRA ..."

Stevie swallowed the lump in his throat. He paid for the weapons and walked out. He wouldn't be back in that shop or, for that matter, in Canada, again. He had missed the curfew and the first shots fired at the British Army and he was kicking himself.

Angela had returned to Belfast two years earlier as if there had never been a family row. They all welcomed her back and said nothing. Although she was thinner, Mary had to admit to Maureen that she had been correct: she now appeared more contented, so London and going away had done her a world of good.

She got a job in a tie factory, typing invoices and taking calls, but was made redundant when the factory closed and the contract went to Crumlin Road Jail. She then moved to an accountant's as an audio typist for a year until she got tired of it. In the summer she started work as a clerical officer in the Royal Victoria Hospital.

Angela sat sipping her tea in the packed canteen of Bostock House, looking jealously at a postcard from Patricia who was holidaying in the Costa Blanca. She sighed. Not only was the deteriorating situation in Belfast depressing – the riots, the recent curfew, the raids and arrests, and shops being set on fire in town – but romance had recently gone out of her life as she and her boyfriend had just broken up through sheer boredom.

Colleagues would talk about boyfriends and dances and holidays and she began to feel excluded. Or they would idly speculate about which young doctors were having affairs with staff nurses.

"Excuse me, may I join you?"

Angela looked up at the young man, who was tall and casually dressed. He held a tray and obviously had trouble finding a space in the busy canteen.

"Yes. Sure. Of course."

He carefully buttered a piece of wheaten bread and cut a piece of cheese to fit. He looked from side to side, either nervously or mildly curious. Angela snatched quick glances of him. He was good-looking, not stunningly handsome, but also had the demeanour of the vulnerable.

"Busy, isn't it?" he said, nervously. She noticed his English accent.

"Yes. Always is at this time. Have you not been here before?"

"No. It's my first time, though I'm based in the complex."

She looked at her watch.

"Oh. Are you late?" he asked.

"Just a few minutes."

"Maybe I'll see you again," he said, politely, standing up as she began to leave. "My name is Roger. I'm from Yorkshire." He held out his hand.

"Oh," she said; thinking, that was quick. "Angela. Angela McCann."

He shook her hand and smiled.

The following Monday she was again finishing lunch when he showed up and asked could he sit beside her and her friends. When her company saw that the two knew each other they cleared off, ignoring Angela's assurances that they weren't interrupting anything.

Roger was not a trainee doctor nor a laboratory technician, as she first thought, but worked in communications. They hit it off and she found herself talking quite a bit about herself as he made a good listener and didn't dominate the conversation. The following day he asked her out. They went for a drink in the Washington Bar then to a dance in the Romanos Ballroom. He told her he was an only child. That he spent his childhood miles from nowhere, on a sheep farm in the North York moors, where a bus ran once a day. She supposed that was why he was shy and a bit strange and he had probably consciously struggled to be well-mannered and was proud of that trait. Another night he took her to the cinema and he laughed throughout. She let him choose the film and he chose *Doctor In Trouble*, probably, she thought, to please her, though she found the film awful.

She suspected he had a secret. He said he was going back to England for a week and arranged to see her when he returned.

Late on a Friday afternoon and by sheer accident she and some of her friends called into the canteen for a snack. Roger walked over to her table and her friends made excuses and left. As he sat down Angela at first laughed at the British Army uniform and at the thought of how silly she had been not to make the connection. Roger produced a diamond engagement ring from a box and suddenly she found herself in a bizarre situation.

"This is for you, Angela. Please take it."

She was shocked. It was all so ridiculous.

"Look Roger, this is all a mistake. I can't. We barely know each other ..."

People were staring at them. The British Army were billeted in an old building at the edge of the hospital, near the ambulance depot, and although soldiers occasionally frequented the canteen, nationalists had for many months, especially since the curfew, stayed well clear of them. Catholic girls who went to British Army discos had been attacked by republican supporters for being "soldier lovers" and some had been publicly tarred and feathered and photographs had appeared in the newspapers of girls tied to lampposts with their heads shaved.

"Roger, I'm sorry. It's all been a big mistake." She rose from the table.

"It's okay. I know it's just early days but my mother would like to meet you on my next leave. So, I'll see you on Monday or Tuesday and we can tell your family." Instead of shaking her hand he leaned over and kissed her on the cheek.

Angela was shaking.

Trust me to attract a nutcase, she thought. She went through her bag for a cigarette but found she had no lighter. She walked over to some men whom she knew to see but they had no light. She found it unusual that they claimed to be out of matches when there were was a packet of Embassy sitting on their table and butts in the ashtray.

Catch yourself on, she told herself. You're falling to pieces.

Back in the office she felt that those who hadn't gone home yet were whispering about her. The snack rumbled sourly in her stomach and she ran to the bathroom where she was sick. She calmed down. Any half-wit who saw or heard about what happened would realise her surprise at a man, a soldier and practically a stranger, proposing an engagement! She laughed at the thought of just how ridiculous it was. The girls from the Falls Road to whom she urgently wanted to explain the whole matter were not among those still on duty.

"He did what!" said her mother when she told her what happened. "Angela, I'm going to ask you one more time. Are you sure you're telling me the truth because to be honest it just sounds like something you would do, leading a fella on ..."

"Mammy!"

"Well, what do you expect me to believe? You have brought more trouble on this house down the years than five daughters."

"Thanks a lot! Some mother you are!" She stormed out. Walking through Tullymore Estate Angela felt that all eyes were on her. She was extremely uncomfortable and fearful on her way to Coolnasilla to see her Aunty Maureen. Maureen would contact someone in the IRA and sort it all out. She had heard through the grapevine that her old boyfriend John O'Neill was in the IRA but she could hardly approach him.

"How did Roger's letter go down at the dance," he might say with utter justification and cynicism. "Did they laugh at it?" Although West Belfast was a small village, you could go many years without meeting an old acquaintance, and she hadn't seen John's face at all in the crowd or on the bus.

Angela recalled how, before moving up to Andersonstown some years earlier, she had despised the close-knit streets of the Falls, the narrow, dirty entries, the dogs and cats, the lack of open space or greenery. Men spitting in the street. Drunk men urinating in the entries. Parochialism, narrow-mindedness, choked her. She had just been coming around to embracing it as *her* home, as true life, warts and all, then this happened. Despite her bad experiences in London she relished the sense of freedom and anonymity it offered and she now wished she had never come back.

"How could you have been so stupid!" said Maureen. She had been expecting nothing but sympathy from her aunt and was taken aback. "You saw that he had short hair. Did you not realise he was a radio man in the British Army? And all that time you didn't know he was a soldier? Are you sure you weren't seeing him somewhere else? Back at the base? You know they take girls back there, have special rooms?"

"I swear to God, Maureen. The whole thing is so incredible."

"It is incredible. I believe you. Tomorrow I shall go and see someone. So you can relax and set your mind at rest."

"Two girls came into the club last night and asked if we knew where you were. But we told them you hadn't been here in weeks… Are you okay? You've gone completely white."

Angela told her friends everything.

"Jesus, you don't think they were gonna shave your head, do you? You know, don't you, that there's a rumour going around that you're pregnant?"

"And that you're getting married to a soldier."

"Who told you that fuckin' rubbish?" She was angry but she was terrified.

"Everybody's saying it. There's talk that it's gonna be a military wedding. Angela, I think you're in big trouble."

"I know. I know," she said, biting at her nails.

"Mammy, I can't settle and I want to go."

"But what would you work at in England. You've nobody to go to."

"Bloody IRA!" said Frank. "Who do they think they are? Just let them come near this door. So much for your sister being able to sort it all out!"

"It's okay. Everything's been cleared up," said her mother, reassuringly, on the phone from Belfast.

"But mammy I've only arrived and I've another interview tomorrow for a job."

"Angela." It was her father's voice. "The right people have been seen. Only one side of the IRA was told. The other group had it explained to them and everything's okay. They even laughed. I'm sure you're glad?"

"Yes, daddy. But I'm shattered by the whole thing. And if you and mammy don't mind I think I'll stay here for a while. To tell you the truth I was getting fed up with Belfast anyway."

CHAPTER 9
9 AUGUST, 1971

A double-decker bus driving down the Springfield Road slowed down at the British Army post. Suddenly, from upstairs, a man opened fire through the window and sprayed the observation post, cutting chunks of masonry out of the brickwork. The soldier inside dived for cover and when he felt sure that it was safe he peered out to see a number of armed men jump from the abandoned vehicle and disappear into the Kashmir Road.

"Well, did you get him!" John shouted to Stevie as they and another Volunteer ran up the street.

"I dunno! I dunno!"

Two youths with nail bombs were in the side streets to deter any patrols which may have been in hot pursuit, but no soldiers came immediately. They would wait for reinforcements before entering the Clonard area.

"You should have drove slower," said Stevie to John at the debriefing in the meeting place, the call-house, the home of a supporter.

"I wasn't used to the thing and I was afraid of it stalling," said John, under whose command an active service unit had been set up to carry out special operations.

The news on the radio announced that no soldiers had been injured.

"They're probably lying. Wait till you see," said one of the Volunteers. "Tomorrow's papers will announce that a soldier's been killed in a car crash in Germany. That's how they cover it up."

John wasn't convinced. Many of the Volunteers exaggerated and would claim to have seen not one but two or three soldiers fall wounded when shots were fired.

Every day the IRA was in the news as its activities intensified.

John had just arrived in Southampton for a meeting to discuss new means of smuggling weapons from North America when he heard that a republican feud had broken out in the Falls and learnt that his leader and friend, Charlie Hughes, had been shot dead by the

Officials. He missed the funeral and by the time he came back the feud was over and had been resolved through mediation.

He visited his friend's grave in Milltown Cemetery, read the list of the patriot dead going back over a century which were memorialised in the inscriptions, and he wondered how many more names would be added to the list before there was freedom, justice and peace.

Would his be among them?

John's active service unit had been to the fore in a series of bomb and gun attacks. It had bombed the RUC and British Army barracks at Queen Street, Roden Street, Springfield Road and Henry Taggart Hall. It had killed two British soldiers and seriously injured several others. The Volunteers were confident of closing down Roden Street barracks which was undefendable and would represent a huge propaganda success. Two of his Volunteers had been killed and three had been wounded and moved over the border for hospital treatment.

Their actions created a flow of new recruits who had to be trained and disciplined, though 'bad' operations in which civilians were killed or injured hurt support.

John and Stevie were interviewing some new recruits, looking for a particular type of character.

"Why do you want to join the IRA?"

"*Gabh mo leithsceal. Abair sin aris, le do thoil.*" [Pardon me, Could you repeat what you said please.]

"Oh, a *gaeilgeoir*! Certainly, I'll repeat it." John was pleasantly surprised and engaged the young man in Irish.

"Speak in English. I don't understand," said Stevie, churlishly.

"I've always believed that Ireland was a nation long before England. I believe that we are entitled to our own heritage and to freedom. I am a great admirer of Padraig Mac Piarias and have read all his poems ..."

His starched white shirt annoyed Stevie.

"Could you throw a nail bomb? If I told you to shoot somebody could you do it?"

"Well, if I was trained properly I am sure I could throw a nail bomb at a specific military target but I would not shoot anyone unless I was absolutely convinced that it was the right thing to do ..."

"Could you take being hated?"

"What do you mean?"

"If an operation goes wrong your ma or girlfriend could be calling the IRA "a pack of bastards" and it might have been you who was responsible. You'll hear it from the priests during Mass. You'll read it in the papers that we're wrong. When you're arrested the Brits and cops will hate you with a venom you've never experienced before. They'll kick your bollocks in. The screws in the jail will detest you. So, could you take being hated?"

"Ommm, I shall have to think about that."

Stevie gave him more cold treatment.

But not all potential recruits were so naïve, or sophisticated.

"Why do you want to join the IRA?"

"The Brits won't leave us alone when we're standing at the corner playing Pitch 'n Toss. You know, they're always fuckin' us about. Now I want to fuck them about."

"Why do you want a united Ireland?"

"I'm not that fussed. Haven't thought about it much. Like, generally, I don't have a prob." He shrugged his shoulders to show that he had no burning enthusiasm for politics. "But every time you stand at your corner minding your own fuckin' business they come along and tell you to get up against the wall and spread your legs and arms. They use fuckin' bad language in front of your girl. So, as I said, I'm fed up with it and just want to have a blarge at them."

"Could you throw a nail bomb? If I told you to shoot somebody could you do it?"

"I'm your man!"

"Could you take being hated?"

"For fuck's sake the only two people who love me," he said, grinning, "are my girl and my ma. And I'm not that sure about the ma."

"What do you think?" John said afterwards to Stevie.

"You know me. I'm not into the language thing, the culture. We'll make a fighter out of the last one, and his politics can come later, but I wouldn't be for the first one."

"Yep. We'll go with Ali La Pointe."

"Who?"

"This new Prime Minister Brian Faulkner's a joke! He says, 'The IRA's on the run and will soon be crushed'. Pass me a nail bomb, somebody," said Stevie, laughing as he put down the newspaper.

There were about six of them in the call-house, there to plan business for the following week. One of the men was told to go to Ardoyne to be part of an IRA court-martial of a Volunteer who was appealing dismissal for "loose talking". A man and a young woman were to borrow a car and move weapons to a safe house. That night a bomb was to be prepared for Springfield Road Barracks and a van was to be got for the next morning, Saturday, when they were supposed to kidnap two RUC men from the city centre, bring them up to the Falls Road and tar and feather them outside St John's Chapel. The Brigade Officer Commanding said it would make "good propaganda" and show the world that they didn't always kill but gave the enemy a chance.

The bomb was to be made up of ten pounds of gelignite with a 12-second fuse.

John was dropped off in Crocus Street. He lifted the holdall out of the car. A scout went to the corner; there were no soldiers in the vicinity. He broke the phial of acid to start the fuse, turned the corner and hurled the bomb over the barbed wire fence towards the look-out post that had been strengthened following an earlier attack which killed a paratrooper. As he ran away the soldiers opened fire and he tripped on the ground, lying there for a few seconds. There was an almighty explosion and the buildings appeared to momentarily shimmer.

Two women shouted, "Run, son! Run!"

He ran into Colligan Street but at the bottom corner soldiers were dismounting from their vehicles, unaware of what exactly was happening, but cutting off his escape route. John's father, Peter, had been leaving Maguire's Bar when the bomb went off. He saw John run down the street and was almost sick with dread, thinking he was going to be killed or captured.

Soldiers streamed out of the barracks and began forcing people – women and men – up against walls, ordering them not to move. Peter started a hullabaloo and encouraged others to engage in punch-ups. Somebody got bottles from the bar and threw them at the soldiers, and a small riot began.

John burst into the first open door he found and ran upstairs. His ankle was twisted and sore. The elderly owner, realising what his unwelcome guest had been up to, was terrified and John calmed him down.

"Can I get out the back? Can I get out the back?" he shouted, and attempted to open the bedroom window but it was jammed. There was loud hammering on the front door and John was convinced he was captured.

"Don't open it! Don't open it!"

"I have to, son. I have to ... Who is it?"

"Open the door. It's okay," said a woman's voice.

The old man opened the door and she stepped into the hall. She shouted to John: "Are you one of Liam Hannaway's men?"

"Yes," he said, still agitated.

"Quickly. Come with me." She took him out, across the street, which was still in uproar, and into another house. He was helped over a yard wall, into a house in the next street and then out the front door and into a car. Stevie, chewing gum and blowing bubbles, was behind the wheel.

"Bet you thought you were a goner," he smiled.

Peter walked home. He was shaking from tensions he swore to God he was never placed on earth to experience. Violence repulsed him, even the throwing of a bottle at an armed soldier. He could never do what his son had just done. He knew it was useless talking to him. Catherine just couldn't cope with being acquainted with the details of their son's activities even though deep down she knew. He just wished that it was all over and that there was peace.

And yet strangely he felt closer to John than for as long as he could remember.

"Something has to give." John was at a brigade meeting in Ward Street.

"British Home Secretary, Maudlin, or whatever's 'is name, has declared war on the IRA. That is, you, would you look at you! If you ask me, somebody's going to get their mascara stolen, then there'll be an almighty row," said Dominic.

"Anyway, the info is that they're going to introduce internment, you'll be glad to hear, so any bad boys in the room are henceforward ordered not to sleep at home. Any questions?"

"Can I stay in your flat?"

"Fuck off. Any intelligent questions?"

"Like what's the chances of them lifting you, Dominic?" joked one of the Volunteers. "You haven't fired a shot since the 'Fifties."

In late July there had been scores of dawn raids in Belfast and other towns but all those arrested were later released and a certain complacency arose.

John was at home only at weekends, usually if he was out socialising with his parents. Back in March he had had a furious row with his mother over the killings of three off-duty soldiers, two of them teenage brothers, who were lured to a pub then shot dead.

"That was murder," she said.

"Tell me a killing that isn't."

"Do I know you, at all?"

Their argument was kept from Peter.

In the July raids his home wasn't searched. He was a bit surprised they hadn't raided for him and he concluded – from other reports he had received – that their intelligence files were not that good, given that many of those arrested in the swoops were not active militarily, and that some others were active only in the Civil Rights' or Student movements.

"A man's been shot dead outside Springfield Road Barracks!"

"What happened?" said John to the young Volunteer who had brought the news.

"He was in a van, driving past. It backfired and the soldiers opened up."

"Anybody seen Stevie? Is he back with that van yet? Jesus, anybody seen Stevie!"

The kitchen door opened and Stevie walked in.

"I know. I heard. The Brits are saying they were fired on but they weren't. There's crowds gathering. We'd need to cancel that op on the two cops, there'll be bigger trouble now."

Rioting broke out on the Falls, in Ardoyne and Ballymurphy. A crowd of three hundred attacked Springfield Road Barracks. On Sunday a soldier was shot dead in Ardoyne and six others wounded.

"The Sticks have five .303s out in Raglan Street," Stevie reported.

"How many have our people out?"

"We've two Armalites, a Thompson and a .45. Whoever's in charge of the Brits hasn't a clue. Snatch squads armed only with batons are chasing the rioters into the area. The 'Dogs' are out at Lower Clonard Street and Spinner Street waiting to cut the dung out of them."

The trouble lasted well into the night and since most of the shooting was of an opportunistic nature John's unit was not needed after 10 p.m. Some of the men stayed around just to be in the middle of things but John left and phoned up Geraldine to see if she fancied a drink.

He had been introduced to Geraldine at a *scoraiocht*– a fundraising party – three weeks previously. She was good company but he wasn't serious about her. He met her as arranged and they called into a club and joined Peter, who sat with a pint of Guinness in front of him, and Catherine who sipped at her tomato juice. For years Catherine stayed at home and rarely ventured out to socialise, but since the children had grown up she occasionally went out with her husband and found that she had enjoyed the sing song and lighthearted banter, though she would certainly never allow alcohol to cross her lips.

Peter immediately made the two welcome and gave his order to a passing waitress.

"Big round of applause for Tony now," said Maxy the guitarist, "and a bit of order because he's not wearing his teeth. Come on now, a bit of respect, Tony's one of the nicest fellas you'd ever meet."

The singer, a small elderly man in a faded shiny suit was a well-known favourite of the audience. Clutching a cigarette, which acted like an informal baton, he incoherently mumbled the words of an old song but was drowned out by the chorus from the floor who then went on to give him a rousing ovation.

"More! More!" they shouted. "Sing again, Tony. Go on, sing again!" He got back up and as bold as brass proceeded to sing the same song to much applause.

A woman in her late twenties lifted her handbag from a table near the stage to visit the ladies. She had had too much to drink but thought she was sober. She knocked over a glass. As quick as a shot Maxy responded facetiously: "Watch you don't knock that glass over, love," but she continued on her way oblivious.

John was enjoying himself, relaxing after the feverish activity of the last few days.

"I saw you," Peter whispered to him when the group resumed the stage for the final half hour.

"Sorry? What do you mean?"

"On the Springfield. You know my views but I was really worried for you. I hope you young people know what you're doing. Be very careful," and he winked at John. It had taken so long for them to arrive at this understanding, he thought. So long.

"Will you have a whiskey, daddy?"

"Aye! Why not! What about you Geraldine, will you have a wee vodka?"

"Yes, thank you, Mr O'Neill," she replied, even though it was John who was buying.

John sat next to his girlfriend with his arm around her chair, whispering to her in between sipping at his pint of beer and glass of whiskey. A ginger-haired youth entered the club with the doorman who pointed out John. He came over and gave him a message which irritated him.

"I'm sorry folks, but I have to go. Something's cropped up." His father despite being philosophical just seconds earlier, now felt as if he had been showered with cold water, felt the Republican Movement once again reach into their lives. Catherine grabbed John's hand.

"No. It's nothing like that. It's just that I've got a message and I have to find various people before the morning. Geraldine, are you coming?"

"Look, why don't you let Geraldine stay if you are rushing off," said Peter. "I'll walk her home. She's still got a drink in front of her."

This appeared to suit everyone.

John had received word that ten new recruits were to be ready to go to a training camp, leaving early the next morning. The brigade training officer, who was a personal friend, had gone to a billet and only John could trace him so he set out to deliver the news. It was after 2 a.m. before he got back to the Falls. He was to stay in a billet close to his parents but walking past the house he noticed their lights still on. He called in and discovered that his mother was ill, she thought that one of the tomato juices had given her some sort of food poisoning.

"Shouldn't you be somewhere else?" said Peter.

"Ah, they're probably well tucked in now. I'll stay the night if that's all right with you?"

"You know you're more than welcome."

Before John had time to recognise the crashing sounds, the noise of boots on the stairs and Sheila's and Monica's screaming, the paratroopers came in on top of him. They had sledge-hammered the front and back doors and had left their armoured cars on the main road to ensure surprise. Raymond was away in England and Jimmy was staying in his granny's house so there was no disputing who – Peter or John – was the 23-year-old.

"What's going on? What's going on?" demanded Peter.

"Never you mind, old man. John O'Neill, I'm arresting you under the Special Powers Act. Tie him up!"

Catherine was shaking, Monica and Sheila were crying.

"Leave him alone! Leave him alone!" his youngest sister protested but she was pushed aside.

His hands were tied behind his back and a rope put around his neck.

This was the price that had to be paid, John kept thinking, but cursed himself for being at home having chided the others who had fallen back into the habit of creature comforts. If only the house had been raided in July then I wouldn't be here now, he thought.

Peter ran out into the street and stuffed a packet of cigarettes into John's trouser pocket. But the escort wouldn't accept John's shoes and socks. Though it was still dark, people had gathered and were shouting abuse at the soldiers. There was a sudden, hushed silence when the noose around John's neck was tightened and he began choking.

"Get your bin lids out and start rattling!" shouted a neighbour, Peggy Carson. Another, Mrs Clarke, comforted Catherine. John was made to lie on the floor of the armoured car, soldiers' boots on top of him.

"What about Donnelly?" he heard an officer ask.

"We missed the bastard."

They arrived at Mulhouse Street Barracks. He was taken inside and roughed up. Radios were crackling, and Armoured Personnel Carriers were arriving and departing in a frantic commotion of shouting, cursing, and horns being blasted. The place tasted of fear. He was brought into what appeared to be an assembly hall where there were many other prisoners similarly bound. A soldier was appointed to each prisoner.

There was a loud explosion close by; probably a nail bomb, thought John. They had planned what to do when internment was introduced. As soon as the crowds came on to the streets the units would begin moving weapons out of dumps. They were to attack the soldiers and demonstrate that the IRA was still intact; but it was also part of the plan to move the struggle onto a new level.

The sun came up to reveal in the sky palls of black smoke rising from nationalist areas as the rioting spread. John was bundled out of the hall and placed on plank seating with others in the back of a canvas-covered lorry. Of the eight prisoners only John was an IRA Volunteer, while a few were supporters and the rest had a small local profile in street politics. The lorry drove out of the base and turned down the Grosvenor Road. Shooting from the Leeson Street area could now be heard. The soldiers fell quickly to the floor but jabbed the muzzles of their rifles into the prisoners forcing them to sit upright.

"Boys, this is Pocky Logan, Pocky Logan! Don't be shooting! Hold your fire!" shouted a prisoner sitting closest to the back flaps. John felt disgusted at the spinelessness and noted that the soldiers who had slapped them for asking questions or speaking earlier didn't interfere or interrupt Logan's screams.

At Girdwood Barracks John was thrown out of the lorry. There was a queue of silent prisoners waiting to go into a gymnasium. Many were badly injured, blood pouring from head-wounds. One complained that his fingers were broken and was struck with a baton across the shoulder blades. There was an old man, stiff in his movements, who had just received a black eye from a military policeman for refusing to comply with an order. Another soldier protested at him being hit.

"This is feckin' desperate, corporal. Look at 'im – he's only an old man."

"Mind your own business and carry out your orders," said the Military Policeman, who was his senior.

In the gymnasium several hundred prisoners were sitting on the floor, some in pyjamas, with their hands on their heads. The Military Policemen were in control. Fractious detainees were hit with batons and ordered to do press-ups. Names were called out and then those persons were marched out to interrogation rooms.

John's wrists were still behind his back. He was photographed and taken to a room for questioning. As he approached the room he heard a loud groan. Two RUC men in plain clothes, whom he took to be Special Branch officers, were interrogating a prisoner who was handcuffed and hanging from a round iron bar cemented into the wall. On the other wall was a framed colour picture of Queen Elizabeth and the Duke of Edinburgh, smiling.

"No more, no more, please! I'll talk. Let me down, please!"

The fear in the room was palpable but John was suspicious of the quasi-crucifixion. Activity in the room had only begun when he was a few yards off and there was too much blood on the prisoner's face. He had heard from old republicans about being put in the same cell as someone who would claim to be from another IRA Brigade area but who was actually a plant, trying to get information. He decided that this was a set-up.

One of the RUC men flicked through a thick file: "Ah, so you're John O'Neill. Take him away!" He was surprised that that was all that was said. On the way down the corridor he had to pass MPs who were standing about.

"Here's the bastard that shoots our mates in the back!" one shouted. They began punching and kicking him. He ran as fast as he could but two of the MPs had their arms through his and they slowed him down. He was put back on the floor. The beating had helped restore his faith in his convictions. The bruises were sore but he was not bleeding and he stared ahead of him, curiously enjoying the thought of a cigarette, inhaling the stream of blue smoke like it was an intoxicating draught. He was also more anxious about his family than about himself because at least he knew what to expect.

The cord around his wrists was cut off and he was ordered up off his feet and taken to the toilets. "Here, clean them!" he was told. He let the scrubbing brush fall to the ground.

"Clean them!" the voice roared – bad breath – inches from his face. John refused, was punched in the stomach and grabbed by the scruff of the neck. He was flung to the floor and caught some of the kicks before they did him harm. He was brought back to his previous position. Hours passed. The prisoners were called up to a table for tea. There were only about twelve cups for the entire hall and the fact that they were being re-used without being washed put John off. Since his days at sea he had a fastidious attitude towards delph and cutlery but he was so thirsty that he drank the awful concoction. Out of the side of his eye he caught sight of other prisoners washing windows, brushing the floor and two carrying mops and buckets out of the toilets.

"O'Neill! Out here!"

"Cah! Out here!" When prisoner Kerr realised he'd been called he wasn't long responding. Another four were ordered out. John was escorted out the door into the daylight and fresh air.

"Hands out front!" He was tied with plastic cuffs.

The engines of a Wessex helicopter were started up and the men were ordered to climb in. John was last. Behind them the doors locked like a vacuum seal. They took off and the flight lasted about fifteen minutes. An MP grinned at John.

"Can you swim?" he shouted. "I said, can you swim?"

John nodded.

"Well then, can you fly?" The prisoners were worried. "Did you ever see the Viet Cong getting thrown out of the choppers? Eh? That's what's gonna happen to you fuckers."

The door roared open and air shot in. John was kicked out and his heart gave one last hard pump, but he fell only a few feet into a dog compound where whorls of faeces sat like deposits of giant lugworms. The other prisoners landed beside him and the helicopter quickly rose into the sky. Snarling Alsatians came running at them and the prisoners formed a group with their backs against each other, kicking at the animals who were on leashes staked beside their kennels, but long enough to present a danger. A gate opened and handlers rushed in, grabbed the men by the hair and trailed them through the barking dogs. Other soldiers, standing about as observers, shouted their approval of what was happening.

The men were taken back into the gymnasium where the number of prisoners had significantly fallen. They were then individually called for stew which turned out to be cold. It was covered in a white layer of grease and was unappetising. Anyone who refused to eat was beaten, so John was again pummelled.

His name was called. An MP grabbed him and frog-marched him out of the hall. He was taken into a large hole, which soldiers had blown in the wall dividing Girdwood Barracks from Crumlin Road Jail, and was led through. In the basement of D wing his hands were untied. The RUC found the cigarettes and confiscated them. John's watch and ring had already been stolen.

"These will be placed in this bag outside your cell and you can collect them when you're going," an RUC man said, whilst a prison warder locked him up in a cell. John was jubilant and was singing to himself, "I've survived! I've survived!"

His cellmate stared at him: "My God, what have they done to you?"

The young man, whom John didn't know, tore some linen from the bed, wetted it with water and washed the wounds. He rinsed out the makeshift flannel in the cup which instantly turned bright red. John thanked him. He then realised the extent of his injuries. His lips were split open and the air was like acid eating at them. Both eyes were black, one was almost closed over. Blood had clotted on his scalp and had dried over the skin creases. The door was unlocked and an RUC officer appeared.

"You, get out! You shouldn't be in here with him!"

He was left on his own and pondered over what sort of arrangement was it that had RUC men and MPs in charge of prison warders, telling them where to put prisoners and when to open and close the cells. The door creaked open again. He recognised a senior officer in the Special Branch. He had been shown his photograph. The IRA had been planning to kill him. They had nicknamed him the Bouncer. The Bouncer introduced himself.

"You must know where there's a few guns knocking about, John, my old friend. I'm not after names, just guns and bombs, you know the sort of things. I want you to think about it, son. You look like a nice fella. I know everything about you but I'm a reasonable man. There's £20," he said, extricating two £10 notes from a thick wad. "No, just you think about it. There's plenty more where that came from, as you can see. I'll call back later after you've rested."

John placed his ear to the door and listened carefully until the Bouncer had finished his rounds. Then he banged on the cell door until a warder opened it.

"Any chance of a smoke?" he asked. "I've fags just sitting outside in a brown bag." The warder gave the bag a glance.

"Piss off." He proceeded to close the door.

"Wait, wait, wait! Just a minute!" John dug his hands deep into his pocket and pulled out the two £10 notes. "This is no use to me in here. Here take them, go ahead, but give me a smoke."

"Let's see," said the jailer. "Okay, what's the harm." He gave him the packet, lit him up one of the cigarettes and pocketed the money in his breast pocket, fastening the silver button. The barefoot prisoner lay back on his bed, one leg over the other, smiling at the high, yellow ceiling.

When the Bouncer returned John had enough smokes for a week.

"Well, have you thought about it?"

"I've thought about it and I'm not interested."

"You'll be sorry. I have something special in mind for you. You're one of the lucky ones. Now, give me my money, I mean, our money back."

"I haven't got it."

"Where is it then?"

"He has it," said John pointing. "That screw has it in his top pocket. I gave it to him to mind for you."

The warder began stuttering.

"Oh yes, here you are, sir, here you are."

"Why wouldn't you take the money?"

"Money wouldn't buy my pride."

"Well, you'll have plenty of time to think about your pride."

All that night the lights were kept on and the cell doors were banged. It was only possible to lightly doze.

On Tuesday morning MPs took John out of the jail and forced him to run an obstacle course made of barbed wire and broken glass. He was once again confused and afraid because he had thought it was all over once he was in jail. His moods swung between spiritual highs and demoralised lows.

What if they're right and I'm wrong? Could we really have expected to take on the British government without retribution? Were we upstarts, dreamers, doomed from the outset? Then he would draw upon his convictions which were buried under the weight of the brutality, and he felt an inner peace. I am right, I am right! he said aloud.

And when they saw the trace of that defiant smile they beat him all the more.

Late on Tuesday night, shaken and hungry, he was brought outside into the darkness. There were three other prisoners whom he recognised but did not acknowledge. Their hands were tied behind their backs with plastic cord. The MPs stood in front of them, silently. Slowly and deliberately they produced eight hoods – hessian-type bags – and put one hood inside the other. Then they walked behind each prisoner and pulled the hoods over their heads. The man on John's right began to scream and he heard the dull thuds of fists pile-driving into a stomach. The terrified prisoner quietened down after that.

Someone twisted the bag at the back until it tightened and John felt as if he was choking. A helicopter landed and they were pushed and kicked on board. Within seconds it took off. It flew for over three-quarters of an hour. When it came to ground they were again kicked and forced to run over rough terrain. The length of the journey made John think he was in England or Scotland.

He was brought into a brick building. The floor was cold and bare. From the echo of his escort's boots he felt that they were going down a corridor. He was brought to be medically examined. He could hear the doctor turning in a swivel chair.

"Any ailments?" said the doctor. He was English. John guessed he was fat, from the compression in his voice.

"I've a bad heart," said John.

"Uncuff him and take his clothes off." He cursorily examined him. "He's all right for interrogation."

The hood was wrenched tight and he was forced out of the room. He was bundled into a boiler suit, two sizes too big for him.

"Up against that wall!"

He didn't understand the order because of a loud hissing noise and was forcibly spread-eagled by two or three people with English and Scottish accents. He tried to reduce the angle by a few inches, and thus ease the pressure on his limbs, but his feet were kicked even further apart.

"Now, maintain your posture or else ..."

Hours dripped by and he felt as though a snow-plough went through his brain, scattering cells, splattering red flakes into the ditch, returning and churning up more furrows, shaving his brain smooth, opening the road to allow the interrogators' traffic through.

"What time is it?" he asked.

"It's August and don't you leave that wall!"

He fell and was beaten, then he was helped into the spread-eagle position and told: "Resume the posture!"

More hours passed by.

"Come with us."

He was taken into a room. The hood was removed and a number of men sat behind arc lights which were trained on him where he stood.

"You asked to see us."

"I didn't ask to see you," he whispered.

"What did he say?"

"He said he didn't ask to see us."

He was hit across the head and fell on the concrete floor, but got on to all fours. His interrogators wore track suits and plimsolls and their faces were hidden. He was frog-marched back to the wall.

"Resume the posture!"

Hours passed. More beatings each time he fell. The noise drove excruciating pain through his head.

"Can I go to the toilet?" he asked.

"You are shit, so shit where you are!"

He had no bowel movements and had been given no water. He dreamed he was urinating against an entry wall and urine dribbled down his leg, hot and stinging, chafing his thigh, and he was reminded of dribbling as a child when he thought he had finished.

"Out!"

Corridor. Room. Lights.

"You asked to see us?"

"I didn't ask ..."

Another beating. Back to the wall, back to the Devil's screech.

"Out!"

Corridor. Room? No room. Air. Lorry. Drive. Helicopter. Sky. Earth. Jeep.

"Get him through the hole in the wall."

Crumlin Road Jail?

The hood was removed. Three RUC officers sat in front of him.

"Are you John O'Neill?"

"Yes."

"Here is a removal order empowering the RUC via the Civil Authority to remove you to any place where your presence is required and question you for any length of time. As you can see it has been signed by the Minister of Home Affairs, Mr Brian Faulkner. Okay? Here you are."

It was stuffed into the top pocket of the boiler suit.

He was taken back out through the hole in the wall, hooded, placed in a jeep, driven to the helicopter, flown to the place of interrogation and was soon back up against the wall in the spread-eagle position.

Hours. Hood removed.

"You asked to see us?"

– Silence.

"I told you he asked to see us, didn't I!"

"Yes, you did! Do you think is he ready?"

"I don't know. Let's ask. You did ask to see us."

His convictions were hanging on to the edge of a cliff with one finger nail. You were a tout before, O'Neill. Are you going to be a tout again? What about Paul McShane? Paul McShane . . . Paul McShane, McShane, the shame; the shame of squealing on McShane. School days, so long ago, so innocent, before all this. He hauled his mind up from where it perilously dangled, used the pause, the silence, as breathing space and muttered: "I didn't ask to see you ..."

"Fuck you, O'Neill!" The lamp was knocked over and one of the figures kicked him in the groin. The whole world went dark.

"And what do you think you'll be doing in five or ten years' time?" Angela asked. It was late August and she was lying with her head in his lap, staring up into his eyes. His hand circled her right breast as it rose and gently fell.

"Oh, who knows? Living in Paris, London, Berlin? Why do you ask? Would you come with me? Would you live in a spacious garret with me, and in the winter mornings I would go out and buy hot croissants? When I came back you'd have the coffee made. We'd spread butter and strawberry jam over the hot rolls, eat and drink, and then we'd climb under the continental quilt and make love as the snow fell outside our window."

"Where's the guns?"

"Where's Stevie Donnelly?"

"Where's Dominic Gallagher?"

"You blew up the jeep in Brougher Mountain!"

"You killed the three Scottish soldiers!"

"Two of them were brothers, you bastard."

"Yeh, and seventeen years of age."

"You blew up Roden Street Barracks!"

"You blew up Sergeant Wallace in Springfield Road!"

"You planted incendiaries in Anderson and McAuley's!"

"Where's the guns?"

"Where's Stevie Donnelly?"

"Where's Dominic Gallagher?"

Some of the questions and statements meant nothing. He wasn't talking but most of the time there would have been no time to have answered before the next question or statement came.

"You blew up Roden Street Barracks!"

"You blew up Sergeant Wallace in Springfield Road!"

"You planted incendiaries in Anderson and McAuley's!"

"You blew up Bronco McIvor!"

"Outside his house! That was nice!"

What? What was that? Did he hear that? John wanted to tell them that they had got it all wrong, that he didn't blow up Bronco. They had worked together. Shared cigarettes. Had become friends. Bronco wanted him to stay. Not go on the boats. But then he knew that that was a lie. Was there a police reservist called Bronco blown up in his car? Whatever the truth, John now experienced a mix of emotions as if he were just learning for the first time that his comrades killed Bronco, old Bronco McIvor with the King Billy tattoos, who had gone on to join the Police Reserve, who wasn't just a mouthpiece, who somewhere along the line, because of a word or a deed or an emotion, had been tipped over the edge… like John …

Did they know they had shaken him, might have had him? They could see his face because the hood had been removed. But they could not read the expression of sadness and regret beneath the blood and bruising.

"Do you want to go back to the music room, John?"

The music room, that's what they called the room where the high-pitched hissing sound, the 'white noise', went on and on and on.

Days passed, days of more blood and bruising.

John turned the minute hand of the chubby alarm clock back, to give the workers an extra half-hour to get out. Stevie covered the doors. As John ran to make their escape Stevie dropped his gun and grabbed him in a bear hug, like a madman.

"For fuck's sake Stevie let me go. Let me go! This place is gonna go up! I've planted bombs. It's gonna go up, up, up!"

"What's gonna go up? What's gonna go up?"

He awoke, handcuffed to a radiator – the rest room.

"Okay, back to the wall. Resume the posture! You'll talk. You'll talk!"

The doctor saw him twice more: "Fit for interrogation!"

"Where's the guns? Where's the guns? Where's the guns?"

"Where's Donnelly? Where's Stevie Donnelly? Where is he?"

"Where's that cunt Gallagher? Where's Dominic Gallagher?"

John sat at the top right hand corner of the ceiling, out of sight, impish, giggling, as they punched him in the ribs down below.

Next, he was being rolled about on the ground. They were rubbing his neck, massaging his muscles, restoring his circulation.

They lifted the hood up and he sipped some water through his parched lips. They gave him a piece of broken bread which almost choked him.

"Right. Resume the posture!"

Spread-eagled again. Legs kicked out. He tried to cheat by using his head to take the weight off his arms but they fired shots which forced him back on his fingers. He thought of his mother and she appeared before him and he felt happy. He did not feel like a person, he was either a mind or an aching, sore body, never the two together.

He felt like crying, he had just shit himself. It had been a painfully slow bowel movement and the little warm balls stuck between the cheeks of his buttocks. They gave off, he imagined, a dreadful stink and reduced him to a baby. He was helpless.

"John? John?" It was a friendly, soothing voice. "John, it's okay. The hooded treatment is over."

His eyeballs returned to his head. His head, arms and legs returned to his torso from the distance to which they had been kicked. He listened hard. His eyes shot from side to side within the darkness of the hood.

"It's over, John. I'll take the hood off in a minute and tidy you up but I'll have to put it back on when you move back to Crumlin Road Jail. These people don't want you to know where you are or to see their faces. Okay? Now, take it easy ..."

It was a Belfast accent. He was worried that his mind was playing a trick on him. The RUC man's assurances made him even more afraid. The hood did come off and John stood trembling. He couldn't move his arms. His legs were cramped in a standing position.

"Come on. I'll help you. It's over. You have my word. I'll be travelling with you."

John burst out crying as he shuffled barefoot down the corridor and into the toilets. His ankles, knees, were swollen, his hands, wrists, elbows and shoulders were in great pain. His friend shaved him, cleaned and wiped his backside. He rubbed and softly chopped at his arm and leg muscles.

"John you have to be photographed. Come with me. It won't take long."

He was photographed in the nude and the cameraman appeared to be hundreds of yards away in the distance. He was taken back to the corridor. He couldn't talk but hung on to the man who was showing him mercy. He held onto him when he thought he was leaving him.

"Look. It's okay. It's time to go. Trust me. Help me put on the hood. We'll do it together. That's it. Now, I have to handcuff you. Then we'll get on board the helicopter. When it lands I'll remove the handcuffs and the hood but don't look back. You're going away from here, back to your mates. When you go to jail there'll be a tribunal. You're not a bad fella, you know. After thirty days you'll be able to go to this tribunal and sign a form and you'll be out. If I ever meet you in the street would you buy me a drink?"

John spoke for the first time: "I'll buy you all the drink you want."

"We're going now."

When the helicopter landed the policeman said: "Don't be looking back. Good luck," and he pulled the hood off and pushed him out. The doors whooshed closed and other RUC men put him into the back of a Land Rover and then drove him to the jail.

He was brought into the basement of D Wing. The prison doctor weighed him. He had lost 16 lbs.

"What day is it, doctor?"

"It's Tuesday."

"It couldn't be. I was here on Tuesday. It must be Thursday or Friday."

"No. It's Tuesday, Tuesday the 17th August."

John shook his head in disbelief. He just shook his head.

CHAPTER 10
LONDON II

When Angela left Belfast she went back to London in search of a new life. She found a job and threw herself into work with absolute commitment and few distractions.

Even the other typists in the law firm of Stevenson, Scott & Bevins had to admit that she was conscientious. An agency had arranged the interview and Mr Bevins' supervisor took to Angela right away. The different jobs she had had before could have been interpreted as flightiness, but her references were impeccable and Miss Richards was impressed. Angela's shorthand was excellent and she could speed type at 65 words per minute. But Miss Richards did warn Angela that, despite being with Mr Bevins for over twenty years, she still found him cantankerous.

When Mr Bevins and his wife had had an argument he would be in a foul mood. He would lock the door of his office and dictate letters, including swear words, onto his recorder. Then he would simply slide back the glass window, hand out two hours of tapes without comment and later slide back the window expecting the letters to be typed up. If they were not finished by five he didn't scream or shout but coughed loudly and then simply sat on, loudly drumming his fingers on his desk whilst the girls typed away, doing overtime without pay.

"When shall I ask for a rise?" Angela said to a colleague after three months.

"You'll not have to. He knows you're a good worker."

Angela had been promised that her wages would be reviewed, depending on her proficiency, after three months. Time passed and when she had been there six months she spoke to Miss Richards. Miss Richards told her that Mr Bevins had personally to clear all increases in salaries for his girls with the exceptions of those in the typing pool who worked directly for Misters Stevenson or Scott.

It was now time to knock on his door.

"Mr Bevins, as you know I've been here for six months and pay-wise I am still below some of the other girls who have less experience. The new girl who started last month, Maggie, is getting exactly the same as me. So I was just wondering ..."

"Don't worry, Miss McCann, I'll discuss it with colleagues and let you know."

One week and then two weeks passed.

"Excuse me, Mr Bevins, but have you had any chance to discuss the matter of my pay with ..."

"No, I haven't. But I'll organise it."

A month passed and there was still no rise. She then heard that he had booked a fortnight's holiday for himself and his family at the end of the month. Angela grew increasingly irritated. One morning she had difficulty getting out of bed. Her hip still occasionally gave her trouble from the time Jonathan had hit her. She decided to see a doctor. He gave her the all-clear and she arrived in work just after eleven.

At the end of the following week when she examined her pay slip she noticed a shortfall. She thought it was a mistake and checked with the bookkeeper who told her she had been docked for being off.

"But I've never been off. Not once in six months!"

"Nothing to do with me. See Mr Bevins."

"I will."

"What are you coming in here for? Can't you see I'm trying to get away?" He threw his briefcase into a corner.

"Mr Bevins you have docked me for going to the doctor and you have been promising for weeks now to give me a pay rise. What about the extra hours I have worked? I even worked on a Saturday so as you could get your legal aid money. If that's all you think of me then you can keep your cheque!"

She threw the cheque on the table and stormed out.

The whole office, including Mr Scott, heard the commotion. Angela began clearing her desk and packing her handbag. A few minutes later Mr Bevins, slightly embarrassed, emerged from his office.

"Here. Take this cheque. It belongs to you."

"I won't take it until you rectify it. Maybe you want me to hand in my notice. Is that it?" asked Angela, feeling sorry for herself.

"Don't be silly, girl. I'll sort out your increase when I return. Meanwhile, take your cheque."

She stood stubbornly before him and he stared at her until his patience ran out.

"As from now we'll take it, Miss McCann, that you are on a month's notice! Now, if you'll excuse me!" He thumped the cheque on her desk and walked out.

"I'll not be seeing you again!" she shouted after him and whispered, "you baldy bastard."

Mike Scott came over to her.

"You'll be cutting your own throat if you leave. Come over to my office for a talk."

He ordered coffee and Angela explained what had happened. Outside, the leaves on the trees were turning green to catch the bright, warm April sunlight.

"I know he's hard to work for. But don't commit yourself to leaving. I could do with someone extra. June is leaving to get married and is intending to become a proper housewife, which she will regret, but that's her decision. Come and work for me."

"Oh my God!"

"What? What is it?"

"He's written a new cheque. It must be for all the overtime. I'm scundered. What am I going do?"

"What did you say you were?"

"Scundered. It's a Belfast word for being embarrassed."

"You certainly are scundered, especially since most of the office heard you referring to him as having no hair!"

They both laughed.

"Think about it," he said. "Think about coming to work for me."

"How long have you been married?"

"Ten years. But it's been stormy, as I said to you before. Having no kids hasn't helped either."

This was the third occasion in just as many weeks that over-time had kept them in the office together and that they had subsequently stopped for a drink, she having accepted his offer of a lift to her flat. She had only been working for him for two months when he made her his personal secretary. She suddenly then found that she was in a position to buy clothes and save at the same time.

Angela sipped at her drink and Mike ordered another for himself.

"What about you? Any steady boyfriends?"

"No. Not this long time. I'm working an evil past out of my system!" she laughed.

"I don't believe it," he said.

"Well, I'm not joking."

"Tell me please. I'm really interested."

She thought his expression was of genuine concern.

"Well, before I do," she said, pinning him with a comically raised eyebrow to denote that if he should betray her he would suffer indescribable retribution. "Before I do, promise me you're not a British soldier!"

"Pardon?" he said, baffled but smiling, and realising his privilege in hearing the confession of this intriguing woman.

She told him about school life under nuns, her wild teenage years in West Belfast, about her first lover, John. She omitted the story about his letter and humiliating him. She spoke about living rough in London, in the squat, being on drugs. About the Troubles in Belfast, her terror at being mistaken for a 'soldier lover', her coming back to London. About taking 'a fancy' to him shortly after starting in the firm. At times his jaw dropped.

"Now, what do you think of all that?"

"You've lived three lives and you're only what is it? Twenty-three? Twenty-four?"

"Twenty-one! It wasn't that rough a life."

"I'm sorry," he said.

"It's all right!" she laughed, turning her empty glass around and looking at him.

"Waiter!" he called. "Waiter!"

Angela went back home for a holiday in late July. For some days she had been trying to gently break the news to her mother and father that she was living with a married man. She confided in her sister Mary Ann but she just listened without commenting, as if there was nothing that Angela could do would surprise or appal her.

Frank's sister and her husband were visiting and Frank was boasting about the success of his daughter in England.

"Yes. She's doing very well for herself."

Angela smiled and passed the sandwiches.

"She's a private secretary and has moved into her own house and even has her own cheque book!"

Mary was very proud of her and Angela couldn't shatter the illusions after so many disappointments. But she was determined that her days of being deceitful were over and just as she and Mike faced Vera, his wife, with the announcement of their love – even before they began an affair – she would tell her parents by the time she was set to leave. The day approached and she decided to wait until the last possible moment so as to minimise the time available for tears and rancour.

"Mammy, I've something to tell you. Where's daddy, I want him to be present."

"He'll be back in a second." Her mother sat down slowly, perched on the edge of the sofa. She bit her lower lip. "I think you better tell me before you tell your father. Are you pregnant? Is that it, Angela?"

"No, mammy, I'm not expecting."

"Thank God for that. What is it then? What's wrong?"

"Well, actually, I don't think anything's wrong. Not in my eyes."

Despite this being a shot at prevailing moral prudery, as well as a hint of what she was getting at, she saw the cloud lift from her mother's face and a ray of relief beginning to show.

"I'm sharing the house with someone."

"So?"

"We're buying it together."

"It's a man, isn't it? You're living with a man. My God, what's your father going to say!"

"He's married."

"Jesus, Mary and St Joseph, that's all I need. That's all I need. How could you? We'll be the talk of Andersonstown." Her mother started to cry. Paul wandered into the room, saw the tears, and quickly backed out.

"I am ashamed of you. You're nothing but a brazen hussy. You've brought me nothing but shame and trouble ... Shame and trouble ... What'll your granny think?"

"But mammy he loves me and I love him."

"And what about his poor wife. Think of her or are you so full of yourself."

Frank came into the room.

"What's all this then, eh?"

"Go on, tell your daddy what you told me. Go on, tell him."

"I'm living with a fella, daddy."

"Well, you would be, wouldn't you, you selfish bitch."

"That's not all Frank. Go on, tell him."

"He's married daddy, but he's getting divorced."

"Fuck, I've heard it all. I've heard it all."

It was the first time he had ever cursed in front of his daughter, or inside his home.

"Get."

"What? What do you mean?"

"Get! Get going and don't come back."

Angela was too stubborn to cry and went upstairs to pack. There, she made no attempt to rally Paul, Sean or Mary Ann to her side. She wasn't asking anybody to support her, nor was she going to be a cause of division. But what annoyed her was that, whilst communications had now broken down between her and her parents for the foreseeable future, they would lie on each occasion someone asked after her and her circumstances.

The taxi pulled up at the door and sounded its horn.

"I'm going now," she shouted into the sitting room. Paul grabbed her case from her and took it out to the car.

"Thanks," she said. Mary Ann and Sean stood about the hall at sixes and sevens and bid her goodbye. She kissed them both.

Paul opened the door of the vehicle. "I'll see you big sister. Take care of yourself."

"You too. Tell mammy and daddy I love them."

"I'll do that okay. Time will sort it out, you'll see."

153

The small house in south London which they shared was one of several properties owned by Mike's father, the others he had converted into flats and sold them off.

The firm had been handling the conveyancing when Mike had his marital crisis. His father never got on with Vera and lost no sleep over the break up. He had no hesitation in selling his son the house at a knock-down price.

Mike felt that Angela's parents would eventually understand though he couldn't understand their opposition, their morals. Living with someone you loved was no big deal. A bigger deal would be living with someone you didn't love.

Angela enjoyed cooking for her partner and looking after him. She bought ties to match his shirts and in the office prioritised his interviews and supervised his workload. The other girls respected and liked her because she was loyal to them, arguing their interests and representing them in disputes. The only person who avoided her and kept contact to a minimum was her former employer, Mr Bevins. But Angela would tease him at every opportunity.

"Beautiful weather for September, Mr Bevins, don't you agree?"

He would huff and all the girls would laugh as the dumpy little man waddled down the corridor.

Whilst Mike gently snored beside her she stared at him. He wasn't handsome, indeed was plain-faced and gangly-limbed. She used to take a fancy to men with good looks and only afterwards consider their personalities. She stroked his black hair with its premature silver streaks and he awoke and smiled in the dawn light.

"Okay?"

"Yes, I'm okay," she whispered.

I am contented, she repeated to herself. I am contented. But she knew there was more beyond her; another view of the world.

There was one girl in the office not prepared to keep the secret and that was because Angela had been especially friendly with her and had taken her out to lunch a few months before to discuss a personal problem. Angela lent the girl money and told her to pay it back when she could afford it.

"Angela. This may hurt you but you should know. All the other girls have been talking about it and I don't think it's fair."

"What are you talking about?"

"Mr Scott is seeing his wife again."

"I know. He sees her occasionally. They're sorting out the divorce."

"Angela, it's not like that at all. There's going to be no divorce. He was seen two or three times in the same bar and they were clearly intimate. I thought you should know."

"Have you been seeing Vera again?"

"No! Who told you that?"

She gave him one of her let's-be-honest looks. He went and poured himself a drink.

"Angela. I'm sorry. It's true I have seen her. She's been really hurt and upset since I left. I know you have given up everything for me, your home, family, you've accepted my friends, and what can I say? You have been wonderful to live with, we've never argued and you're a great lover. I have been happy, really happy, with you but I have never been able to cope with the guilt of leaving Vera."

"Be honest with me Mike. Is it just guilt?"

"I think so," he said. "I feel so responsible for her. I was her first and only boyfriend and my leaving shattered her. I love you Angela, I really love you."

They made love there and then on the rug, more passionately than ever before. They spent the next few days kissing and exchanging intimate glances at every opportunity but by the fourth day something inside both of them knew that the furtive activity was not a sign of eternal bliss but was really the clock counting down.

Angela was annoyed and hurt but not shattered. It was ironical.

"Vera and I have a lot to thank you for. In many ways you brought us back together and we have learnt many lessons."

Even Vera had begun talking to her in friendly, sisterly terms.

"You know I can no longer work for you, Mike," said Angela, a few days before he removed his clothes and belongings.

"I've thought about that. I've sorted things out. Here," he handed her papers.

"What are these?"

155

"The deeds of the house. It's yours. Stop! Don't say it. I know what you're thinking and it's not like that at all. You deserve it. You've had nothing but hardship. And anyway you have no choice. Mr Bevins handled the small print and it's yours to knock down or sell. What will you do? Will you stay here? It has its memories."

"Oh, I don't know. Life's a bit of a challenge. I've been homesick a lot recently. My friend Patricia from Belfast will be staying with me for a few weeks. I've a lot of thinking to do. In fact, I've to sort out my life. Don't feel guilty, Mike. We had a good time. A short time, mind you! But a good time."

"I'll never forget you Angela. You're a great girl. Kind and understanding."

"Shut up. Or you'll have me crying over this girl whom I've never met!"

CHAPTER 11
AMBUSH

Stevie arrived at the house first, he was always on time. The others followed separately, through the back door, down the steps, through the small kitchen and tiny living room and up the stairs, where they stunk out the back bedroom with the constant smoking of cigarettes which steadied their nerves.

This call-house was new: a young husband and wife appalled by the torture of prisoners had decided to support the IRA. More homes were opened to the republicans after soldiers shot dead thirteen people on a Civil Rights march in Derry.

"Dominic Gallagher's been caught," said Stevie to the men who comprised his unit.

"When did this happen?" said Joe.

"Brits raided a house in Iveagh Parade this morning, he was using as a billet. Anyway, life goes on," said Stevie, as he fanned his face. "Joe, open that bloody window, the smoke in here would kill you."

There was a knock at the door. It was opened and the woman left in a tray of buttered baps and mugs of tea. The baby's room had recently been decorated and carpeted. It had a Magic Roundabout lampshade hanging from the ceiling and curtains patterned with scenes from a zoo.

"Do you want an ashtray?" the woman asked, sounding a little bit anxious.

"My apologies for these men," Stevie replied. "They should be put out in the yard!"

She smiled and returned shortly afterwards with ashtrays.

"By the way, I'm making a fry for Eddie later if any of you would like one. He's to go to work at two, he's on a shift."

"I'd love a fry," said Stevie. "I'm starvin'." He munched at his second bap.

When she left, Patsy let his envy be known.

"How the hell could you eat a fry? I'm having trouble keeping down this tea." He had also been to the toilet twice because of his nerves.

"Not only could I eat a fry, my boy, but I could eat yours as well. Anyway, down to biz. I've cleared a float with the Operations Officer. If we don't 'touch' we have to wrap up before half-three."

"Why's that?"

"Never mind." In late afternoon a car-load of nitrobenzene explosives was due in the Falls and Stevie needed the area to be quiet by then.

"Joe, I'll be on foot and you float behind me with the gear until we get a foot patrol. I'll stay around the front of the road. We'll 'touch' quicker there. Tell Marian to take the thirty-eight and for her and Liam to take a car at the zebra crossing. They're over in McDonough's but they need to get another house to hold the driver. Hold his licence just in case he's an Orangeman and bolts. Tell Marian not to be hijacking any women – they'll only scream and things'll be fucked up."

Stevie pulled out various articles from the parcel he had asked Joe to bring.

"What do you think of this?"

They all began laughing. He had pulled on an old cardigan and put on glasses with round metal frames which gave him a silly appearance. From beneath the bed he produced a pair of hedge-clippers. Finally, he dipped his comb in the tea and within seconds stood his hair on end.

They admired the lengths to which he went. Some of the Volunteers experienced a thrill, unmasked, undisguised, running through the streets, armed.

"The Brits don't wear masks, so why should we," conceit would foolishly dictate, as they took the chance that the soldiers, the eye-witnesses they faced, would not survive their sniper fire.

I see the patrol and I smile to myself. They haven't been shot at in two weeks and they have relaxed. They probably believe the bloody know-all intelligence officer who put Gerry, Peter and Sean in Long Kesh and thinks he has cleaned us out. The second foot-patrol – what are they thinking of – home, the IRA? – is about five hundred yards behind, too far to be of help in our maze of streets.

"Joe, get the gear ready. Tell Patsy to put the car beside Murray's house, facing up the street. We'll get them from the corner against the hoardings."

They stop outside the post office – the Englishmen, Scotsmen, Welshmen, the uniforms, I don't give a damn. One stops a woman and rummages through her bag. I can make out her protesting, giving off, and, like a cat baring its fangs, a vengeance flushes through me that tautens every muscle and sinew.

The radio-man stops a young lad. I can almost hear that jarring British accent ordering him to put his arms up higher and get them legs out. He's feeling his jeans, frisking the body of the frightened kid.

Oh, I'm in control okay. I run my finger along cold steel. I stroke the smooth wood. Here they come, their sight of me bordering on curiosity, wary, until I raise both hands and, with a clip of my shears, level the last section of the hedge. And the soldiers relax. I whistle The Rifles of the IRA, *so cheekily, so contemptuous of their ignorance, with so much daring, almost challenging them, that it excites me and I am pleased with the aura of deception I have carefully fostered.*

Soldier, don't say we didn't warn you.

Here they come. They don't see me even though they are looking directly at me. I look a fruitcake, so happy and serene and domestic, standing with my hedge-clippers now tucked under the arm of my woolly cardigan.

"You Paddies! 'Greenfingers' is hardly going to cut our heads off! No self-respecting English kid would be seen dead wearing that kite-sized tie and polka-dot shirt! He must have been dropped on his head when he was born!"

And because with my glasses I look a twenty-year-old gawk, and because this is a strange land, because this is Ireland, I know they shrug me off. Innocence oozes out of me. The leader of the patrol does not mentally mark me down to be p-checked. He comes up to me, me with the clownish grin, specky four-eyes, and I use our exchange of glances to impart a duplicitous trust and friendship. I have that brotherly respect for both of us that opposing combatants share in war, but I cannot confide in him in the way that his battle fatigues mark him out for me. Fraternisation, communication, pity, restraint, humour, is always their *gift, depending on* their *mood, depending on what side of the bed they* crawled out of. *Favourable responses, replies, repartee, and their eyes sparkle as if they've just seen light at the end of the tunnel.* "Mama, we're winning their hearts and minds! They smile at us! Are almost talking to us again!" *But these are never sentimental exchanges across no man's land. There's no football at the Christmas front. The Brits remain implacable and we remain cunning.*

As he now passes me, me whom he'll never see again, I turn into the side-street of my youth and run across the cobblestones. From here I can almost touch the house I was born in and the entry where standing in darkness we fumbled at first making love.

I move as naturally as this sunny afternoon's light breeze blows across the Falls Road, an imperceptible shift of air that would hardly tickle a fly. I am honed for the delivery of this stroke like a sharpened pencil between the fingers of an artist.

I am immortal. I shall see tomorrow. This will be that corporal's last day.

I have already thought about him, even before he left England. Many times him. And the rest. He is somebody's son, perhaps a good man, maybe even a loving husband. We both speak the same language, could have stolen the same type of bars of chocolate from the corner shop, told the same juvenile jokes to our mates, and sheltered from the same storms as they fell a few hours apart on our lands. I listened to the same music and watched the same television as he did, The Beatles and Coronation Street. *But his people – his ma and da, their government – didn't even know we existed and cared nothing. When I pieced things together for myself, when I listened and watched, I understood it all – the police batons, the burning of homes, and then my decision to roar back. Sitting with the patience of a prophecy was my Irishness, waiting to be tapped and to explode.*

"He didn't even want to be there."

Already I can hear the familiar sermon echoing all the comparisons and lecturing me, the killer. I can see those comparisons myself right down to our mutual likes and dislikes in food, Granny Smith's apples, flowing butter on warm white bread, plenty of salt and vinegar on the fish and chips.

We may even support the same team for the FA Cup.

He probably doesn't even want to be here.

Everything can conspire to scream at you, to weaken your resolve. Everything I've been taught, from the words of my mother, to my schooling, my religious teachings, my own beliefs, were all part of a moral system whose effects are to cripple this action and stop me. Then there is the smug power of the status quo and the awesomeness of existing authority.

My bowels could give way as a sign of cowardice, a warning of the danger, a call to self-preservation. A twinge of conscience, yesterday's bloodshed, can become a black nightmare. I have seen that in comrades who fell away because the ghosts broke their health or mind. In others it was because of a flawed commitment to begin with, or "because of the wife," or because of a suddenly discovered political disagreement or a personality clash.

He probably doesn't even want to be here...

But he is! Rewards for soldiering, too tempting. Worth the chances he takes.

You're no peacemaker. You and I know that.

And that's my edge over him, over all their arguments. That's why I have blood like oil lubricating my steps which take me through these close streets and into Murray's street, ahead of the Brits.

He has no right to be here and if he doesn't want to be here then he shouldn't be here. He can kid himself, and may well have done so, but when all is said and done here he comes, sauntering up my road with his gun in his hand, doling out his mood to pedestrians, ever nosey and curious, ever the law, on top, dashing for his survival across open spaces because he knows we don't want him here. He would just as quickly rob me of life if ordered or if the fancy took him. But I am just too smart for the poor bugger. Governments may have us, the foot soldiers, at each other's throats but I am a soldier and a general, a politician and a civilian. I am my own government, but without him there is no government, no rule.

I am not claiming God's blessing for my actions. I am not that conceited. I believe in a god. I see the beauty of God's creation all around me, especially in this man with the clean face and short hair who'll never shave again, in the red roses over there bathing in the floating warm air, in this demonstration of power and fate unfolding and the tragedy of trapped people.

I entertain doubts precisely because they strengthen my single-mindedness, my convictions. The fact that I am doing this in spite of myself, *against the grain, against my nature, and not because they ever killed anyone belonging to me but because I have rationalised this confrontation and carry it out on behalf of others, shows that it isn't personal. I take up a gun for every intimidated Irish man who fucks the Brits up and down. I am here on behalf of all those who are weak, who lack the stomach for violence or lack the courage.*

I am the history maker.

This is my power, this is my cause, and behind me lie centuries and centuries and a thousand lands where similar foreign fuckers with rifles or bayonets, not ever wanting to be here or there, were around just the same, doing their missionary work, civilising us natives, maintaining their peace.

Oh, they have their criminality well packaged, well wrapped in law, literature and morality, whose duplicity only the likes of me can really appreciate, because the rebel knows the thief beneath the wig and the waistcoat.

It's even harder for us. The Brits were nurtured on superiority, on empire building, that others were Coons and Paddies and bloody Kaffirs.

The pulpits say I'm for hell!

We were reared to conform, to obey, to roll over, so it doesn't come easy to copy the killers and kill and even-up history a bit. I'll even stretch my imagination and allow that a Brit can be a relatively innocent being. So I snuff out an innocent life and – bingo – he goes straight to heaven. I've done him a favour, before he committed any serious sins and sentenced himself to eternal damnation. On the other hand, if he's a bastard and was heading for hell anyway, the most I've done is put him there prematurely. So where's the sin?

I'm being silly.

I'm not as callous as this and there's always, always, always, unease, a sense of violation and wrong, about killing this man and the ones before. Experiences and intellect, the slide into violence, eliminate the compunctions and Time absorbs the inhumanity. If I go to hell for this, I'll go to hell. My soul will burn eternally not for something I did only for myself but for what I did for others. And God's not up to much, if he'd burn anyone forever and ever. Imagine having those screams on your conscience!

I pass the garden shears back to one of our supporters, an old man who sits on a chair at his front door reading The Irish News.

"Good luck and be careful," he says.

"The Gardens are clear," Joe shouts. "So is the Drive and the Road." He opens the boot of the Cortina.

"Wait a minute," I order.

He snaps it shut. I walk out to the corner for a last look. I am on stage. The cobalt blue sky, the blazing sun focuses on me, the main character, me with the magic forefinger, fate-maker, sorter-outer of British soldiers come to do you harm.

"Quickly, they've stopped some fellas again."

But as I turn I see two armoured cars come down the Falls Road.

"Wait!"

They whine. They trundle past, beeping their hooters to their comrades, their drinking buddies, who wave back. The air is pungent with the foreign smell of their fumes. It all becomes so real, so critical, so deliberate.

My comrade opens the boot again. I pull on my gloves, place the silly spectacles in a side pocket of my trousers, pull on a cap, and lift the Garand. Patsy, our driver, turns on the ignition. Joe takes up a position with an Armalite to cover my back. The area is not too busy. Traffic is light.

I peep around the corner. At this corner we used to sit when school was over and play cards and whistle after the girls from St Louise's – the 'brown bombers' we called them. Little did we know the use of corners.

Mr Corporal is just about one hundred yards from me, down on his hunkers, finishing the frisking of a young lad. A colleague holds his weapon. Another soldier leaning over a wall and pointing his rifle directly at me, concerns me, but I am gone from sight and I have made him doubtful I think by the time, a few seconds later, when I re-appear with my gun raised, the butt resting comfortably into my shoulder, into my spine, down to my firm feet, like it's a part of me.

And it is now that I make my thunderous finale. The corporal's back is broken under the severe punch from a bolt of lightning lead but I also feel an unusual recoil as the top furniture of my rifle is splintered by the shot returned from the marksman.

We turn and run, Joe firing a burst into the air, which keeps the Brits pinned down under fake fire. It's a good excuse for some of the yellow bastards to stay put. A woman has fainted but some kids start cheering and clapping our performance. *The weapons are thrown into the boot and my two comrades drive off; Joe to hide the weapons; Patsy to leave the car in Clonard for use as a lure.*

I run into side streets, air streaming across my brow, blowing through my hair, curving my body. I run up an entry where a stout woman, her grey curls loosely pinned around a falling bun, is brushing some rubbish from her back door.

"Jesus Christ, what was that son?"

"I don't know missus, but I think somebody opened up on the Brits."

She blesses herself and rolls her eyes. I cross into another entry and push open a back door. My clothes I put into the washing-machine and turn it on.

I climb into the shower and in the distance I can hear armoured cars and Land Rovers.

They don't even know where to begin.

Pellets of water pummel my face.

I hear on the news that the corporal is dead, that he was married with two children, aged four and one. I clench my teeth and swallow hard and I will often think of this man.

I regret the life that has brought me to this.

Then I focus on the British government. I think of the corporal who might have hated his job, who might have been buying himself out of the army.

I'll live for him and in some sort of communion with him.

One thing is for sure.

I'll think about him more often than his commanding officer.

I'll maybe even be still thinking about him when his widow has stopped.

Who knows?

CHAPTER 12
SOMEONE AT THE DOOR

A battered, blue mini-van, which Catherine did not recognise, arrived outside her house and Peter got out from the passenger side. Hair unkempt, he was furtive, odd looking, as if he was a six-year-old creeping to the biscuit tin in the middle of the night, or a gun-runner. No, he definitely wasn't a gun-runner. One IRA man in the family was enough, she thought.

"Is she about?" he said.

"Is who about? What are you talking about? Have you been drinking?"

"Sheila. Who do you think! I've got a present for her but I don't want her to see it."

"She's out somewhere. What did you get her?"

But he was off, rapping the driver's window and Catherine saw Anthony Stewart and his cap appear.

"Hiya Catherine. Not a bad day."

Men never failed to amaze her. This was an occasional, just an occasional, drinking companion of her husband's. Years ago Peter had been labouring on new housing sites in and around Newtownards, work which had actually lasted almost a year, and when extra labourers were needed he got Anthony started. She couldn't recall from where they knew each other – probably some betting shop – though she had a vague recollection that like Peter he had attended Slate Street Primary School but had been in a different class. It was difficult to keep track when at least two dozen people and several old teachers had been pointed out to her over twenty-five years, some perhaps ten or twelve times, as having been "in my class" or "he was a real, wicked bastard." Case-hardened by such reminiscences, the next two dozen schoolyard acquaintances thrown her and her husband's way through weddings, and, as they got older, through funerals, hardly commanded her attention. To her the owners of the bald heads, the paunches, the shining suits, never looked qualified to have once been young-faced. To her husband they hadn't changed a bit.

God only knows where he found Stewart, she thought.

Anthony opened the back of the van into which he disappeared and Peter spat into the palm of one hand and then the other, as if sparring for a fight. A bag of cement had to be removed and placed on the footpath to allow a comfortable negotiation. Catherine's first thought was to raise objections to "that heirloom" coming into the house, but the dusty, dirty object, which resembled a small upright piano, held a certain fascination. Peter was exuberant, even though he was puffing as they carried the desk – he called it a Davenport – through the house and out the back into the yard. She could see by his one-word responses to Anthony's drawling questions about the whereabouts of old acquaintances, which Anthony then went on to answer himself, that Peter was growing impatient. He was even more agitated when Anthony stayed for a cup of tea. She knew Peter was anxious for his old friend to disappear and so she teased him.

"Now which one was Nipper Henderson?" she asked the visitor, who munched at his fourth biscuit, driving her husband to distraction.

When Anthony eventually left, his van had hardly turned the corner before Peter had removed a hinge and, with three screws attached to his lips, repeated to his somewhat ashamed wife that "the heirloom" was an old, but solid desk, and was a present for Sheila. The week before she had received her O-Level results and had passed all subjects, with distinctions in English, French and Geography. She had been talking about leaving school but was now, like Jimmy, going to take her A-Levels.

By dinner-time Peter had sanded down the drawers and left the hinges and other metal strips and plates to soak in some stripping fluid overnight. Before hiding the parts underneath old sacking he realised that surgery was required to a large portion of gangrenous panelling at the back.

"Where's Jimmy?" he asked. "I need him to go to McDonnell's wood yard."

"Don't you remember, he and Mary Ann are away up to the Kesh to see John."

Peter muttered and headed off on the errand himself.

The next morning after Sheila left to go down town with some friends, Peter was once again covered in sawdust. Through the kitchen window Catherine watched him. Like a craftsman he used a small chisel on one or two knots for about half-an-hour. She came out to the yard and handed him a cup of tea.

"Ah, that's great!" he said. "Thank you. Well?"

"It looks nothin' now but I'm lookin' forward to seeing it finished."

"I must say woman, you're looking well today!"

"Catch yourself on!" Catherine looked up to the sky, ignoring the compliment. She continued: "Have you seen our Sheila's boyfriend? He looks far too old for her . . . God, in our day your mother would have killed you if you held a fella's hand."

"Ho! Listen to you. The cow forgets she was a calf! Come here and give's a kiss."

She smiled. "Leave off. Anyway, Jimmy's come in. He stayed in Micky Conlon's last night. He's upstairs in his bedroom. Probably heard every word you've said! He's going out again if there's anything you want him to get."

"No. I'm okay. Right, break's over. Back to porridge."

For four hours Peter worked unremittingly, grinding the remaining surfaces to a glass finish with first rough, then smooth, sandpaper. He shook himself down and cleared up the shavings, brushed the sawdust into a shovel, and stared at the sky. The afternoon was dull, the air cool and still, but he imagined the yard was teeming with small flies and, although few houses had their fires lit, he swore that atoms of soot were falling so slowly as to deceive the naked eye. He ran a damp cloth over the wood which he, with his own hands, had meticulously brought to light. As it dried he scratched his head as if that would help him decide whether to varnish it here or indoors. Catherine was washing fish at the sink. He asked her advice. She said she would prefer if he used the yard. She watched him thinning down scumble oil in a jar and with a little brush and a little love he accentuated the contours of the grain.

There was a song on the radio in the living room and Catherine found herself day-dreaming. She enjoyed this harmless activity which was almost always provoked by music. Hanging laundry on the clothes horse, or whilst making the beds, an old number from the 1940s would come on the radio. If she concentrated really hard, her mind would suddenly roll over on itself and for an instant she would experience the past with a rush of pleasure. Sometimes she would even cry for the past or for lost youth, then she would reprimand herself and think of Peter, think of the kids, and think of Jimmy. She thought of her seventeen-year-old son, her favourite child, though she felt ashamed to think that. She knew that God saw into her mind, and saw this intense love, but God would also know that her affections for the others were not in the least diminished.

The varnishing over, she watched as Peter surveyed from all angles the body of the desk, and, separately, the top which had to be again attached to the hinges, and the drawers. He smiled at her.

"What do you think?"

"It's lovely. Beautiful. She'll be very pleased ... There's someone at the door. Could you get it, my hands are wet."

Yes, he thought to himself, slightly grumpy because he was tired. And mine are covered in varnish, but I'll go anyway.

They were there but neither of them could believe it. Jimmy's mouth was in a snarl, such as one sees on the face of a dead dog whose guts have been scattered by a passing car. Tubes were in his mouth, wires were running from his bare chest. His left eye was black, his head was scored and scratched. But he was alive. The staff in Intensive Care checked him every five minutes. The priest had been. Catherine and Peter kept vigil.

The dinner had been abandoned, the desk left in the rain which had suddenly started after six. Sheila had heard about a shooting when she was coming up the road and then she was stopped by a neighbour and she knew by his tone that something was wrong.

She was in tears in the corridor outside, sitting along with Raymond and Monica. Sheila jumped up and threw her arms around Mary Ann who had just arrived. Peter said he was taking Catherine to the lavatory. Sheila and Mary Ann went in to be with Jimmy.

Catherine gripped Peter's arm. She was cried out. Her husband was almost insensate. The smell of chloroform created a small, concentrated terror at the back of his mind. He could observe nothing around him and simply kept praying for his son to live, to survive this calamity, to come out of it. He thought of his own faults and moodiness, how only yesterday he had been short tempered when he couldn't find him.

Catherine came out of the toilet a few minutes later, her cardigan unbuttoned. She was ashen-faced.

"We've lost him Peter!" she screamed. "I felt him go!" They hurried into the ward. Mary Ann was stretched over her Jimmy, placing a farewell kiss on his cheek and wiping her tears from his face. The rest of the family had formed a group at the bottom of the bed and were sobbing.

In the corridor their huddled group moved with the slowness of a funeral cortege. Catherine stopped.

"Oh Peter – ah Jesus! ... He was the most beautiful soul I ever knew," and her husband understood what she was saying. He began blubbering uncontrollably and his head felt as if it had been smashed open like the shell of an egg and his scrambled senses were flying in every direction.

Wave after wave of Jimmy's image flooded his mind, the smiling face, his humour and innocence. A wave of guilt overpowered him. All he could think about were the things he had denied his son or the times when he punished him as a child. The acoustics of their small house was such that every little noise from above was amplified through the floorboards. When the kids were younger and diving in and out of each other's beds he shouted to them to keep quiet. When they continued he would race upstairs to chastise them. He would tell them to shut up but Jimmy would continue to giggle. He would smack him and warn him that if he found it funny he'd get hit again. Jimmy would snigger and he'd smack him again and he'd giggle again with that infectious laugh of his, until Peter burst out laughing and they would all give each other "a huggle", their description for a cross between a hug and a cuddle.

The couple stood with their arms around each other crying. Catherine knew that part of her soul, not just her own flesh and blood, had been wrenched from her by something diabolical. Of the five children she had carried inside her there had been a special, glowing feeling during his pregnancy. She recalled excitedly waking up her husband when life was first felt. For Peter the novelty soon wore off. She was tickled and fascinated at the shape of his tiny knuckles and heels knocking on the wall of her womb or punching it. Some of her others had almost put their feet through her kidneys and had her constantly running to the toilet with the pressure on her bladder. John had stretched so hard she felt as if his feet would come out her mouth! But Jimmy had been playing a game with her and moved about as if for her comfort. If she talked to her navel he was listening. After he kicked around she said, are you quite finished? I'm tired. She swore she felt a sigh and then he would become passive. He had helped her decide upon dinners or to make up her mind on a whole range of matters.

Undoubtedly, as a child, a boy, and a young man, he had got up to much mischief, but nothing evil, she knew. And despite her possessiveness, she was happy when he was happy, and wasn't the slightest bit jealous when he looked into the eyes of girls his own age or when he brought Mary Ann into their home.

She knew there would be no recovery for her from this crime committed by someone against her son and her family. Life would go on, but every hour of every day she would cherish his picture in her mind and would drive back the tears. Oh the treadmill would go on okay, but life was ... She became hysterical, pulled out lumps of hair and was overpowered by a madness, into the depths of which her mind desperately ran, seeking to reverse time, hoping to find sanity, hoping to awaken from the nightmare.

She punched Peter several times, then rolled down the wall and onto the floor. Peter and a nurse tried to help her but she pushed them off with an abnormal capability and screamed.

"No! No! No! It's not true! It's not true! Jesusssss! Jesus! It's not true!"

Peter was distraught. He hugged her. He begged her. He lied to her. He kept saying, "It's okay, it's okay," as she sat on the floor like an hysterical toddler, her fists flaying. Eventually they calmed her and gave her some Valium.

She woke up, drugged, lying on her own bed, hating everything, every person, the wrinkled face of her mother before her, the ugly, masculine hairs from a hive on her mother's chin, the hand with its bony, transparent skin stroking hers, their wedding rings rubbing, the useless gold. This attention and the crying of her other sons and daughters were of no comfort. What right had they to cry? They who stole his sweets, pushed him around. They never loved him the way she did. *Had.* A convulsion, like a shadow, darkened her and made her shiver. If they want to help me, she thought, then make Jimmy walk through that door.

Suddenly, she leaped out of bed in a panic and ran downstairs, past her family who were confused and on edge. She went straight to the bathroom and desperately pulled at the soiled clothes in the laundry basket, scattering them over the floor.

"Oh no! No!" she cried. Then she found the shirt Jimmy had worn a few days earlier. She pressed it to her lips and breathed through it. She wrapped up the shirt in a cellophane bag and went back upstairs, saying nothing, and locked it in a wardrobe before returning to bed.

Then she began crying and grabbed her mother in an embrace, begging for some solace, for some respite from the black, unending chasm inside her.

"Oh mammy, mammy, mammy; why, why, why?"

"Come on Catherine. Let's say a prayer."

John applied for parole and was allowed out for four hours, unaccompanied. It was accepted that republicans honoured the terms of their parole. He returned to the jail in a deep depression. He wanted to walk on his own. He was still walking around the exercise yard fifteen minutes after the time for lock-up had been repeatedly called.

Dominic came over to him and told him he would have to go in. John sharply withdrew his shoulder from the friendly hand, turned on his heels and stomped into the hut where he sat on the edge of his bed. Attempts were made by some of the others to break the silence or involve him in some distracting conversation. Then he suddenly apologised and several men crowded around him for comfort, gave him a mug of tea and started a game of cards.

In bed, when the lights were out, he quietly cried and thought about Jimmy. Schooldays, holidays, Christmases. What they were doing together – pulling crackers, fighting with the girls, swimming. Their re-unions when he would return from sea.

He thought about his naive young brother, and now his broken-hearted mother and father. Each time he seemed to be drifting into a light sleep the words "he's dead" would explode in his head and his heart would beat rapidly as if it were ready to burst.

At about six in the morning, before the warders unlocked the doors, he rose and dressed and sat with his head in his hands.

He had no appetite. He would feel hungry, would sit down to some food, would have two spoonful's and would then rush off to the toilet to be sick. He knew he had to pull himself together and he knew that were it someone else in mourning in similar circumstances he would be lavish with advice. Advice which bore absolutely no relation to the reality of grief.

His parents and Monica visited him. He sat next to his mother. His sister across the table fidgeted in the plastic chair, and the three of them held hands. There were more tears and his father, his old, greying father, swayed in agitation, his fingers dancing with nerves.

John had several other visits with his family over the next few weeks. Each member was trying to come to terms with the death. Nobody mentioned to him the arguments in the house, the cruel words slung – the furious rows which would lead to Peter walking out, slamming the door and coming in drunk in the early hours. Or Peter's attempts on other occasions to meet Catherine three-quarters of the way, only for her to lie on the sofa, suffocating the atmosphere. Or her refusal to come out of the gloom, to communicate with any of them. Her days on end lying in bed.

Things eased, but very slowly.

Sheila never went back to school. Peter stopped drinking. Catherine went shopping and in conversation with those she met appeared to make sense. But when she walked home, heavily burdened by the lightest of messages, she would look up to the sky and for her the clouds would form his face and she would say, "I love you Jimmy, I love you."

This deal with life, this arrangement, kept her sane and gave her time to put meaning into her existence. He was always there.

Memories long since forgotten kept surfacing.

She recalled her fortieth birthday when Peter and even her own mother had forgotten to send her a card and she felt a bit neglected. It wasn't until the afternoon that Peter understood why she was in a bad mood. He apologised and said he would go and get her a card immediately, and a cake, and flowers, but belated patronage was no use to her and she gave off to him and then burst out crying. The kids cleared out and then Peter stormed out, muttering that he would never understand women.

Half-an-hour later she was peeling potatoes when Jimmy came in, his face beaming, hands behind his back as he circumnavigated the furniture rather than turn. Suddenly he declared, "De Daaaaa!" and produced a birthday card – signed in his child's scrawl – which he had bought from the rewards of several errands he had solicited from neighbours. When she saw the forty 'X's she burst out crying again and hugged him.

Then she remembered the cat.

One day she had answered the door to find Jimmy and his pals extremely agitated. Her son gently placed a kitten on the ground. It was too well-groomed to be a stray but from its endless cries it was clearly in agony. Jimmy was visibly upset.

"Mammy, mammy, mammy. A big dog bit the wee cat and it's crying. Can you help it?"

"By the looks of it it's dying," she said as she bent down to examine the little thing. Its legs went stiff and then suddenly a stream of urine shot out. Then it died.

Jimmy began crying, even in front of his friends, and she held him close to her.

"Ach son, come on now, it is better dead and was suffering too much. Don't be crying. What's wrong?"

"Theresa the cat's died on me." He was choking back tears. "I was going to call him Geraldine but I forgot its name so I called it Theresa."

"There now, it's gone straight to heaven and is happy now."

"You mean to say he went straight to heaven?"

"Yes, straight to heaven and is happy now."

"But Mammy he didn't bite. Theresa didn't know how to bite and he didn't scratch."

His innocence gave her a lump in her throat. She wrapped the kitten in newspapers and then in a bag and sent the gang over the fields where they buried it and said prayers over the grave.

John had begun eating again but still had troubled nights, though jail-associated dreams were once again beginning to dominate.

He was looking forward to seeing Big Stevie and was standing on his tiptoes at the fence, trying to catch a glimpse of him. Two country men and three other city men were also in the prison hospital, where it was routine for new prisoners to be held overnight.

The six new internees appeared with their guards at the hospital gate and had a long look at the inside of Long Kesh, or the Lazy K as the warders called it. Their first sensation was the greyness and the smell of metal, an iron-greyness in the nostrils, followed by the dissonant noise of bolts on bolt-holes, keys in locks and the clanging of gates.

A helicopter, chopping at the air with a vehement power, was arriving at the nearby British Army base on the outskirts of the camp. Two soldiers with Alsatians on leads crossed over a concrete road and pretended to set the dogs on the prisoners. The soldiers laughed as prisoners and warders tried to hide behind each other.

Shouts of recognition came from the directions of the several cages.

"You oul fuckin' eejit! Imagine getting' caught!"

"What Cage are you going to? Hey zombie, what Cage is he going to?"

The warder ignored the abuse and one of the country men shouted, "I think I'm going to Cage Five. Is your Cage, Five?"

"Naw. This is Three. But sure you can get a transfer tomorrow or get a Cage visit."

They walked along, separated by high fencing from their comrades.

"How's things going on the outside? Everything okay?"

"Sure I'll tell you when I see you!" shouted one of the new men, unable to get the feel of the place or a clear understanding of how far the authority of 'a screw' went. The others repeatedly encouraged him to loiter at the fence.

"Fuck them 'ens. Stand here for a while. I haven't seen ya in a year!"

"Move on! Hurry up!"

John saw Stevie and waved frantically, beckoning him. A broad grin appeared on Stevie's face and he ignored the warder ushering him onwards. They shook fingers through the wire. Stevie dropped his few belongings and his strong hands clawed at the fence. Standing akimbo his leg muscles stood out – those legs which had leaped walls and strode streets in bounds. The tiger in him had been tethered at last.

"Well, comrade."

"Well, comrade."

"Fancy meeting you here!"

"I've just dropped in to say hello and then I'm off."

John laughed for the first time in a long time.

"Where are you for? Do you know? Hold on. Hey, Wright? Where's he for... Donnelly's the name?"

"If he'd move on he'd find out. He's in with you lot."

The prisoners were being dispersed. The large gate opened in front of Stevie and another young man from south Derry. A uniformed, non-political prisoner, a teenager serving time for burglary, pulled a trolley on pneumatic tyres loaded with mattresses, blankets, clean sheets and pillows into the control area, a small square section in which all human traffic was halted and checked, before the next gate was opened.

"Two from reception!"

"Two on!"

The log book was marked. The large, inner gate was then unlocked, bolts withdrawn, and the two men were met by many friends who took charge of them and their bedding, and who were overwhelming in their hospitality. Other Falls' men were anxious to hear the latest from Stevie but he ushered them away.

"We'll get a yarn later. I want to have a yarn with John first."

"I'm sure you're sick of walking round the Crum. We walk anticlockwise here as well, you'll be glad to hear!"

"I'm tellin' ya, Belfast Prison is something else. There's fellas walking round the yard talking about just getting ten years if they recognise the court and sixteen if they don't and they're all obsessed with their own cases. 'The solicitor says this,' 'The solicitor says that.'

It would frighten you and they can't wait to get sentenced so as they can get settled. I'm telling you, I brought guys into this movement six months ago and told them it would be over before Christmas! The internees would be out, there'd be an amnesty and the Brits would be talking again. What's worse, I believed it myself. Well, half believed it."

John laughed.

"What's things like in here?" asked Stevie.

"The usual. There's random screw searches and we get a heavy Brit raid about once a month. That can be nasty."

"You know what I saw in the Crum? The death cell where Tom Williams was hanged. I got into it one day and had a good look. It's swept and washed out at least once a week and is always prepared. I saw the trap door. It was kept behind a door like a wall cupboard, only when you opened it you were on a platform and above you was the gallows. The trap door opened into the basement."

"I'll tell you better than that," said John. "There was a screw, a Catholic, who took part in the execution and who gave Williams a rough time. Afterwards he left the jail and became a merchant seaman. I think he worked on coal boats. He was so remorseful, or sick of what he'd done, that he threw himself overboard and he was never found again."

"Here, we'd some good times on the boats," said Stevie. Then he immediately brought up the subject John had been waiting to talk about.

"I'm very sorry about Jimmy."

John shook his head.

"It was me who went to see your da. He hadn't a clue what we were talking about. We were out in the kitchen. It was just before the body came home. He told us to fuck off, that we must have got him killed, and then he cooled down and apologised and agreed to a military funeral."

"I had no idea he was connected, Stevie, and when I heard it I blamed myself. He was so quiet. I still can't get over it ..."

John sniffled.

"Was it my doing? Was it because of me, because I got put in the Kesh or sent him on messages for us?"

"Naw. Nothing like that, though it all could have played a part. He was active for months, even lied about his age to get in. He was good, very courageous. He joined the First Batt so that nobody down the Road would know. I operated with him. I was too hot down the Road, a couple of Brits in particular were on to me, knew what I looked like, so I moved to Andytown and it was there I found out he was a Volunteer.

"The Brits messed him about for being your brother, okay, but no more messin' than anybody else was getting."

John felt a glow of pride line the edge of his desolation.

"When the Brits arrived outside your house there was panic. I had asked to be on the guard of honour. We got the berets, belts and gloves off okay, and we didn't think they'd raid the wake. But the bastards surrounded the place and came in, apologising – you know the shit. I suppose you heard all this when you got parole?"

"Only some. They didn't tell me everything."

"There could have been uproar but your ma, the poor woman, was hysterical and screamed at everybody for no trouble. I had bum ID but a Brit who knew me came up to me laughing and I was hauled off to Mulhouse Street, then Castlereagh, then the Crum' and the Court. They dropped the charges – they actually gave me three berets when I was leaving the Crum! Outside the jail they had the doors of the jeep opened and ready for me. Up to Castlereagh for round two and then here.

"But I'll never forget your house so long as I live. The Brits were walking through your living room, nodding to each other to have a look at Jimmy. Their radios were crackling, the Saracens' engines were running in the street. Your oul dog Cocker was in the yard going mad. People were gathering outside but they were pushed away and Johnny Kelly, ya know Johnny with the bad leg, he must be near sixty, he was arrested for hitting a soldier.

"And through it all your da was sitting in the corner beside the coffin, crying like a big child, holding two broken pieces from an ashtray a Brit knocked off the mantelpiece. Somebody said Jimmy had made it at school."

Stevie stopped talking, uncertain of the effect of the conversation on John, but feeling his own dander rise.

"What were the actual circumstances when Jimmy was killed? I've heard a couple of things."

"Well, you know we were out on a snipe. Nobody had seen the Brit patrol. They must have spotted the comings and goings, moved in from behind, and as soon as Jimmy appeared at the corner with a weapon, they shot him ..."

Now it was Stevie's voice which was broken.

"The Brits were dancing and whooping and a soldier held the captured rifle above his head like a scalp. Then another Brit lifted Jimmy's head by his hair and shook him. He was the one who was clocked. We were still in the area and one of the boys popped up from behind a garden wall and blew him away."

They had stopped in the yard. Just stood there in silence for a few moments.

"Come on in," said John, "and I'll show you where you are. You'll get a visit today, so if you want to get washed and changed into some of my clothes, go ahead."

"You think I'm that thin!"

CHAPTER 13
THE LETTER

"Close the bloody door!" someone up the hut shouted at the last one out. The imprints of boots and shoes were wettest around the inside of the entrance but tapered as they vaporised further up the floor. Four blow-heaters were meant to service the concave, corrugated iron hut with its thirty-one inmates, but the icy December draughts criss-crossed between cracked windows and along the length of the hut between the two ill-fitting wooden doors at either end.

A number of men were still out on the afternoon's visits. For some this was their last before Christmas. There had been a rush in smuggling for the past two weeks after the last British Army search. The contraband – mostly vodka in balloons – survived the cursory frisking by warders, making some of the prisoners believe they were turning a blind eye.

Vodka also came in through the parcel censors disguised in jellies. The prisoners had also been collecting fruit to make 'jungle juice'. It gave them a huge hangover and diarrhoea but was thought worth it.

Stevie, John and McGurk had been walking around the yard for over a half hour and were talking about going in. McGurk, a swarthy man nearing thirty, came from south Tyrone. At night they would sit around the beds talking into the early hours about history, books, world politics.

It was bitterly cold. The wind whistled through the coils of barbed wire on the fencing and rippled across the many puddles in the exercise yard.

"We'll do another few bouls," said Stevie.

McGurk pulled on his pipe and drew comfort from the warmth of its bowl. Hands now plunged into pockets, fingers turning over pocket dust, they were walking at a brisk pace, overtaking others every second or third lap.

Two fences away and below the wall was the catwalk – an inside perimeter link between the look-out towers. Blurred, uniformed figures in marching formation approached one of the posts and were called to a halt. One fell out and disappeared into the turret to relieve one of two colleagues who, seconds later, emerged to march off with the others. A group of prisoners shouted at the soldiers, questioning their prowess, baiting them about the latest IRA action. When they drew a response from one of the privates losing his temper they delighted in drawing this to the attention of the officer as a breach of discipline. Stevie laughed into the wind at the carry-on and the wind blew back into his lungs.

When the patrol disappeared out of sight the two sentries in the watch tower slid their window open and at first poked fun at the prisoners. But when the mutual abuse subsided the inmates struck up a conversation.

"How long are ya here for?"

"Taw months, then we're off to Germany."

One inmate, who suggested they were all internees of Long Kesh, was clouted on the back of the head by a comrade who was not amused. The two soldiers smiled.

"Lass time we was 'ere we was in The Ahdoyne. Do you know it?"

"Know it. I was reared in it, ya bastard."

"Niaw, niaw Paddy, what about discipline!"

"Well, tell us this – I can hardly see ya from here... what age are you?"

"I'm twenty-eight. Why?"

"And what rank are you?"

"I'm a private, why. Why do you want to know?"

"A fuckin' private and you're twenty-eight! My mate here was a battalion commander and he's only twenty! A fuckin' private! Would you ever catch yourself on!"

"Catch meself on! You're the feckin' fool, Paddy," he shouted, as the dialogue trailed off into curses, exchanges which both sides thoroughly enjoyed.

An army helicopter which they had heard lifting off about fifteen minutes earlier moved down from the top end of the camp and hovered overhead. Suddenly, it began broadcasting through its tannoy *Good King Wenceslas* and *We wish you a Merry Christmas!* Moving backwards it performed a large circle in the sky so that all the Cages received seasonal greetings. Stevie shook his head in bewilderment and the three men, warmed-up by their exercise, turned in for the evening.

John tossed and turned in bed. He looked at his watch. It was half-two. Somebody had a rattling cough. Half-a-dozen snores were competing. There was a smell of sour socks close by which the cold hadn't managed to freeze. The rats were scurrying in the timbers. From the bottom bed a glow from another insomniac's cigarette described a parabola and then there was a sigh of smoke, some of which became a wide, grey bar for a few seconds as it was caught in the sharp light filtering through from outside lamps. Water from the tank of one of the two latrines at the bottom of the hut continually trickled. At night the noise could become eerie and would tug at the slumbering mind and pull it back to consciousness. But even the trickle had frozen and was now silent.

John stared at the bunk above him; the flat wire spring which provided the suspension was embossed with little sags of mattress, and the discoloured sheets had become loose. A pair of trousers and an overcoat, used to provide additional warmth, were close to falling to the floor. John sat up and tossed them back up as best he could over the body in the bed above. One of the bed's spring hooks was broken and was swinging to and fro every time the man above turned over. It was life. Even in here it was life.

For some reason he thought about Angela McCann, where she would be now and what could have been between them. He even quietly laughed when he remembered her bitchiness and the incident over the love letter in the dancehall, which at the time had shattered his pride and morale. Had they not broken up he probably would not have got to see 'the world'. He recalled their first kiss and he felt warm inside for having known and loved her.

You still love her, you fool, half of him said to the other half. Oh, I know. I know, I know, I know, he answered.

So he lay with her again, snug, nestling up close to her naked body, a thousand miles away from fences of barbed ice, frosted panes of glass and a gale whistling through a prison hut.

Before he knew it he was sound asleep.

There was a sharp shriek from the thick metal hinges. He was familiar with the first sound. Secondly, was that running? He heard no barking. He stirred. The doors being unlocked every morning was so routine to all but new inmates that they didn't wake. But when there was a raid the warders would steal up to the entrance of the three huts in advance of the soldiers and, as silently as possible, unlock the doors so as to spring surprise and create fear, a fear which sent the Alsatians into a frenzy.

The doors burst open, the lights were switched on and a line of soldiers in riot helmets ran up the centre of John's hut banging their batons off the beds as they went. The reveille continued until an officer strolled up the aisle.

"This is a raid."

"You don't say." There was a loud crack, a baton blow to a knee, the noise not muffled even through the blankets.

"You will do as you are told. You will stay in your beds until told to get out. When told to arise you will indicate which are your clothes and which locker you own and you will identify yourself when asked. You will then be allowed to dress and will be taken to the canteen until the search is completed. Oh yes, before I forget, don't forget to tell your Mums that I send my regards."

He smiled and the other soldiers laughed.

"You! Get out of bed!" screamed an NCO into the face of a scared teenager. He jumped to the floor, shivering. He was wearing an old, checked shirt, underpants and two pairs of socks.

"Get them pyjamas off! Let me see."

He gave the soldier the shirt which was searched before being thrown back at him.

"Okay. You can put it back on. Now the socks."

As if they were diseased the soldier held them at arms' length and shook them. Others were searching lockers, taking no care with the neat piles of clothes, were reading letters from wives and girlfriends, scrutinising family photographs, probing mattresses and shining torches up bed-ends for contraband.

Prisoners who were searched and processed were each escorted out by a soldier. There were scuffles at the door and Dominic, who was half-dressed, pushed past a soldier and confronted a senior warder.

"We were told we were being taken to the canteen so why are we being put against the wire?"

The warder appeared embarrassed. Before he could explain an army officer stepped forward. He had no beret but had a cravat around his neck which smelt of cologne. He wore a windcheater – which didn't appear to be of British Army issue. He tugged at the wrists of his leather gloves. He was quite tanned, given that it was winter; and spoke in polished tones.

"I am in charge here while the major is out and I say you go to the fence. We have to search the canteen."

"But there's fuck all in the canteen. It's an empty hut."

"Soldiers. Take this man out."

Dominic was led out of the hut, shirtless, his teeth chattering, two soldiers digging their fingers into his arms.

Chilled by the winter's night the morning air made straight for the bones. Seventy-nine prisoners were spread-eagled against the fence. Stevie refused to tremble even though the rime-covered metal mesh was draining his palms white. He turned over in his mind the option of just refusing to continue with what he considered in part to be self-imposed humiliation. He would be batoned, the dogs would be set on him, to get him to conform to the orders. But if he still refused he could only be beaten so far and would be removed to the punishment block or the hospital. If they all refused then the Brits would have a major problem. He knew that a general burning down of the camp had been talked about but, unfortunately, given the mix of the prisoners and the various levels of commitment, it was impossible to expect such disobedience. Besides, he could start something and there was no guarantee that the Brits would concentrate their reprisal on him. One of the older, less able men could end up bearing the brunt of a bad beating.

Someone collapsed. It was 'oul Joe'. A young soldier kicked him and told him to get up, suspecting that he was acting. Stevie turned on the soldier, fists knotted by his side.

"Kick him again and I'll knock you back to fucking Liverpool!"

The soldier grabbed him by the collar and forced him against the fence but Stevie pushed his throat against the soldier's grip so that for a second their faces met in sheer hatred. A warder came between them and another soldier, clearly with some authority, ordered Stevie and the next prisoner to carry Joe to the canteen.

They laid him down on the floor and a warder fetched a cup of water. When they were left alone in the canteen Joe winked.

"You're definitely a countryman!" joked Stevie. He surveyed the empty canteen. "Look at this. No search at all." The door opened again and prisoners, two or three at a time, filtered in. The main points of concern among them was the extent of the damage to handicrafts – the wooden harps, jewellery boxes and miniature spinning-wheels they had carved for friends and relatives as presents, and the survival of their Christmas alcohol.

Some four hours after the raid had begun somebody watching from a window reported that the raiding party was pulling out, although a line of prisoners against the wire in the adjacent cage was plainly visible. It was a half-hour before they were allowed back into their huts. The place was in a mess. Bedding and clothes scattered everywhere, boot marks on sheets. A bottle of ink had been spilled over a shirt. Most handicrafts were smashed. Photographs were torn or missing. Christmas cards had been scrawled on by Petes and Mikes and Bobs. Sugar had been poured over cheese and meats, salt over sweet things. Lighter fuel had been sprayed into the water container.

The place reeked of vodka and the floors were soaking from over-turned creamery cans, which normally contained milk but had been pilfered for the brews. Dominic went immediately to a spare locker which was in a no-man's-land between two beds, the exact position it had been in earlier. He smiled and was joined by two others. They tilted the locker and the grins fell off their faces. Splinters of wood from a false panel indicated that the pair of bolt cutters and the camera had been found.

"Well, fuck that," said Dominic. "Back to the drawing board."

Some prisoners were called for visits. They had no time to fuss about their dress or about being unshaven and while they were away the others cleaned up the huts. The only food which had been spared was a large home-baked Christmas cake covered in icing and marzipan which had been thoroughly probed for the proverbial file and hacksaw when it had been handed in to the parcels' office.

'To Pat and his comrades. XXX Pauline', the icing read.

Later that night, after lock-up, John's hut decided to have their party. They were taking no more chances. Some of the lost stock of spirits had been replenished on that day's visits but there still wasn't much.

John called the hut to attention. He stood on a bed and wrapped in a blanket, toga-style, began a speech: "Friends, Roman Catholics and Countrymen" – he winked at McGurk and the South Derry men. – "Lend me your ears. Stevie!"

Stevie stepped forward. He had two large red fire extinguishers under either arm. No one knew what to expect. There was no sign of smoke.

"Stevie, open the champers."

He twisted the seal and took off the valve. The men cheered and then lined up with their mugs as Stevie began pouring jungle juice from the fire extinguisher.

"To Freedom!"

"Freedom!"

"To Victory!"

"Victory!"

The cake, crumbling at the circumference, was laid out on Pat's bed, and sliced. Inside two minutes three-quarters of it had been devoured.

Pat crossed the hut and offered the last piece to be divided between John, Stevie and McGurk. They were sitting on beds in deep conversation in an area partitioned by blankets draped between lockers and bunks which offered some privacy. Stevie thought the weather had turned mild or else the alcohol was beginning to take effect because no one any longer complained of the cold.

To the right of Stevie's head, pinned to a locker, was a large newspaper advertisement which contained the names of all the republican prisoners, reminding them that they were not forgotten and wishing them a Merry Christmas and a peaceful New Year.

"Hold it!" Stevie shouted at McGurk as he was about to sink his teeth into his slice of the cake. Stevie's finger and thumb handcuffed him at the wrist and forced his hand back from his mouth. John stared on, perplexed. Stevie revealed a razor blade which had been inserted length-wise into the cake. He had seen a glint of light reflect off it, just in time.

"The bastards!"

"Thank you, Mr Donnelly," said McGurk.

"Not at all. You can buy the next round," said Stevie, pointing to the fire extinguisher.

Men were playing cards or having a sing-song.

McGurk produced a big balloon, swollen with whiskey.

"Where the hell did you get that?" asked John.

McGurk tapped a finger against his right temple, indicating intelligence.

"I heard the Brits coming in this morning and had the stuff ready, just in case. As soon as the row started I dropped it into my trunks beside my balls. The Brit was either too flustered at the commotion to notice me or too embarrassed."

"You can say that again."

"This is going to be some night."

"You can say that again."

McGurk spoke about his wife and his three children. He said his family in Tyrone were great and gave material and moral support to his wife. By now they were slightly drunk.

"Never hear you talk much about women, John, though I see plenty of different ones up on visits," the countryman said.

"They're just friends. And some are up on Army business. No, as soon as I was arrested I stopped seeing my then girlfriend. It wasn't fair on her. The joke is that she now visits a fella from Cage 4! But, I'll tell ya. I really fancied this one years and years ago. We went out a lot and I thought one day we'd end up married but we never got anywhere. Maybe I was too serious."

In deference to some men who had turned in, half the lights were switched off.

Although matchsticks were banned McGurk produced one from his jacket's top pocket and ran it along the floor. In the dim light the match hissed into flame and the splinter slowly shrivelled across the mouth of the pipe bowl. The tobacco lost its moistness, tensed and sparked.

"Visit for O'Neill. J. O'Neill!" the warder shouted across the yard. Although it was only March he wore just a shirt and tie on top, as if he was trying to impress everybody that he was impervious to the cold. The message was sent into the hut. John was already washed and dressed and ready to see his sister Sheila. Having been processed and searched he stood in the corridor of the visiting area, a long prefab hut, talking to a fellow inmate but was motioned on towards Box 7.

There was a latitude granted by the warders which often allowed one or two visitors of one prisoner to go into the box of another prisoner to have a snatch of conversation. A large crowd of people – wives, children, girlfriends, parents, brothers and sisters, friends – passed up and down the corridor. Amidst the exchanges of banter was another scene – a married couple clinging to each other, the woman in tears.

A warder knocked on the door of the visiting box opposite John. A young man, vaguely familiar, came out.

"Two minutes!" said the prison official. The young man suddenly acknowledged John with a loud "Hello!" and within seconds his visitor, a woman in her twenties, came out from behind him.

"Lord, what are you doing here?" she said, with a trace of her old confidence. Though taken aback, John smiled at Angela. Despite his confusion he took in the attractive figure before him. He gazed at the soft bridge of her nose and noticed that the freckles had gone. She had kept her hair as he had remembered it, tucked behind her ears and long. She skipped her first remark which wasn't really a question and asked, "How are you keeping, John?"

"I'm okay. How are you doing? How long have you been back?" He then realised that the other prisoner was her brother, Sean McCann. Sean made himself scarce and struck up a conversation with some friends further along the corridor.

"Ach, I've been back a while." Just above her right eyebrow was a little pockmark or birthmark which he had always found attractive. He was embarrassed at finding himself looking her up and down.

"It's been a long time," he said at last.

"Over six years. A lot of water …"

"Yes."

"You haven't changed a bit. Made a name for yourself too. Your case about being tortured was on the news. I read about you in England."

So she took an interest in me, he thought.

"Listen, John, I was sorry about Jimmy." Her tone suddenly changed. "It was terrible."

"Yes," he replied, hearing his name, being reminded of the heartbreak. "He was going out with your sister, Mary Ann. She was up to see me once. Her and Jimmy. In fact, it was in this very box that I last saw him alive ... Mary Ann's a nice girl."

"Not like her older sister... Are you really keeping okay?" The question was asked with some intensity.

"Yes! I'm okay. What about you? Have you made your first million yet?"

"Huh, that nonsense," she said.

One warder was growing impatient with Sean, ordering him to move on. Another was shuffling just a few feet away from the couple: "You're well over the time. The visit was up ten minutes ago."

"I suppose I'll have to go," she said, looking around. Sean came back and was kissed on the cheek and for an instant the barely audible smack caused John to sigh. She turned to leave and unexpectedly pressed John's arm with her hand. "All the best," she whispered, gently. He didn't know what to say. She wore a black leather coat against the March weather. It was fastened by a slim belt in a simple knot and he would have loved to have grabbed and held her, despite the past.

He watched her walk down the corridor to the locked door, beyond which was freedom, through which only visitors and warders could pass. He finally shouted, "All the best, Angela!" His use of her name made him feel awkward for some reason.

The door was open but she suddenly stopped and looked back. By now his head was in a whirl. She gave him a meaningful glance and, in a flash from the past, winked at him. He began laughing and saw her smile back. Then the door was closed.

The next day John was still in a euphoric state but had kept telling himself to calm down, to measure his steps. He came into his hut that afternoon and saw a letter lying on his bed, her handwriting even familiar from a distance. He lifted it to his nose and his heart pounded when he smelt the scent of her perfume, *Youth Dew*. He clenched his teeth but would be patient, very patient. He placed it under his pillow and went out to the yard for a walk. He wanted to relish reading it. He strolled over to Stevie's hut. Stevie had, surprisingly, moved out of John's hut about six weeks before. He hadn't been in any rows and John felt a bit aggrieved since he felt that there was a real bond of comradeship between them. Stevie was already out walking, so John joined him.

"I was looking for you!" he said.

"*Na bí ag caint i mBéarla!*" (Don't be speaking in English!)

"What?" said John. "What did you say!"

"*Dúirt mé leat, ná bí ag caint i mBéarla! Tá mé ag foghlaim Gaeilge le mí anois.*" (I said don't be speaking in English! I have been learning Irish for over a month now.)

"*Maith thú, ar fheabhas. Anois tá fhios agam cad chuige ar bhóg tú amach. D'fhoghlaim tú le háthas a chur orm!*" (Very good, that's brilliant. Now I know why you moved out. It was to surprise me!)

"I'm sorry," said Stevie. "I don't understand. What did you say? I was taking classes outside but missed many of them."

"Well," replied John enthusiastically, clapping him on the back. "I said, '*Beidh lá file ag na b'Paorach go fóill*'. There is hope for old Ireland yet. '*Beidh lá file ag na b'Paorach go fóill!*'"

Dear John

Once again, or should I say, at long last, I put pen to paper to write to you. As I write I cannot help but cry both tears of sadness and of relief. I have been such a fool all these years, have squandered so much, hurt so many people and degraded myself.

When you left Ireland my friends told me how much of a bitch I was and this hurt me. I wrote to you two or three times. I don't know whether you ever received those letters. I heard you were back in the Gulf but I wrote for the wrong reasons! I said I was sorry and apologised but if you read them you probably saw how hollow and hypocritical I was being. Maybe that's why there was no reply. I was just wanting you to get me off the hook for what I had done.

My Aunty Maureen used to keep talking about you and praising you. I was a little bit fed up one day and light-heartedly told her what happened between us at the dance. She was very angry and didn't speak to me for weeks!

In 1966 we moved up to our present address in Andersonstown. But despite the move I still couldn't stick Belfast. In '67 I went to London and got involved in a lot stupidity for a while. I was home for two years but then left again over an issue, which I understand you know about, or knew about and I since heard that you helped sort it out. A belated thanks!

I had a good job in London for some time and eventually ended up owning my own house. Into property, at last! Some other time I'll tell you all about it but let me say dearest John that I have never gotten over you.

Last August I was listening to the news one day when I heard that an IRA man and a soldier had been shot dead in West Belfast. My stomach turned and I couldn't get it out of my head the thought that it was you who had been killed. It was a crazy notion because, believe it or not, I had followed closely your goings-on from writing to Patricia and knew you were still interned in Long Kesh. When Jimmy's name came out that night I sobbed my heart out. Do you remember we brought him down town to the Wimpy Bar one day and he had us on the edge of our seats with laughter?

I tried to phone home but couldn't get an answer and when I did eventually get through it was only then that I learned that he had been going out with our Mary Ann and that my family had been down at the wake. John, nobody had ever told me about Jimmy and Mary Ann such was the gulf between my family and me. I had become a complete outsider, a stranger. I spoke to my mammy on the phone and actually made up with her since the big argument we had had some time before. I decided to come home and by Sunday night I was in Belfast.

I watched the funeral and I caught a glimpse of you for the first time in all those years. You looked wretched and I felt so sorry for you and your family because of what you had come through. I knew then that my home and heart lay in Belfast. I went back to England to sort out my things and eventually sold up my house and came back to Anderson-stown. Then four weeks ago our Sean got interned.

I suppose I should finish off now but I just can't help pouring my soul out to you. John, have we really changed that much? I can understand life having made you harder but I feel that I have really sorted out myself at long last. Throughout all those years I have thought of you. Do you remember that afternoon at Maureen's? They were the most wonderful moments of my life.

I have to confess that there is still a bit of the schemer in me. It was no accident that we bumped into each other in the visiting boxes. I was out with your Sheila two weeks ago for a drink and she told me how we could try and get the visits to coincide. I was panicking when the warder said that the visit would be over in two minutes. We thought you still hadn't come out. Our Sean had been up and down getting a light, asking the warder what time was it, were his letters through the censor yet, and was he allowed raw meat in parcels. I'm sure the warder thought that jail was cracking him up. And then Sean nodded to me that you were through. That's when I got up to leave. God, I was really nervous, even though I may have appeared differently.

It was wonderful seeing you again and that is why I have been so relieved and full of hope. At the risk of completely offending you I would like to repeat the warmest, most sincere words I have ever come across. A love letter from you to me: "Let me know through a shooting star, or the buttercup yellowing my throat, if you are for me! You showed me heaven and passion and the lights of love. Now you have gone and every bright day is dark night and it is literally killing me."

I hope upon being reminded of that night that you have not torn this up. After you left the dance I retrieved your letter from the stage. I always carried it around with me. It got me through some very, very hard times, and I would think of the courage and love behind it.

John, I wasn't all bad, I was just lost.

I would like to see you again, or, at least, to hear from you. But if you don't wish to see me I will understand, it is perfectly understandable. But please write to me, at least, and let me know.

Love
Angela
XXX

P.S. I now have a view of the world which, you'll be glad to hear, includes more than myself!

– Angela
XXXXXXXXX

CHAPTER 14
DIARIES

Extracts from the diaries of Jimmy O'Neill saved by Sheila from a British Army search

1968

January 1st: I do not think I shall write things of privacy in this diary. Of those things I have, this is private. Later, I suppose I shall write madly but until then I pray that it should come.

Friday 5th: Didn't go to Mass or library as I usually do. Look before you leap – must remember that.

Sunday 7th: St Louisa's start back tomorrow. I'm glad. I'll see somebody I like.

Monday 8th: This morning it snowed and settled. Seen Margaret McGorrian this morning but was too nervous to say hello. Got two Victorian pennies. That's ten I have, plus eight Edward the Sevenths and two George the Fifths silver thrupenny bits. Did eckers early. Have a geog test tomorrow and I have no idea about mining in Durham and industry in the north of England. O God help me tomorrow.

February 12th: Sheila, if you ever read this I'll kill you, yes you!

February 29th: Jimmy Saville on *Top of the Pops* was great.

March 2nd: Radio Caroline went off the air.

March 9th: Handball is back.

March 19th: In butchers for mammy after school getting sausages. There was an argument about England. I joined in. Jimmy, the butcher, backed me up. Very interesting, even though I was laughed at.

April 5th: Martin Luther King, king of the downtrodden Negroes, has been assassinated.

April 23rd: New decimal coins came out today. Five new penny equals a shilling, ten new penny equals two shillings. Trolley buses are going off the Road soon. Thinking of joining weight-lifting to build up my biceps.

April 28th: Louis Armstrong – "What a wonderful world".

May 6th: Britain's first heart operation took place the other night. Donor an Irishman. First heart op took place, I think, on the 2nd of December.

May 12th: The trolleys went off the Road today, very sad.

May 13th: Dirty, stinkin, smelly diesel buses on the road.

May 14th: Cousin Tony can get BBC 2 on their TV.

June 5th: Today Senator Robert Kennedy was shot thru the head. He is critically ill. They took the bullet out.

June 6th: Today Senator Robert Kennedy died of yesterday's gunshot.

June 7th: I went to the library and got a book called *Farewell Flying Saucers*. The man who shot R. Kennedy was arrested.

June 8th: Somebody was arrested in London in connection with the assassination of Martin Luther King. Daddy didn't come in until 5 this morning.

June 25th: Tony Hancock committed suicide today.

June 29th: Our John gave me a pound after he won the races. Lester Piggot won the Irish Sweepstakes Derby. Sir Ivor came second but I don't know who was riding him.

August 8th: My mate Noel and I cycled to Helen's Bay. Noel's cat caught his second bird yesterday. UTV is still on strike.

August 15th: We had a great bonfire and Noel got off with Deirdre Masterson. He said she's a dirty baste and put her tongue right into his mouth. He said he felt like throwing up. Swapping spittle, ugh!

August 21st: Russia invaded Checkyslovakia and they're still there. Practising self-hypnosis.

Saturday October 5th; Derry civil rights march today. Gerry Fitt, our MP, got hurt and we prayed that he would be okay.

October 6th: Fighting broke out in Derry today again. Police were appalling during the fighting. A petrol bomb was thrown at police in Deny. Blood boils. Feel awful.

October 7th: I was made a prefect in class today because my work has improved.

October 8th: The Cabinet support police action in Derry.

October 9th: Queen's University students march today. Also Paisley in Shaftsbury Square. Last night a petrol bomb was thrown at the Protestant church on the Falls Road, up at Broadway. No clash between Paisley and the students.

October 11th: Biafra reduced to small size. Got a book on E.S.P. and after I read it lent it to Micky Conlon. We are to do an experiment.

October 14th: This morning I was told to take Jackie Hunter to the head master to be slapped. But instead I took him for a walk around the school for twenty minutes. This afternoon my form master sent for me and slapped me and I lost my prefect badge.

October 25th: Studied Conlon in sleep and got results. Asked him did he dream of a girl, yes. Did he sleep on his left side, yes. Was the song, *Wheels on Fire* but it was *Those Were The Days*. 66 out of a 100, not bad.

December 24th: Came sixth in class, highest in class at English.

1969

January 2nd: Peoples Democracy march set out for Derry. Major Ronald Bunting, a friend of Paisley's, was waiting for them and there was some fighting. Started back to school. A OK. Got out at 2. Went up to the chippy tonight and stood at corner.

January 4th: Snow expected. Fighting in Derry. 59 injured. Bunting's car was burned.

January 13th: Master Armstrong kept Doke, Dick and me in after school. I had to count in thousands all the people in Norway, but when I was half-way through he told me to go on home and that would teach me not to be "facetious". He's used that word about fifty times this week.

January 28th: Late for school. Paisley got 12 stitches in his arm today. Did English test.

February 4th: Late for school. There is to be a general election this month. Unionists unstable. We went to St Clement's Retreat House. Seen films on the Holy Shroud of Turin. Having a great time. From my bedroom window, room 86, I can see across the Lough and the lights of County Down opposite. My mate Kieran tells me all his worries and I listen. He is troubled.

February 24th: Tonight is election night and at Bannside the Rev Ian Paisley came very close to Captain Terry O'Neill.

April 22nd: Got haircut. Micky Conlon and myself kidnapped Linda Gormley and brought her down town then over to the museum. I think she fancies him. Bernadette Devlin made a historic maiden speech in Westminster today. More fighting tonight. No 1 Beatles. *Get back to where you don't belong.*

July 1st: Do not try to find fault in God's plan. There are none. Evil and sin do not exist on earth but in the mind. The nights are warm and we spend them playing handball and later standing at the corners. There is a light mist in the evening and sometimes a heavy smell from the dry drains and sewers.

August 10th: Having a brilliant time in Donegal. Our family is the best family in the world, okay!

August 13th: There is fighting in Derry. A huge riot and the fellas have hoisted the tricolour over Rossville Flats. Tonight at about 12.30 gunfire broke out in Falls Road. Fighting in Belfast, Derry, Dungiven, Newry, Omagh, Enniskillen, Lurgan, Coalisland.

August 14th/15th: B Specials went mad tonite shooting all night. Snipers all over the place and gunmen in a blue mini. Saw petrol bombs being made. Our John was to go away but stayed because of the troubles. Conway Street was burned to the ground. Troops moved in. I helped the men lift flagstones and put up barricades at the top of the road. Remember 1916!

August 17th: Latest news at 5.30. Troops to stay as long as the P.M. says so.

September 3rd: Our John secretly brought me into Radio Free Belfast in Leeson Street.

September 20th: Barricades came down today at about 3.30.

September 27th: Our John came in and said loyalists burned down five houses in Coates Street and the British army didn't do a thing. The barricades were put up again.

October 10th/11th: Hunt Report came out. Heard shooting at 11.30. Continued all night. Protestant sniping on Shankill Road at cops and army. Constable Arbuckle shot dead and two civilians dead. About 100 injured. Civilians were Protestants.

December 19th: The Scottish soldier at the billet told us to Fuck off and called us Paddies. On Thursday night Noel Cassidy and I had bunched together and bought him five cigarettes as a present.

December 1970: I have decided to begin a diary again. It is almost a year since I wrote and a lot has happened since then. There was big trouble on the weekend of June 27th and many people were killed, including an IRA man defending St Matthew's Chapel in the Short Strand. A week later was the Falls Curfew when more were killed and I got caught in CS gas. You can hear bombs plenty of times now. At school you are either an Official or a Provisional. I'm not in anything. Go to the youth club on Tuesdays.

December 3rd: Had bad dream last nite. Dreamt that the soldiers were chasing me down our entry as I had a .303 rifle. We are collecting groceries for the old age pensioners at Christmas and I had to make a speech in the Assembly Hall. Was a bit nervous. Went up to mate's house in Whiterock and walked home over the football pitches. Behind me was our mountain and I looked over our beautiful city which at that time was clear with just a few lights being switched on in homes.

Tuesday December 8th: This morning was awoke for 'school' at eight but managed to fight off my ma to explain it was a Holy Day of Obligation. It's not like her to forget.

When I have fears by John Keats

> When I have fears that I may cease to be
> Before my pen has gleaned my teeming brain,
> Before high-pilèd books, in charactery,
> Hold like rich garners the full ripened grain;
> When I behold, upon the night's starred face,
> Huge cloudy symbols of a high romance,
> And think that I may never live to trace
> Their shadows with the magic hand of chance;
> And when I feel, fair creature of an hour,
> That I shall never look upon thee more,
> Never have relish in the faery power
> Of unreflecting love – then on the shore
> Of the wide world I stand alone, and think
> Till love and fame to nothingness do sink.

Wednesday February 3rd: Called over to Mickey's and heard that soldiers were raiding the Kashmir Road area for guns. We walked up to see what was going on. Eileen Austin who goes to our youth club, and her sister and other girls were fighting the Brits with hurls. Feelings were very high.

February 4th: There was more trouble again, also with a few gunners taking pot shots at the army. Nail bombs, acid bombs, jelly bombs, hand grenades at the duck patrols. There were a hundred arrests.

February 6th: ¼ to 2 a.m. (Sunday morning): Tonight's trouble is bad with 3 civilians dead and one British soldier. I counted at least 25 explosions and you couldn't count the shots, there were that many. This trouble really annoyed me. Our John came in late and I heard my mammy say that he had blood on his hands and she abhorred hate. Our Monica shouted, "You have no right to say that to him!" and there was a big row which ended in tears all round and John asking did she want him to leave the house and she shouted back "do you want me to leave the house!" Anyway, when my daddy came home it was all kept from him.

February 7th: Went to Mass with the lads. During Fr Murray's sermon, which was against the jelly bombers, a man stood up and condemned him for being one-sided. He then left mass and the woman behind us (who was really well-dressed) shouted out that she agreed with the man and she then left with many others and if anyone else had left so would we have. Everybody was later talking about what happened and somebody said the same thing happened in another chapel up the road. Later we went to the youth club. After this week I would say that my sympathies lie with activist republicans. (This is nothing to do with our John.)

Tuesday February 9th: Went to school early and came home and heard news. First time ever I cried for my twisted country and the complicated situation. It seems solutionless and this time I was realistic. Last night a child of five was knocked down and killed by an Army jeep and the riots started again with guns out again. Today brought news of five civilians blown up at Brougher Mountain in County Tyrone. They are all dead and I don't know the circumstances surrounding it but when I listened to it on the BBC I cursed the English announcer but then I blessed him and thought, "Let he who is without sin cast the first stone." Everything is wrong. I too. And I also prayed that God would show the people which way to go and for him to direct me. Later went down the road from school and spent the afternoon until 5 at the IRA funeral. Crowds of about 3,000 were there.

February 13th: School was terrible and I couldn't study. In the afternoon I was determined to work. There is 17 weeks to my exams and that doesn't give me much time.

February 24th: Got our ashes and then Noel and I again visited oul Willie in Slate Street and Mr McCarthy in McDonnell Street. A friend of my daddy's, a chiropodist he knows, had called in as arranged and did Willie's feet. We were also able to present Willie with a second-hand TV, which we had got repaired. I am reading a book by Robert Graves. It is called *King Jesus*.

February 26th: Heard at one o'clock that forty-eight women were arrested in Chichester Street protesting against the prosecution of a fella who had marched in the IRA-style funerals. Later had an argument with my Uncle Harry over the troubles. He adopted the real Christian attitude and he was right and I know it but I was arguing from the passion angle. At about 12 midnight, at the height of the shooting, two policemen were shot dead and again I was stunned by the actions of men. Shooting has continued, especially in Ardoyne and in Cromac Square which up to now had been quiet. There was plenty of places set on fire and also nail and gelignite bombs were thrown. Later on the British army said that they had shot two civilians dead but tomorrow will tell the truth.

March 1st: The news this morning was of a soldier being killed. It happened in Derry. An army Land Rover was patrolling part of the Bogside area when it came under petrol bomb attack. The jeep went on fire and ran out of control crashing into a wall. The soldier, an 18-year-old youth, was killed. Although this was terrible we become used to it. Life, which originally was precious, loses its value after the first dozen or so killings . . . Mammy shouts in, "Kids, did you hear that?" She is referring to an explosion which took place thirty seconds ago. "Yes, I heard it." I shout back, and I think, God help us.

Thursday March 4th: Went to the youth club to watch *Top of the Pops* in colour.

March 5th: Heard of trouble in Leeson Street so left school at 3 and went to observe. The soldiers baton-charged the people and my rage built up. Our John came along and ordered me home. Have since heard that the rioters have hijacked a 2,000 gallon petrol tanker. Petrol bombs galore. The riot started when the soldiers raided the Long Bar. (There goes another explosion. And another one.) Whilst at the top of Leeson Street I heard three nail bombs go off. Have heard on news that one civilian was shot down by the army. Our John is not in yet and I am down on my knees praying. Please Jesus, it's not him. I can hear more machine-gun fire.

When our John came in I asked him could he shoot somebody thru the head and he said what was I talking about, there's a war going on. I think he could but it's okay for him, he knows his mind and what he's doing. I wanted to press him further but didn't because I know he's got a lot on his mind and anyway I admire him and I didn't want to upset or annoy him.

March 9th: We were all at the corner and heard two very loud explosions and then we heard of the shootings. The IRA were fighting each other in Leeson Street and Cyprus Street. One fella was shot dead. Others were wounded. Fell asleep about two o'clock.

March 10th: 10.15 p.m. After some studying was called for my supper and on television there came a newsflash. Three men were shot dead tonight. They were found in Ligoneil and they had been shot thru the head.

10.25 p.m. Mother has just shouted up that the news announced that they had an unconfirmed report that the three men were British soldiers in civilian clothes.

10.45 p.m. Went downstairs again and heard the news. The three men were from a Scottish regiment. I again felt like crying. This is wrong and I am moved for the man who thinks this right. This brings the total number of soldiers killed to six.

March 12th: Was coming down the Antrim Road in a bus today and there were two girls sitting in front of me. They were laughing and one turned around to me and said to her friend: "Well, what do you think?" She replied, "Umm, seven out of ten." The first one said: "No, ten out of ten. He's real sweet."

I tried to say something mature but was spellbound. I followed every turn of her head and was excited by her hearty laughter. I was with her for five minutes and was so happy.

I got off at Carlisle Circus and said: "Cheerio now!" and touched her on the shoulder. She turned around, as if real feeling had passed between us. She had the most luscious eyes and lips and said: "Bye, bye now." And I will probably never see her again.

March 28th: Had more talks with daddy – these on the troubles and republicans. He being a moderate, and right, cut me to ribbons. But can I help it if at this age I am caught up and have these ideals which I know to be a natural product of my time. Is it my fault that I like to think that I cherish this land, that I love this place?

Later: Sooner or later I asked this girl, Patricia, home and sooner or later she said yes. So I left her home to Cawnpore Street. She told me she was sixteen and worked in Boots chemist (and had muscles to prove it!). I walked her up from the club at 11 and didn't get home until ¼ past 12. We stood lumbering in Dunmore Street entry and she wore a maxi coat like Anna Karenina. When we got to her door she said: "By the way, I'm nearly 14 and in your Sheila's class." I was mortified but I ran the whole way home and let the rain wash my face. I'll be arrested for baby-snatching.

No. 1. *Hot Love* – T-Rex.

Easter Saturday: Came home to an argument between mammy and daddy and John over the display of the Tricolour from our house. I think John was right. But he was told in no uncertain terms that the flag wasn't flying.

Easter Sunday: Me and my mates went to watch the IRA parades from Beechmount Avenue which turned out to be brilliant. The British Army were taking photographs from the roof of Broadway Picture House but some fellas spoilt their film by shining mirrors using the sun at them.

Saturday April 17th: Sheila brought me the *Irish News* in bed and sure enough they had printed my letter. I was really pleased!

Friday April 23rd: I thought I was limited but more comes up from below and there must be a reservoir in me. It is damp and I look out upon the wet roof across the way. I think I should try to leave school and become a library assistant. Whilst working there I could do A-Level English, then I could write about life and what I feel. It is truly frustrating being imprisoned by ignorance.

Wednesday May 5th: Today an immersion heater was installed in the house and everybody was trying it but the electrician put the switch round the wrong way so that it's on when it's up and off when it's down, but that's only being bitchy.

May 21st: There was trouble in the New Lodge Road involving Scottish soldiers. On *News at Ten* I saw brutality. Four Scotch soldiers beat and kicked a Catholic man from one side of the street to the other. The regiment involved was that which lost three soldiers in the killings a while back. My feelings were ones of crying at the lostlessness or else of anger and future retaliation. I again was tempted to sign up. Help this country, God.

June 24th: After *Top of the Pops* we went to Noel's bedroom and yarned. At about 1/4 to 10 the drizzle had stopped and we went to the corner where we viewed the world. We offered tissues to the crying girls coming out of the Broadway pictures where they had watched *Madam X.* Some more were walking past, talking about something and one said to her mates: "So say a wee prayer for me," and as quick as lightning we all said in unison: "Our Father who art in heaven … " They started laughing. The night was great and urgeful. Got the habitual battered fish and bottle of milk.

June 29th: Gave pint of blood in Durham Street. The nurse said: "You've a very young face," and I said back, cheekily: "You've beautiful, bursting blue eyes." And I think I embarrassed her but didn't mean to.

July 5th: 1.15 a.m. As I write now I hear an explosion – the cause. What of the justice? The rights and wrongs are tortuous. Frustration in belief. I think those violent on our side (technically non-Catholic) may bring about an end to this. Is God in liaison? 1/4 to 2 a.m. Two explosions, one after the other, have raked the land. I have got a summer job in Fleming's groceries. Start when I come back from my holidays.

July 7th: I was lying in the yard enjoying the sun when Splaasshhh! Our Sheila upstairs threw a cup of water around me.

July 11th: Went hitching with Noel. We got a lift to Dungannon and from there to Bundoran, then Salthill but went back into Galway and bedded down on benches in the city square. Now outside Oughterard. It is very bare and lonely countryside. The sun is out and the wind high in the sky is whistling.

July 14th: We got into Bundoran and Noel went off drinking. I told him I'd see him in the morning. I left the bar and wandered down the town. Went on to the beach. Listen, I am lost. I need somebody's help. There was a snake in my gut, twisting my bowels into knots, and I wandered with this pain in me and took myself up the cliff path beside the golf course. I bedded in a small shelter on this path and have just woken and walked to the top, looking out over the Atlantic. I became detached yet I thought, why am I always *here*. A unique happiness came over me. I have ended up here alone. Because Nature is here I come close to God. I wanted company earlier: I am now content. I know that when I leave this place I will have happy associations with it. The wind and the sea imbue the growing man. White foam shivers. I sit at the edge of the world. Miles out a lone beam travels to the water. I feel related. There is something *rare* about me. Before I had doubts but now I know.

I am cold – it doesn't matter. A stream of happiness bursts its banks into my soul and I cry to God for experiencing the long thrill of life.

July 26th: Mr Fleming was not at work today because he got a kicking by the British Army last night so I was more or less in charge of the grocery section.

August 7th: Was out doing deliveries around Springview Street and there was still badness in the air. A man in a van was driving past Springfield Road barracks when it backfired. A soldier shot and killed him. This is terrible and tragic. I wonder whether all this trouble is worth the loss of life?

August 9th: The news is awful, really awful. My brother John has been arrested and nobody knows where he is. I'll begin at the beginning.

I was minding granny's house and had Noel Cassidy with me. We woke early, very early, and could hear screaming and Saracens. We went down to the bottom of Clonard Street and the people were out banging bin lids, building barricades. We stopped a fella and asked him what was going on. He said: "They've introduced internment; we're all gonna go to jail. It's internment!"

The place was black with people and every time the Saracens raced down the road everybody scattered into the side streets and hid behind cars and the fellas fought them with stones and petrol bombs. The community is like a chicken with no head. I was glad that our John hadn't been staying at home. We went back to my granny's and didn't know what to do though Noel says he's definitely joining. On the five to eight news we heard that one soldier is dead and that there is rioting in all nationalist parts of Belfast, in Omagh, Derry, Newry and other places. The barricades are going up again, on my own doorstep and I thought – this is my country.

I went home through the crowds which were milling about with stones and bottles, even women, and just knew before I saw the people around our door that something was up. It was one of the Walshes told me, "they got your John in your house."

The Brits sledge-hammered the front and back doors at around four o'clock and John for some reason had gone home last night. They kicked him down the stairs and put a rope around his neck and bound his hands. They wouldn't say what they were doing with him. When my mammy saw me she ran over and clutched me and held me so tight. My daddy phoned an SDLP councillor and he said they've rounded up hundreds, civil righters, the students as well as republicans. We heard that in Andersonstown they took away a son when the father wasn't at home.

Later: My ma would hardly let me out of the house at all but I promised her I'd be round in Noel's and anyway she said she knows I'm sensible but she said she doesn't know what she would do if anything ever happened me. I told her she could buy a new one and she sort of smiled.

The pirate radio stations have returned and it is back to Radio Free Belfast days. I spent the anxious evening running about listening to news bulletins, mostly RTE, which has good coverage.

August 10th: Still no word about John but Faulkner has announced the introduction of internment. I hate that man. I put on the news and broke down. Fourteen shot dead, rioting in many towns and many people have been wounded. The soldiers have been trying to take the barricades down and they have met with resistance. Jesus! This fuckin' place won't let me live in peace. I'm shattered.

Later: I have done it. I lifted stones and fought the Brits. I was out at the Springfield and then Beechmount and at Broadway. At first I ran with the crowds, protesting by occupying and filling our streets. Then I stayed with the rioters. My stone was with a thousand others and I thought, we're all in this together, and I asked God's forgiveness.

We were out in great numbers and it seemed very successful until the soldiers started shooting live bullets. Their first plunged into the wall at the corner of the chemist's. Later they stopped at the Avenue and were out on foot. We replied with bottles and stones and I was against the right-hand wall in the Drive when a bullet lifted a lump of masonry above my head. Two seconds later another bullet ricocheted off the ground into the sky two yards from where I stood. Eventually they got us pinned down in the side streets but a republican sniper opened fire along the Avenue and the Brits returned the fire everywhere. I fell to the ground with my arms around my head and lay crumpled till the shooting stopped. It is worse than '69 and there is a real war-time feeling. Yesterday Noel and I speedied up one of the telegraph poles and erected the Tricolour. Swanzey, who was arrested, was released from the barracks. The soldiers cut his long hair off with a dagger. He said the screams in Girdwood made him nearly shit himself. Our house is like a morgue and Ma and Da haven't slept. Monica's looking after everything. Raymond phoned from England to find out what's happening as it's all on the news over there. I caught our Sheila making petrol bombs in the entry and told her to get home as this wasn't for wee girls.

August 11th: Seventy people have been released and two hundred and thirty interned. We are waiting to find out where John is. In Ballymurphy Fr Hugh Mullan was shot dead by the British Army when he went to administer the last rites to an injured man.

August 13th: I haven't eaten. I'm sick with worry and I've prayed every minute. My mammy's been crying non-stop. The RUC and British army have both denied having our John in custody. They said he must have been released if he was arrested at all. All of those arrested last Monday have either been interned in Crumlin Road Jail or on the Maidstone Prison Ship or released. My daddy and Uncle Harry began visiting the morgues to see if he had been released and perhaps killed in crossfire. Twenty-three people have been shot this week and some of them haven't been identified.

August 18th: Jubilation at home! John has been found to be in Crumlin Road Jail. He and a number of other men were separated from the rest. My mammy was so relieved when she found out. They saw him this afternoon and after the visit she was still crying. She said to us all. They tortured your brother. They tortured him. And then she cried again. But we bucked her spirits up by thanking God that he'd been found. My daddy then gave me £5 for doing well in my O-Level results which came on Monday amid the crisis. Tomorrow I'm going down to buy *The Irish Republic* by Dorothy Macardle and *I'm Still Waiting* by Diana Ross.

Saturday August 19th: The mystery of the night has been discovered. Earlier walked up from town through the Loney and up Leeson Street and I thought of what the people are going to *rise* to. Britain, this is where your power in Ireland will be broken. This is the barrio that will break you!

Tonight my mammy made me swear I would never join the IRA and I swore for her. Tonight also I met a very old friend. It was very funny. I used to knock about with my cousin Tony O'Neill and knew Mary Ann McCann from then. She's since moved up the road. She was at the Holy Child dance and was wearing a jumper, zipped up at the front. She's got really nice. I said to her in my usual stupid goat-way: "Do you fancy going fishing?" and she replied, tuned-in right away, "Naw, you'd only catch ammonia," and we laughed. I walked her home, held her hand and kissed her at her corner against the hedge. I told her that my brother was one of those arrested and interned and she said that she has an older sister in England who used to go out with him way, way back. So there you have it, not a coincidence but a real connection. I believe in connections. I think I remember her too. She's agreed to go out with me again and had actually thought it was her friend I was trying to get off with. I'm on top of the world. Yes! Life is presenting itself. And there I was searching for a bed in which to rest this mind.

August 27th: The Provos have now admitted responsibility for the explosion at the Electricity Headquarters on the Malone Road in which a man died and 35 people were injured. I know all about our John and those other men and what happened but I cannot agree with this.

August 29th: More people walked out of Mass tonight when a priest condemned the IRA.

Tuesday the 31st, the last day of August, 1971: This month has been the fastest one so far in my life. It went like a flash. Our John was arrested, tortured and interned. I used violence and I have fallen for Mary Ann. But I am left holding the same problem. This country and I may survive together and see bright days when we can lead others in the arts and in fact every aspect of life.

September 2nd: More city centre explosions and 42 people hurt. If that was the IRA there is no justification and any support will consequently diminish.

September 7th: Saw our John in the Crum' today and he is fine. What spirits he and his friends have! A hundred people have now died in the troubles since August 1969. Noel got a loan of his da's car and he and his girl and me and Mary Ann went for a spin over to the Floral Hall up by Cave Hill. The two of us went for a short walk and kissed and cuddled and I felt her right breast and she looked so longingly into my eyes that my heart was fit to burst with joy. I put my arms around her and we looked at the lights from Holywood shimmering on Belfast Lough.

It is interesting to note how memories are formed. Last week, for example, has not solidified yet. But internment week and the July holiday have set and they shall remain the same forever, never to change.

September 15th: There was near riots and then a man in a combat jacket and wearing a hanky over his face asked us to clear the corner. He had a gun. Mary Ann whispered to me that she knew him from round her way and I so admired him. It was him okay, Cuchulain reincarnated. I once saved him in a fight on Black Mountain when we were kids! It's a long story.

Faulkner signed 219 internment orders this morning. Curse that man. But God loves him as much as he loves you.

4 a.m. I can't sleep. I can't get over seeing him blaze away at the Brits. He was prepared to die. And he roared: "Up the IRA!" at them when he emptied his gun before running into the entry.

September 16th: Is he to be left on his own? What happens if he dies or goes to jail? I admire the republicans but there are just certain things I am not capable of doing.

Mary Ann and I have talked about it. She at first laughed at me but apologised when she saw the look on my face and says it's up to me. But the morals of it wreck me.

September 24th: Was asked to accompany my great Aunt Rita to England this weekend, all expenses paid! She is going to see her brother for a few months before they both die. He left Ireland in the early 1920s because of the troubles. So we got the Ulsterbus coach to Aldergrove and we passed the burned-out ruins of Squire's Hill Tavern where the three Scottish soldiers were killed back in March. The skies were clear and Belfast glinted below us.

8.25 p.m. From observation the Irishman is highly emotional and not as materialistic as the English. The standard of living here is very high. The people are not like us, no sense of community, of togetherness, of having shared strife. Their priorities are different. For us a day is twenty-four hours and bedtime is anytime you choose. In some of our minutes there are seventy seconds!

Sunday, September 26th: Am heading home, thank God. Changed trains at Guildford for Woking. And then there was this lovely bridge (for blowing up). There isn't even a house burnt out and the Protestants and Catholics in Belfast have more in common than do the people over here. And then they are shocked to hear that a man you know can kill. And all *their* fathers were in the British Army! I hear a loud backfire and I smile. I love everybody but I move with a few. I had an argument with this old man in the station who maintained that the world is mad, especially the Irish because of our fight. Yet, he *too* fought in the war!

So the thinker having taken himself off misses his land. I am rooted to this sad land and its people as much as I am devoted to the flesh and blood which gives me life. I sit and think. I remove all distractions and distortions and I wish the self away into the self. Travel deep. Touch the point of life. Into the core. Communicate with the red hot core of life! Once you touch it you are moved. The soul moves. The experience is heaven on earth.

September 29th: Left Mary Ann home and walked down the road hearing shots. Got in and heard bad news. In Shankill Road pub there was an explosion which killed two and injured many more.

October 5th: I never blame anyone. I exonerate most and think that people are never ultimately responsible. Because of this I cannot be an extremist. If only I could in my mind fix properly the idea that there are evil people then I could learn to hate. Listen, I don't want to kill. I must though make a stand for what is right. We have gone through an awful lot.

Made contact with the *Tattler* republican newssheet, Ballymurphy, and wrote an article for it. It's either write or shoot. I am really confused. I want to do that which agrees with me.

October 16th: On news heard of a large arms haul in Amsterdam. Four tons of arms bought by the Provo IRA and destined for here were seized. No matter how I reject violence this frightens me. *Our* guns.

October 19th: There was a big fire in a large building in Great Victoria Street. I stood watching the flames eat up the statelet of N.I.

Later, coming down Malcolmson Street, the soldiers stopped us and a Scotch captain told us we had thirty seconds to "fuckin' get home." We nervously took our time. No wonder less patient people react with guns.

We have six centuries of history and present day oppression. If soldiers are prepared to kill innocent people as well as the IRA then the justification for the IRA killing them is present. Played Seán Ó Riada records and found part of me in his music.

October 23rd: Two women were shot dead by the army in Omar Street. Steeped in this country I feel at times for extreme violence. No. Not yet. It has not got far enough yet. I am soaked in centuries of blood.

October 24th: The British Army shot dead three young men for the simple civilian crime of theft. The soldiers now have licence to murder.

Statistics for October: 27 people died, 150 wounded and there were 150 explosions.

It is a disappointment, a great disappointment, that violence will change the situation. It is the only way.

Mary Ann introduced me to her people who are nice. It appears they had a lot of trouble with the eldest one, Angela, who now lives in England.

The country is almost everything.

I once wrote that we were becoming immune to the deaths. That was a lie.

December 5th: Shocking news this day. Catholic pub, McGurk's bar, was blown up last night. Fifteen men, women and children were killed. My God. It must be loyalist revenge.

December 10th: Our John has been moved from Crumlin Road Jail to Long Kesh Internment Camp.

December 24th: Many houses have candles in their front windows in solidarity with the internees. I put one in ours. I don't know what to do. What should I do?

December 30th/January 1st: Before I write the following words their meaning has died a thousand doubts this day. Perhaps by putting them down I hope to reinforce their meaning.

Anyway, Christ has become country. I have been demented for months, agitated, and Mary Ann says she has got to know me so well she can see my torture. I went into town and got a bus to Dundonald. I had a lot of thinking to do and wanted to be on my own. I walked down the Newtownards Road. I stopped outside the gates of Stormont and had a good, long look at the place and what it represents. I then walked on into town, looking at some of the swanky houses, then other ghetto areas just like ours and at Goliath crane in the Shipyard, a place where our people never knew work. I crossed the Lagan and made my way across the city centre to the west of the city. Looking up in the cold December sunny light I saw the Royal Victoria Hospital and behind it Black Mountain. The day was reminiscent of other cold and sunny December mornings but I felt a change coming on. One of totally bending my life to the cause. I suppose it was only a matter of time. There is nothing left to do but enter into sacrifice and war. I feel so relieved.

Later: Went out tonight with Mary Ann and told her of my decision. She squeezed my arm and told me to be always careful. We went to the dance, had a few drinks and I kissed her at the stroke of midnight when the group announced the New Year. Some girls cried because their brothers or boyfriends are in jail.

I am home now and it is almost 3 a.m. I shall make my mark in this world and I hope I am worthy of it.

I don't know how 1972 will take me but I shall make this my year of years. Your health! To my pledge, to the Republic!

Tonight I felt for the first time that I could justly stand for the *Soldier's Song*.

1972

January

> *Armoured cars and tanks and guns*
> *Came to take away our sons,*
> *But every man will stand behind*
> *The men behind the wire!*

We never could get over August '69. I remember after seeing the destruction, the burned-out homes, walking up Divis Street and the Falls, kicking stones and trying to discover reason.

To die fighting is to cling to real life.

* * *

The years surpass the day, the hours, the moment. Time itself can become a history. A particular time. I shall make times into a particular history. What value my life?

Came home for tea and heard the start of the evening's horrible news. The First Battalion Parachute Regiment went mad in Derry and shot dead 13 unarmed civilians. This was after the civil rights march.

It snowed and we walked the streets, all collected in unity. Clearly, I cannot continue with my studying.

Yesterday was horrible. It was Derry's Bloody Sunday. John Hume of the SDLP has changed the call from civil rights to a united Ireland or nothing.

Rioting broke out and the people fought the soldiers in the snow.

February

The British embassy in Dublin was besieged and has been burned to the ground! Three cheers! Dublin is redeemed. It was great to hear the crowds singing *Four Green Fields* outside the embassy. Support like never before: "'What have I now,' said the fine, old woman ..."

> FLESH
> Her low-cut bra
> Set her breasts
> Out like bubbles.

> Ah! Mary Ann!

> KISS
> That little split
> Middle of her lower lip
> Doubled pleasure.

March

The Provisional IRA have called a three-day truce whilst they put forward peace proposals.

*

The truce ends in one minute's time. One explosion now as the news comes on.

*

Walking up the Grosvenor I heard explosions and a fleet of ambulances passed me. Six people dead and 149 injured in Donegall Street. Terrible.

*

Heard of the announcement of 'Direct Rule' from Westminster. Faulkner and his government will resign soon. A slight victory for the nationalist people.

*

Loyalist power cuts against D. R.

April

I was walking past St Dominic's School whistling and an old man stopped me and said: "Son, it's good to hear you whistling. Years ago you would have heard many people, nearly every other fella on this road, whistling, but recently I have heard no one. It is good to see someone happy."

May

I walk around wearing a grey cardigan, a clean shirt, denims, an anorak and Dr Marten's boots. The anorak, jeans and boots are part of the image!

There is a hunger strike until death by the prisoners in Crumlin Road Jail for political status.

Have completely given up studying but mother and father have no idea. They think I'm sitting exams.

June

We collected signatures in petitions in support of the men on hunger strike in Crumlin Road Jail demanding political status.

Many internees have been released and my Ma's hopes have been raised but John told me that the only time he'll get out is when the war is over, in a year or two.

Saw the lads in our local. It is just like the French Revolution the way they met in pubs and held their meetings and had endless political discussions.

The swallows and the swifts have returned. They conquer the evening sky over Belfast. Their elegant swoops and risings are great to watch.

The IRA offered to the British a chance of peace talks but they refused. The loyalist paramilitary UDA postponed for two weeks their permanent no-go areas.

Had for one minute a great suicidal tendency for Ireland. Felt like assassinating Ted Heath or Reginald Maudling.

I'll give credit where credit is due. God, you made a beautiful evening, a masterpiece – the sun feeding us its glorious light, the sky a blue dress with a white hem, and children, streets of raucous, lively children, each of their destinies a slow sprouting mystery.

A ceasefire has been announced.

Loyalists have a pirate station – Radio Nick. Why can't they become socialists instead of following the blind alley of conservatism and imperialism?

July

11.40 p.m. You want to hear the shooting that is going on now! I'm changing into dirty clothes and going out.

And the truce is over!

Last night there was a big gun battle around the Road with 2,000 rounds of ammunition having been fired. Two soldiers and three civilians were shot dead. Every night somebody dies.

Tonight I was arrested and brought to Broadway Army Post. It was obviously just a routine arrest but I was transferred by Saracen to Springfield Road Barracks. I was determined not to let the side down and though terrified I gave only the barest of details and refused to talk about neighbours who they said were connected. They also said I must be in the IRA because all IRA men they arrested had the Prayer to St Joseph on them, like me. I also had a photograph of Mary Ann in my pocket and they burnt her eyes out with cigarette ends. The place was full of English accents which is really amazing when you think that in every house, in every street around the place are Belfast accents. That's how foreign they are. It was only when I was up against the wall in the courtyard that I realised quite a few others were also inside. Hughie O'Neill from round our way got a bad beating. They had his head in a tank of water and I could hear him drowning and then his head would be lifted out. But he didn't talk.

Before I went in for interrogation they told me I had to have a medical and I was sent into a room to strip. I took my clothes off and then this man came in wearing a white coat and he told me he was the doctor and told me to take off my underpants. Then the door opened and he laughed along with a lot of other soldiers and two RUC men. He wasn't a doctor at all. When I was being interrogated a soldier banged the table and shouted was I not going to open my mouth. There was a lost Johnny Long Legs dancing on the wall, demented and claustrophobic. The soldier grabbed it by the wings and rubbed it against my sealed lips, killing the poor thing, but I never moved. They then whacked me around the head, said I would end up dead or with my brother John in jail. They threw me out after about four hours. How I held on to myself I'll never ever know.

At around three there were many explosions caused by the IRA and there is no escaping the moral responsibility – through association – of today's bloodshed which has so far taken nine lives, four of them civilians. Reaction of supporters is mostly one of two. Some outspoken ones, privately but to your face, criticise you. But most rush to your aid and nurse your morale. "Bloody Friday" has been well-named.

Free Derry has been invaded and there have been many internment swoops again. The Brits are calling it "Operation Motorman".

August
Soldiers are out in strength and it is back to porridge. There were explosions, shootings and robberies and then came the ninth and they had interned us for a year.

500 people have died so far.

> *"Well we got no choice*
> *And we got no innocence"*
> – Alice Cooper, *School's Out*

Mary Ann and I went up Black Mountain today. I said, pointing to a field, this is where we fought the big boys back in '63 or '64, and she said I was wrong, it was over there. I helped her up the steep parts and held her hand and we stood on one of the banks at the Hatchet Field beside the now deserted cottage and looked out across our tortured city. It was quite emotional. Like myself she is a republican. We went on up to the trickling stream which she had fallen into and she insisted it was me who fell in! She said, "God help us when we're together twenty years, what will your memory be like then!" I thought this very sweet and touching, a statement of our togetherness and we lay down on the dry grass and, for the first time, a magnificent dreamy time, we made love. On the mountain top above West Belfast. I love her so much.

Every time we get the chance we make love. Every time their backs are turned, or we can get babysitting, we make glorious love! We're crazy!

Mary Ann and I visited our John today in Long Kesh. I told him to keep his eyes off her! Her family are going on holidays and I shall spend tonight, all night, with her.

I called up at half-seven and later we went down the Shaws Road for a walk. The light was dwindling but it was a hot summer's night and the very tar on the road was as alive as the lawns of Greenan basking in the final warmth of dusk. Before we left her house we heard some Proms' music – Strauss, I think – and Mary Ann wore a long, patterned dress beneath which were her bare breasts, her teenage body into which I fit like a bee's tongue combing the flower's honey. She broke into a waltz on the Andersonstown Road, opposite the applauding poplars in St Joseph's Training College, and in reply I whistled one of my favourite songs. She asked what it was and I told her, *Layla* by Derek and the Dominoes, and, filled with the night, we publicly hugged and kissed and made eejits of ourselves. Anybody who looked at us could see that it was just so much *nature!*
Afterwards we went home and slept in her parents' double bed and made love. As I fell asleep she was still tickling my back! I asked her to set the alarm because today I would be very busy. I didn't even hear it going off but when I awoke there she was with a tray and on it a glass of milk and toasted soda bread which I ate in bed! She stroked my cheek and kissed my bloodshot eyes and from the road I saw her wave from the back window and I blew her a kiss, which I will recapture from the atmosphere and deliver myself tonight.
Went to the place for the business and discovered that we were delayed. Had a few hours to kill and with the okay of a friend, my big friend, I called into our house. From the window of my bedroom where I am now writing I see my Da working hard down below at an old desk which is a secret present for our Sheila. I love that old man, he is a good father. My mammy hands him a cup of tea and they share some joke or other and they smile together.
I have just sat for a few minutes and thought about last night, about my life and the times we live in and the decisions each of us – republican, loyalist, British soldier – make. We can be motivated by love, by noble passions, by fate, by adventurism or by selfishness, and despite our intellects, many of us ultimately fall for our feelings.

I don't have the answers, I know, and I admit that I am a victim of my version of the truth which matured under this sky, in these streets, as I grew up amidst family and friends, in the currents of our small history.

However, I know this much and it's as simple a declaration as I can make, looking down from mine and my brother's bedroom upon the man and woman below who brought me into this world through their own declaration of love.

I look at them with gratitude.

It is great to be alive and I thank God Almighty for having given me a mind of my own, for allowing me to have touched and savoured the beautiful mysteries and quandaries surrounding our existence on this earth, and for allowing me to have seen these years in West Belfast.